MW01258981

# LEVERAGE

# LEVERAGE

A NOVEL

## AMRAN GOWANI

**ATRIA** BOOKS

NEW YORK    AMSTERDAM/ANTWERP    LONDON
TORONTO    SYDNEY/MELBOURNE    NEW DELHI

**ATRIA**
BOOKS

An Imprint of Simon & Schuster, LLC
1230 Avenue of the Americas
New York, NY 10020

For more than 100 years, Simon & Schuster has championed authors and
the stories they create. By respecting the copyright of an author's intellectual
property, you enable Simon & Schuster and the author to continue publishing
exceptional books for years to come. We thank you for supporting the
author's copyright by purchasing an authorized edition of this book.

No amount of this book may be reproduced or stored in any format, nor may it be
uploaded to any website, database, language-learning model, or other repository,
retrieval, or artificial intelligence system without express permission. All rights
reserved. Inquiries may be directed to Simon & Schuster, 1230 Avenue of the
Americas, New York, NY 10020 or permissions@simonandschuster.com.

This book is a work of fiction. Any references to historical events, real people, or
real places are used fictitiously. Other names, characters, places, and events are
products of the author's imagination, and any resemblance to actual events or
places or persons, living or dead, is entirely coincidental.

Copyright © 2025 by Amran Gowani

All rights reserved, including the right to reproduce this book or portions thereof
in any form whatsoever. For information, address Atria Books Subsidiary Rights
Department, 1230 Avenue of the Americas, New York, NY 10020.

First Atria Books hardcover edition August 2025

**ATRIA** BOOKS and colophon are trademarks of Simon & Schuster, LLC

Simon & Schuster strongly believes in freedom of expression and stands against
censorship in all its forms. For more information, visit BooksBelong.com.

For information about special discounts for bulk purchases, please
contact Simon & Schuster Special Sales at 1-866-506-1949 or
business@simonandschuster.com.

The Simon & Schuster Speakers Bureau can bring authors to your live event. For
more information or to book an event, contact the Simon & Schuster Speakers
Bureau at 1-866-248-3049 or visit our website at www.simonspeakers.com.

Interior design by Kyoko Watanabe

Manufactured in the United States of America

1  3  5  7  9  10  8  6  4  2

Library of Congress Cataloging-in-Publication Data has been applied for.

ISBN 978-1-6680-7642-2
ISBN 978-1-6680-7644-6 (ebook)

# LEVERAGE

# PART ONE

## 2015

# LIVING IN THE WORLD TODAY

## *Monday, November 9*

The figurative bloodbath turned literal when my cubemate Keith, prone to stress-induced nosebleeds, sneezed on my monitor. To our horror, visible through the viscous, bloody splotches was a sea of red digits. The Dow, the S&P, and the Nasdaq had plunged by historic, inconceivable levels, conjuring the ghosts of meltdowns past. Keith apologized between gentle sobs, blood streaking down his doughy face and pooling on the collar of his Patagonia. The numbers 1929, 1987, and 2008 buffeted my beleaguered brain as I grabbed a handful of napkins from my stash and tended to the mess.

The market, and the daily, frenetic cacophony that accompanied it, had mercifully closed, leaving an eerie silence. Our polished and pristine offices, situated on the outskirts of San Francisco's Financial District, had morphed into a neoliberalist hellscape on par with the trenches of Verdun, replete with battered balance sheets and shell-shocked stares. Keith plugged his pointy nose with gauze and curled into the fetal position. Dennis drowned his meatheaded sorrows in Red Bull, Reese's Pieces, and Adderall XR. Karen, ever the opportunist, whipped her dirty-blond hair and brilliant blue eyes around the battlefield, snapping countless photos of the carnage and documenting in real time the aftermath from inside Prism Capital—the world's most prestigious hedge fund—for her burgeoning Instagram account.

I ran my hands through my hair, then cupped my mouth and nose, inhaling deeply. *I am completely fucked.* Surely I'd found rock bottom, which meant it was probably time to do the rational thing and kill myself. Then again, my entire existence—from abandoned bastard baby to patronized token minority to Wall Street whipping boy—had been a carousel of catastrophe, and I was nothing if not a glutton for punishment.

While debating the relative merits of a 9 millimeter to the temple or a bottle of Oxy to the gut, I felt a tap on my shoulder. Jennie. My one-sided soulmate. Everything about her was perfect—everything except the Cheez-It-size diamond dangling off her ring finger. Was I okay? she wondered.

"I'm definitely getting fired today," I said.

"You won't be the only one," she said. "*Half* our gains for the year were wiped out. If it wasn't for those Biogen and Celgene shorts you recommended, we'd be totally effed."

"Sounds like you guys made out well."

She scrunched her nose and adjusted her designer glasses. "How bad's your damage?"

"VICE is completely in the red."

Jennie gasped and covered her mouth, as if I told her I'd been

4

diagnosed with Stage IV cancer. "*Holy shit.* You really think you'll get axed?"

I didn't respond. We looked up at the wall of windshield-size LCD screens hovering above the cubicles. They were all muted, all littered with inaccurate closed captioning, all bearing bad news. Farthest left was Bloomberg TV, featuring live, on-site coverage of the business story of the day, month, year, decade, hell, maybe even century. A payday lender called Icarus Management—beloved by Wall Street traders for the 500 to 5,000 percent interest rates it charged struggling Americans of color, which had fueled its sevenfold share price increase—was in immediate need of a new CEO, CFO, and corporate headquarters.

According to rubbernecking reporter Rachel Richards, around 10 a.m. local time, a mob of angry demonstrators had gathered outside the company's Baltimore-based offices to protest its (allegedly) exploitative business practices. The otherwise peaceful gathering took a fateful turn when the building's lead security guard, an Afro-Latino man named Eduardo Vazquez—himself trapped beneath an insurmountable Icarus-issued loan—escorted the crowd to the company's executive offices on the top floor.

"Shortly thereafter," Rachel said, "the rampaging thugs tossed CEO Jeffrey Bull and CFO Douglas Ferentz to their deaths and set fire to Icarus's corporate offices. Police quickly contained the crime scene, although more than twenty Icarus employees remain unaccounted for. Approximately one hundred insurgents, including Mister Vazquez, have been neutralized." Firefighters subdued the blaze by the start of rush hour. The company's stock had plunged 81 percent before Nasdaq management halted it indefinitely "due to extraordinary trading activity."

"I mean, what were the odds?" I asked Jennie.

"Of people finally being fed up enough with capitalism to murder a CEO? That you were unlucky enough to own the murdered CEO's stock? Or that the murdered CEO's company was named after the guy who flew too close to the sun?"

*Touché*, I thought, then wondered if I was truly shocked by the unfolding chaos. Volatile protests had been cropping up at corporate offices around the country for years, and like a lemming, I'd bought into the wisdom of the crowd and discounted the all-too-obvious risk of calamity.

I snapped out of my daze and shifted my eyes to a different nightmare. Jim Cramer was examining Wall Street's autopsy report in gory detail. Commodities finished low. Bonds finished lower. Stocks finished lowest. Every asset class known to personkind had hemorrhaged cash. And, big surprise, according to Jim, it was the *buying opportunity of a lifetime*.

My gaze drifted farther afield, past screens displaying various global terrorist organizations—the Taliban, the Senate Judiciary Committee, the McDonald's Corporation—and fixated on an unexpected appearance from the Weather Channel. Hurricane Consuela was swirling inexorably toward Miami and expected to make landfall by evening. She was "The Big One." Category 5. Tornado-strength winds. Flash flooding. Flying projectiles. Power outages. *Stay inside.*

"I need to check on my mom," I said.

"Not gonna lie, Al," Jennie said, "your birthday's off to an *epically* shitty start."

I wanted to tell her the shittiness started twenty-seven years and nine-odd months ago, when a middle-aged, Green Card–seeking Pakistani immigrant deflowered his sixteen-year-old direct report in a Burger King bathroom stall. "Each year is better than the next," I said.

Jennie flashed her Crest-commercial smile, patted me on the shoulder, told me to hang in there, and said she and Preston would buy my first drink later. *Fucking Preston.* With his inherited colonial wealth, cleft chin, wavy blond hair, and dreamy blue eyes—recessive mutations inbred to perfection over millennia. God was definitely real, and He was definitely a lacrosse-playing frat bro with a kinesiology degree from Duke. Nobody else could stomach being such an asshole.

I shook the thought and ducked into the adjacent hallway to text my mom. I felt little affinity yet loads of responsibility for this woman, who was an abused child burdened with adult responsibilities. Kids weren't supposed to raise their parents, but my childhood home was about to be leveled, and one of us needed to pretend to be a grown-up.

*HAPPY BIRTHDAY SWEEETIE!!!!* she texted back.

*How's the storm?*

*Powers out tree across street knocked down lines im okay tho*

*Do you have enough dry goods and fresh water? Did you board up the windows?*

*Karl dropped off care package Jimmy did windows*

*Are either of them with you?*

An absurd thumbs-down materialized on my last message. Her rotating cast of booty calls would keep her alive, but they wouldn't be caught dead with her during the apocalypse.

*Hang in there. Text/call in case of emergency.*

*Okey dokey Marcia and Will said theyd checkin later*

I added an absurd thumbs-up to her message and returned to my own disaster scene. Brad would come looking for me any minute. I darted down the corridor, past the Klimt and the Monet and around the elevators, then slipped into the men's room on the far side of the office, opposite the Industrials and Internet teams. Industrials had been whittled down to two people and the Internet group was entirely composed of women. This made the men's lavatory on their side of the building solid gold real estate: the perfect place to do your business, mentally regroup, or both.

Sitting fully clothed in my favorite stall, I inserted my headphones, shuffle-played GZA's *Liquid Swords*, and scrolled through my inbox, mindlessly deleting anodyne press releases and breaking news alerts. The writing was all over the wall, bold and colorful like graffiti. A trip to the unemployment line was imminent. But far worse, I'd proved them right. I *wasn't* good enough. I *didn't* belong. The past four years had been luck. Luck that'd just run out.

Fifteen minutes later my thoughts were calmer, clearer, resigned. I went to the sink and dabbed my face with a wet paper towel. I'd been sweating profusely, and my favorite lilac Brioni dress shirt, which accented my silky-smooth, light-roast-colored skin, clung to my damp body like a glow-in-the-dark condom. I cut the music, fanned myself, doused my head with water, pulled out my trusty switchblade comb—the best tenth-birthday present a boy could ever receive—and slicked back my undercut like Michael Corleone.

The face in the mirror told me it was time to see the hangman. But the magical thinker in my brain told me maybe—*just maybe*— this entire day had been one long, awful dream. I simply needed to escape the office, head home, and sleep it off. When I awoke, I'd still be the top-performing analyst at the top-performing firm on Wall Street. Still be the first member of my family to go to college. Still be the guy who told the socioeconomic statistics to go fuck themselves.

Brad greeted me when I opened the men's room door. "Aladdin— there you are! I've been looking all over for you."

"I wasn't, uh, feeling well."

"Given the state of my portfolio, that's not surprising," Brad said. "Dad wants to see you in his office. *Now*."

"Should I, like, pack my things first?"

He sneered his dolphin teeth into a sinister smile. "Where would be the fun in that?"

My guts twisted. That was exactly what he'd told Harold. Poor Harold. I stared through Brad. Willing him to disappear. Forcing this entire day—my entire life—to have been some kind of cosmic misunderstanding. It didn't work. Brad extended a chivalrous arm in the direction of the boss's office. In the direction of a new fresh hell.

# THINGS DONE CHANGED

Paul Kingsley's office occupied the southeast corner on the top floor of the 555 California Street Building. Its floor-to-ceiling windows afforded him a bird's-eye view of the Transamerica Pyramid, spectacular sunrises over the Bay Bridge, and breathtaking sunsets over the Golden Gate. Perks associated with a thirteen-billion-dollar nest egg. When Paul took over the space from a now defunct hedge fund rival, whose demise he helped accelerate, he'd had the building engineers figure out how to knock down two load-bearing walls to ensure he had adequate working space. The room was more than twice the size of my shitty Telegraph Hill apartment, seemingly big enough to house an entire pod of beluga whales.

Walking down the office's central corridor, with Brad skulking behind me like Samwise Gamgee masquerading as Boba Fett, the entirety of the human aquarium came into view. Paul had partitioned the space into four distinct sections. His "retro room" was slotted into the back right corner, complete with a walk-in humidor, wet bar, and leather smoking chair. Sitting opposite was the "relaxation station," where Paul was wont to watch eighties action films, play various first-person shooters, and, when he was feeling randy, call his pal Billy Bismarck, CEO of Allure Entertainment, and live stream the day's shoot. The back left corner was his "productivity hub," which he rarely used, and the front left—the place you *never* wanted to see him lurking—was the section Paul euphemistically referred to as his "leadership center." Everyone else called it the gallows. The place where he reamed your ass out entirely, if you were lucky, or sent you packing, if you weren't.

To my chagrin, but not surprise, the six-foot-two, salt-and-pepper Aryan Adonis sat ominously in the hangman's lounge, sporting a charcoal suit, lavender shirt, and custom wingtips that cost more than a semester at Stanford.

Per protocol, I emptied my pockets and deposited all my belongings in the TSA-style drop box outside the glass door. Brad and I walked through the metal detector, then Paul jumped up to greet me.

"Tough day at the office, huh, Al?" he said, crushing my hand. I nodded. "Take a seat. You need a coffee? Water? Whiskey, maybe?" Paul and I sat across from each other. Brad settled in the chair to my right, a shit-eating smirk plastered onto his chubby red face. "Let's not beat around the bush, Al," Paul said. "What in the Sam Hill happened out there today?"

My mouth started to move but no sound came out. I hesitated, certain he'd explode into a tirade any second. After an uncomfortable pause, I mumbled, "I don't know, Paul. I just, I mean, I've been trying to figure out what I missed. If I didn't see all the angles on Icarus. Or if I didn't do enough diligence. I even wondered if our position was too large. But honestly, all I can come up with is plain old bad luck."

"Bad luck is what happens when you step in a fresh pile of dog shit, Al. Not when you lose three hundred million dollars in four hours. Do you know what I could buy with three hundred million dollars, Al?"

"Uh, a lot of really expensive things, probably . . ."

"That's right, Al," Paul said, matter of fact. "A lot of really expensive things."

"Like, for starters, a whole new analyst team for VICE," Brad chimed in.

"Paul, I'm really sorry. I screwed up big-time. And I understand if you need to let me go, but—"

"Let you go?" Paul interrupted, incredulous. "Nobody's being 'let go,' Al."

"Shitcanned, maybe," Brad quipped.

"Shut the fuck up, Bradley," Paul snapped.

Brad slouched into his chair and the blood drained from his face. I froze in place and stared over Paul's shoulder at the bevy of half-built high-rise condominiums being erected in SoMa. We were more than fifty floors up. If a fourteen-story drop was enough to wax Icarus management, a plunge from here would undoubtedly put me out of my misery once and for all. The bronze bust of Alexander the Great on Paul's desk looked strong enough to break the glass.

"As I was saying, Al, you cost the firm—meaning me—a small fortune today. Whether it was bad luck, bad karma—you people believe in karma, right?—or sheer, utter fucking stupidity, it doesn't really matter. I can't abide such a monumental cock-up. If I let you walk out of here with your job intact, everyone else will think it's fine to piss away our clients' money. Meaning my money. You see the problem, Al?"

"I do," I said. And I did. "If I may, Paul, could I please ask you to spare the rest of VICE? Icarus falls on me. I should own the consequences."

"That's very noble of you," Paul said. "And see, that's part of my dilemma. VICE was your idea, Al. And—excluding today, of course—it's been *by far* our best-performing fund. Better than Internet. Better than Semiconductors. Better than Biotech. Frankly, Al, if I'm being honest, you've been my best performing analyst since you got here—excluding today, of course."

"Of course," I agreed, needlessly.

"So what am I to do, Al? If I 'shitcan' you, I lose my best employee, and fuckwit here loses VICE's golden goose," Paul said, jabbing a thumb at Brad. "Worse, the minute you walk out that door, every hedge fund in the country will offer you a job, making you my competitor. I certainly can't have that. On the other hand, if I let you go with a slap on the wrist, every incompetent pissant in this office will expect special treatment. Really makes you appreciate the complexities of the criminal justice system, huh?"

I wasn't sure if the question was rhetorical, and I had no idea where Paul was going with this soliloquy. I fully expected to be fired when he was done.

"So here's what I'm going to do, Al," Paul continued. It dawned on me he'd never called me "Al" so many times in one sitting. Normally, like every other (obviously) White dude in the office, he'd have defaulted to Prince Ali, Aladdin, Habib, Lion King, or, my least favorite, al-Qaeda. "I'm going to offer you a carrot, and a stick. Bradley will give you the details, but it goes like this: You've got three months to earn back my money, or else your life is over. Clear?"

*My life is over?* If he were planning to kill me, I'd have gladly accepted. "I understand, Paul. Thank you so much for the opportunity to redeem myself. I won't let you down."

"You better not, Al. For your sake." Paul stood and once again obliterated my hand. "Now get the fuck out of my face."

14

$$$

Brad and I walked in silence down Market Street to Super Duper, then took our burgers to the courtyard at Yerba Buena Gardens. I wasn't hungry, but he insisted I order something. A kind of last meal, I'd assumed. Sitting on a bench under a shady oak tree, I picked at the edges of my organic, non-GMO veggie burger. Brad stuffed his ovoid face with a bacon-and-cheese-slathered Super Burger and garlic cheese fries, which he chased with a strawberry-banana Super Shake.

"Okay, Aladdin," he mumbled midbite, "take out your phone and turn it off." I looked at him askance. He insisted, and even though complying boded extremely ill for my future, I did as instructed. "Here's the deal. Today's Monday, November ninth. You've got until Tuesday, February sixteenth to recover the three hundred million dollars you just flushed down the toilet. Dad likes you, so he's giving you some extra time to account for the holidays. He doesn't want to be unreasonable."

*How does one respond to such lunacy?* "That's completely absurd. How the fuck am I supposed to make so much money so quickly?"

"Ask yourself this: *How the fuck* did you lose so much money so quickly?"

An obvious, even reasonable, riposte I should've seen coming. "Brad, I told your dad I screwed up. You should fire me. Honestly, I deserve it."

"If it were up to me, I would. But you heard Dad. He doesn't want you working for the enemy."

"I'll quit, then. If Paul thinks I'm so valuable, maybe I am. In which case there's absolutely zero reason I should be his hostage," I said, this fact suddenly so obvious.

A twinkle lit in Brad's eye as he swallowed another oversize bite. He took a long, methodical drag on his recyclable straw, then set the milkshake down on the sidewalk between his hobbit feet.

"This is the part I've been waiting for," he said lustfully. "You remember how Dad said he had a carrot *and* a stick? So the carrot is this: If you make back the money, you get to keep your job, *and* you get a hundred mil to manage directly for Dad. Pretty good deal, huh?" My heart sank all the way into my scrotum. There was no way Paul would make that kind of offer unless he knew I'd fail. He must've just seen *John Wick*. "But here's the stick—you people like sticks, right? Caning is popular in Derkfuckistan, or wherever you're from, isn't it?" I felt hollow inside, even as I fantasized about jamming my uncivilized thumbs into his imperial eyes. "If you *don't* earn back Dad's money, you're going to spend the rest of your life in jail."

My eyes bulged and my adrenaline spiked. "What the fuck are you talking about? You can't threaten me."

"Nobody's threatening you, Habib. I'm simply explaining your predicament."

"Fuck you, you fat little pussy. I fucking quit." I swiped my unmolested lunch onto the ground and stood up. "You and *Daddy* can go fuck yourselves."

"You better sit right the fuck back down," Brad said in a firm, deliberate tone. I glared at him. It took every fiber of my being not to stomp his head into the pavement. With an eminently punchable smile affixed to his greasy face, he said, "The SEC's investigating us for insider trading. It appears Dennis has been an especially naughty boy. *Allegedly*, he's been buying and selling huge positions in the VICE fund—days, hours, sometimes even minutes before material events have been announced. I have to admit, on paper it looks like a classic case of insider trading.

"But, luckily for Dennis, he and I roomed together at Wharton, and I know his character is unassailable. Unluckily for you, however, Dad and I conducted an internal compliance audit and uncovered some truly shocking revelations. We learned that Dennis had been following the explicit directions of his supervisor, a certain Ali Jafar. And we also discovered Mister Jafar has been diverting these illicit gains through a network of offshore shell companies and LLCs, with the money finding its way to a number of jihadi extremist groups. Who could believe there was a traitor hiding right under our noses?!

"But Dad said not to worry. He said if District Attorney Holloway, who's a close personal friend, found out about such crimes, he'd stop at nothing to ensure a terrorist financier like Mister Jafar was brought to justice. I don't know about you, but I find that last part very reassuring."

Panic, rage, fear, and murderous intent coursed through my veins. A sense of weightlessness took hold, my legs gave way, and I was jarred by what felt like back-to-back helmet-to-helmet tackles. Prostrate on the warm pavement, unable to move, Brad's rambling distant and indecipherable, everything turned black.

# EVERYTHING REMAINS RAW

## *Thursday, November 12*

woke to the gentle whir of hospital instruments. My face and head throbbed and my nether regions were awash in stale urine. The bandage over my left eye was sweat-soaked and tacky. My right eye adjusted to the darkness and homed in on the digital clock on the nightstand: 3:47 a.m. *Where's my phone?* I summoned the nurse using the green "help" button on the hospital bed. She arrived a few minutes later and urged me to go back to sleep, insisting I needed rest.

"I normally wake up around this time for work," I assured her. "Can I have my phone?" She opened the drawer where my things were stored and handed it to me. The battery had dropped to 1 percent, which was annoying, and the date on the lock screen said Thursday, November 12, which was impossible. An incalculable number of banner notifications blanketed the screen.

"What day is it?"

"Thursday. You've been out almost three days. How are you feeling? How's your head?" the nurse asked, with genuine concern. She was fortyish, with blond hair and grayish eyes, and fit snugly into her teal scrubs. Her metallic name badge read *Linda*.

"That doesn't make sense. What happened?"

Linda reviewed my chart, then explained I'd passed out from a combination of stress, hypoglycemia, and dehydration. In the process, I'd managed to bop both sides of my noggin. The left on a park bench when I fainted, and the right when my limp carcass ricocheted onto the sidewalk. The doctors determined the second collision caused the grade 2 concussion.

"How did I get to the hospital?" Linda didn't know. "Did anyone come to visit me?" Linda wasn't sure. "Did my mom call?" Linda thought it was so sweet of me to ask. After handing me my backpack—*who brought it here?*—Linda said if I was healthy enough, my doctor would discharge me when his next shift began in a few hours. Then she said she'd grab a cup of coffee and a bagel for me from the nurse's lounge and departed. I thanked her, sifted through my bag, collected my trusty charge bank, plugged in my phone, and texted my mom. She called back instantly.

"Jesus, Al, you scared the shit out of me. The receptionist said you had a concussion or something. Are you okay?"

"I'm not sure what happened," I said, which was mostly true. I retained vivid memories of a stock market meltdown and a heated conversation with Brad, but I wasn't sure if they were real. Everything felt hazy. I stupidly held out hope this was all just a terrible dream.

"Are you feeling better?"

"My head hurts, but I'm fine. I should be discharged soon."

"Don't rush back to that awful job, Al. Stay and rest as long as the doctor tells you to."

"How'd the hurricane treat you?"

"Power's been out a few days, but our block was lucky enough to avoid the flooding. Everything east of Palm's completely under water, including the casino."

"Wow, that sucks. At least your house is intact."

"I'm doing okay, all things considered," she said. "Oh, I almost forgot to tell you! Karl and I saw a tiger!"

"A what?"

"A *tiger*. You know, a big orange one with black stripes. Karl thinks it belongs to a local drug runner. Hold on, I'll text you a pic."

"Is Karl staying with you?" I asked as my phone vibrated. Incredibly, the image showed a *bona fide* Bengal tiger perched atop an abandoned Xfinity van.

"He did last night. He brought his canoe over and we went all around the neighborhood. It was really romantic. Like Venice."

"Right. Well, at least you're okay. Hopefully things get back to normal quickly. Speaking of which, I have to figure out what the hell happened at work these last three days. I'll text you when I'm out of the hospital."

"I love you, sweetie. Take care of yourself."

*I always have.*

$$$

Linda brought me a second dreadful cup of coffee. It was divine. Being unconscious for three days had led to crippling caffeine withdrawal, which no doubt intensified my head trauma. Linda removed my bandages and handed me her makeup mirror. The left side of my face looked like the inside of a rotten nectarine. I also had a boxer's black eye. I held the mirror still and turned my head, which revealed a large, scaly black scab just behind my right ear. The damage was extensive, but Linda assured me it wasn't permanent.

Sitting there felt surreal. I'd never visited a hospital, let alone been admitted to one. I'd never broken a bone. Never been in a car accident. Never overdosed on pharmaceutical-grade heroin. My appendix remained intact. The only notable injury I'd ever suffered were back spasms, resulting from an awkward tackle in football practice during my senior year of high school. And they were nothing a few muscle relaxants and extra hours of sleep couldn't remedy.

But there I sat. Helpless. Had the gerrymandered elections, financial crises, and endless wars on terror taken their toll? Were the wheels finally coming off? Perhaps I'd simply been confronted with my own mortality for the first time and was feeling overly dramatic. Too much introspection always ended badly. Pretty soon I'd wonder if I could poison myself with my IV.

Linda left to start her rounds and I retreated into my phone. Hundreds of FactSet and Bloomberg alerts bloated my inbox. Most were useless, but some were priceless. I searched for specific messages. Paul had sent a generic "get well" note on Monday evening. Brad had done likewise, but also asked me to check in with him as soon as I was conscious. What a dick. Keith and Karen had expressed similarly tepid concern, though surely the latter exploited my injuries in an inspirational IG post highlighting the dangers of *burnout* and the importance of *self-care*. Dennis had offered his "condolences." If only.

I felt better when I found Jennie's name. She'd sent me an animated e-card chock-full of dancing panda GIFs. Her message was tragically stereotypical and, more important, failed to mention she'd realized she was desperately in love with me, couldn't fathom the prospect of my premature death, and was leaving Preston. *Fucking Preston.* I searched for his name next, because I hate myself, and not only had he wished me a "speedy recovery," but he'd graciously offered to "subsidize any overly burdensome healthcare costs" I might incur.

Next I checked stock prices. Monday's crash was all too real, unfortunately. Icarus shares had yet to resume trading, which meant my once high-flying portfolio remained fatally injured. The stock was clearly on its way to zero. Fuck me. At least the company's twenty-two missing employees had been accounted for. Burnt to a crisp. The news wasn't all bad, though. During a televised interview with Fox Business, Senate Finance Committee chairperson Urban "Snatch" Williams had assured Wall Street that, despite the terrible tragedy, it was "too soon" to discuss "reactionary" regulations for the alternative finance sector. Global markets had undertaken their perfunctory "dead cat bounce" on Tuesday, then slid back to Monday's crash levels on Wednesday. The Sisyphean charade would soon begin anew.

I begrudgingly opened the *Wall Street Journal* app. It was a mediocre newspaper, written at a fifth-grade reading level, with op-ed columns cynical enough to make William Randolph Hearst cringe. And yet, despite these shortcomings, high finance's masters of the universe considered it essential reading. I scrolled past the gratuitous Icarus coverage, the Sinophobic warmongering, and the calls to impeach the president for being Black. I wasn't sure what I was looking for—context? meaning? silver linings?—when the answer hit me like a Stone Cold Stunner. The headline read: "Pain & Gain: How Prism Made $4B from Icarus Tragedy." The story had been published online an hour ago and would be front and center in today's print edition.

The insulting title gave way to a more grotesque lede. I felt sicker with each passing word. By the time I got to Paul's quotes about purchasing "credit default swaps" as hedges against "the tightest credit spreads ever" and the "possibility of massive asymmetrical upside," my eyes had glazed over, and I wished I hadn't survived my fall. My mind briefly turned conspiratorial: When *did Paul buy those credit default swaps? Did he* know *the market would crash? Did he* orchestrate *the crash?*

The insanity proved temporary. I knew never to believe in conspiracy theories because humans were far too tribal and dumb to pull off such incredibly coordinated feats. The real conspiracies—colonialism, white supremacy, regressive taxation—were much more banal, and far more venal. Everything that happened within that framework was random and, thus, meaningless. Not even the formidable Prism Capital could manipulate that fickle muse known as probability.

But then I wondered: If Paul had made an absolute killing from the market crash, why did he have Brad threaten me? *Did Brad threaten me?* My eyes felt strained, and a dull ache echoed deep in the recesses of my brain. A wave of exhaustion crashed into me. I lowered my phone and looked at the clock. The sun wouldn't be up for another hour. Maybe Linda was right: I did need my rest. I placed my phone on the portable nightstand next to a chintzy fake houseplant, buried my head under the single hospital bed pillow, and drifted off.

$$$

I woke up rock-hard—three days without masturbating had also taken their toll—when I felt tapping on my right shoulder. Finally, I thought, the doctor would send me on my way. Brad's orc-ish countenance provided an unwelcome surprise. My heart rate and blood pressure spiked. I sat up.

"What the fuck are you doing here?"

"Glad to see you're feeling better, Habib."

"Where's the doctor? Where's Linda?"

"Linda went for some fresh air. She called a few hours ago and told me you were awake. Nice lady. Very thorough." Betrayed by another White woman. A fixture since birth. I felt nauseous.

"The doctor told me you suffered a traumatic brain injury," Brad continued. "Probably not your first. He said you might have some short-term confusion. Perhaps some temporary memory loss. I came to see how you're holding up. Are you confused, Habib? Do you remember what we talked about before your accident?"

I glowered through him. *Of course I fucking remember!* But playing dumb seemed prudent. "I'm still trying to piece everything together. Why don't you give me a refresher?"

He smiled but didn't say anything, then reached into the pocket of his oversize brown sport coat and handed me a three-by-five note card adorned with a single phone number.

"What's this?"

"People like you never forget anything, Habib. Your ancestors have been slaughtering each other for two thousand years because somebody fucked someone else's goat. The arrangement we discussed still stands. If you need to talk about it, call that number, and that number only."

"What arrangement? What is this, Brad?"

"Rest up, buddy. I'll see you back in the office tomorrow morning, bright and early."

He left without saying another word. There were no nurses or doctors anywhere in sight. Impossibly, I'd slept until two in the afternoon. Someone had slid a sheet of paper underneath my phone. It said my vitals were normal and I was free to leave whenever I wanted, though preferably before three. I *was* confused. My memory *was* spotty. But one thing was crystal clear: My bad dream was just beginning.

# SOLILOQUY OF CHAOS

*Friday, November 13*

My phone alarm went off at 3:50 a.m., an unnatural and inhumane time. Keeping this schedule for four straight years had undoubtedly shaved a decade off the end of my life. Upside to everything. Companies rarely announced news on Friday mornings, even during in-progress financial crises, which was a relief. The prior three trading sessions, which I'd involuntarily slept through in a hospital bed, had done little to increase the value of my positions. Icarus was *still* halted, though Nasdaq announced normal trading would resume the following Monday. *Awesome.*

Emails were otherwise light: a bunch of sell-side spam I deleted without reading and some scattered press releases of the most cynical variety. Nobody alive cared that LaSalle Education Services, a private, for-profit online college with an indicted CFO, a litany of class-action lawsuits, and a market capitalization of $15 billion—

still up 400 percent since IPO and one of my best-ever picks!—had pledged to be "carbon neutral" at a future date "to be determined."

I approached the bottom of my inbox and saw another shit sandwich looming on the horizon. Paul had sent an email at 1:43 a.m. announcing an "all-hands meeting" for nine o'clock sharp. These were almost as bad as visits to the gallows. *Fuck.* Clearly he planned to skewer me alive in front of everyone. That was why he hadn't fired me. Brad's bullshit threats were another layer in one of their twisted games. Fuck, fuck, fuck. If I took the scenic route to work through the Tenderloin, maybe a heroin addict would stab me to death. I was never that lucky.

My head began throbbing again. I wobbled to the bathroom, opened Pornhub in an incognito tab, lotioned up my hand, and scrolled through the menu. Eventually I settled on some DC Comics–inspired anime and temporarily subdued my inner turmoil.

$$$

I arrived at the office just after five. The crowd bustled and whizzed around in panicked silence. Concerned looks abounded and a sense of dread blanketed the entire floor like a damp, sulfurous fart. Everyone feared the worst, and everyone on my team—which was called VICE and consisted of me, Brad, Dennis, Karen, and Keith—expected Ali "Al" Jafar to be flayed alive.

Until our portfolio imploded, VICE had been the top fund at Prism, and I likened our group to my favorite NBA team of all time: the 1995–96 Chicago Bulls. I was, humbly, the Michael Jordan of our franchise, a winner through and through. Karen was our Scottie Pippen, a great player who couldn't win a championship by herself. Dennis thus became a loose but aptly named analog for Dennis Rodman, a high-impact guy who tended to play dirty. We were VICE's "Big Three," which made Keith a pure role player who on his best days was Toni Kukoč and on his worst, Jud Buechler. Finally, sitting above us all was Brad as Phil Jackson, a bad coach who appeared to be a great coach because his team had the best players.

But those were the halcyon days. After Icarus, we'd become the pathetic Miami Heat of my youth, which made me Rony Seikaly: an overrated bum with a strange name and a stupid face.

I settled into my cube and logged into Bloomberg. Beside me, Dennis chewed the end of a Bellagio-branded plastic pen and perused ESPN.com. Keith was absent, and thus likely in the shitter. The only analyst doing any semblance of work was Karen, who busily attended to Prism's professional Twitter account and her personal Instagram. To project an outward image of "openness" and "transparency," Paul permitted Karen to use both accounts at her discretion. Of course, he kept a close eye on her activity, and he loved to lambaste her whenever she was a little too open and transparent for his liking.

"Is Brad around?" I asked after several moments of being ignored.

"He's with Paul," Dennis said without looking up.

"Do either of you know what this all-hands meeting is about?"

They shrugged. I didn't press, because I knew the answer. VICE was on the chopping block, and I was prime cut.

$$$

Karen returned ten minutes before showtime and placed our coffees next to her computer. Fetching them was debasement enough. Distributing them with any semblance of warmth or humanity was beyond her capacity. I leaned over to collect my overpriced, overengineered beverage and caught a glimpse of her impassive profile. Taut ponytail with nary a hair out of place. Sapphire eyes. Diamond-cutting cheekbones. Barbie-doll nose. Unnaturally straight teeth buried under pursed, agitated lips. I, like the tens of thousands of fans who followed her IG @StreetBitch, found her attractive in the Waspiest, most aspirational, most hate-fuckable way imaginable.

I returned to my chair and took a sip of my coffee, which was ruined by a superfluous mint leaf. A superfluous mint leaf I'd specifically asked Karen to excise from my order. I fished out the foliage with a plastic stirrer and threw it in Keith's garbage can.

"Any bets on who gets axed?" Dennis asked. As Brad's power bottom, he knew he was protected, and thus delighted in the forthcoming carnage. *Shitbag.*

"Al's the overwhelming favorite," Karen said, as if I wasn't sitting right next to her. "Vegas wouldn't even take bets on him."

"Damn, that's ice-cold," Dennis said.

"But I wouldn't want to be Dan and Ben, either," she added.

Keith, with his generic brown hair, generic brown eyes, generic pointy nose, and generic oval mouth, looked as stunned as a generic office worker emoji could. "Industrials crushed this week— relatively speaking," he said. "It's also a solid defensive sector to play in while the market's volatile. They're not going anywhere."

"Want to bet?" Karen asked.

"Set the terms," Keith said.

"Ten grand. I'll give you five-to-two odds," she replied.

"Done," he agreed without hesitation. Dennis asked if I wanted the same action. I didn't, so Keith doubled down.

A natural migration began throughout the office as everyone funneled into the central corridor en route to the auditorium. It seated over a hundred people and featured an IMAX-caliber screen with a state-of-the-art ultra-high-definition projector. A queue of dejected analysts and portfolio managers had formed at the door. Sensing an apt metaphor, I waited to join the end of the line.

Ahead of me, each comrade deposited their electronic devices in a large cardboard bin outside the door and filed through the metal detectors. The process had real *Grapes of Wrath* energy. When I entered the auditorium, Paul was pacing back and forth onstage. He was wearing his dreaded black suit with its matching black shirt, tie, socks, and shoes. The same outfit he donned for every all-hands meeting. His spin on Steve Jobs's signature black turtleneck and jeans. I sat with my team near the center of the theater. At nine sharp, the lights dimmed and the room went silent and still.

"During times of extreme uncertainty," Paul began, "a leader needs to take stock. He needs to gather his troops. He needs to look in their eyes. And he needs to figure out who he can trust. He needs to figure out who will fight to the death with valor and honor. And who will panic and flee and put everyone at risk. As I look around this room, all I see is panic. All I see is fear. You're scared. Scared people become irrational. Fear and irrationality go hand in hand. They feed on one another. And their voracious hunger knows no bounds. When they take hold, bad decisions follow. In our business, bad decisions destroy value. Take a look."

A table appeared on the screen. All seven sectors—Industrials, SPACs, Biotech, Robotics, REITs, Internet, and VICE—had lost money. My fund, VICE, had performed worst of all, losing a seemingly impossible 30 percent.

"As of yesterday's close, Prism Capital Management LLC—the firm I founded—has managed to lose two-point-six billion dollars in four days. That's twenty-seven million dollars per hour. Half a million dollars per minute. Frankly, it's astonishing. It's a testament to the mind-altering incompetence of every last one of you.

"This chart? This is what fear looks like. This is what irrationality looks like. Well, let me make something clear: I'm not afraid. I'm not irrational. Do any of you know what the rational thing to do right now would be?" Paul asked.

Nobody dared breathe, let alone speak.

"What do you think, Dan?" he said, singling out his first of many victims. Karen turned to Keith and mouthed, *Told you.*

"Assume I'm rational, Dan. Brutally rational. Tell me: If you were me, what would you do?"

"Uh, well, I, uh—"

"It's okay, Dan. Speak freely."

"Well, um, I would, uh, *probably* fire everyone in this room?"

"Ding-ding-ding! We have a winner, folks!" Paul said with a game show host's faux enthusiasm. "Solid, impartial, rational advice. Dan, you and Ben are fired. Pack your shit and get the fuck out of here."

Dan, a ten-year Prism veteran, pleaded, "What do you mean? Look at the table! We're only down three percent. We're five hundred bips ahead of our benchmark!"

"I'll make note of that in your severance package," Paul said.

Keith's head sank while Dennis and Karen fist-bumped. Somebody in the back—probably Betty, it was always Betty—started crying. Dan and Ben were promptly greeted by a mountainous security guard, and the somber trio made the interminable, ignominious walk up the aisle and exited via the rear doors.

Once they'd departed, Paul resumed. "You people think I'm harsh? Maybe I am. But Dan and Ben were weak. They didn't lose money, but they didn't *make* money, either. There can be no room for weakness! There can be no room for irrationality! There can be no room for fear. I'm liquidating the Industrials portfolio as we speak. Fear and irrationality create opportunity. And opportunity, for those of you who have forgotten, is how we create *value.*"

Paul walked off the stage and fetched a bottle of water. He was taking his sweet time. He was putting on a show, like a medieval executioner. I clenched my fists, teeth, and butt. Paul was just warming up, and everything about that slide suggested I'd be the main event. Maybe I could strangle myself with Karen's ponytail.

"Dan was right about one thing," Paul resumed. "The rational thing to do would be to fire every last one of you imbeciles. Start fresh. But rationality is constrained first and foremost by pragmatism. As you've no doubt seen in yesterday's *Journal*, thanks to me, Prism finished the week *up* a billion and a half dollars. Unlike the rest of you, I'm not a fucking moron, and I hedged our portfolio. FYI, in case you've forgotten, this is still a hedge fund.

"And because of my foresight, I'm going to bathe you useless fucks in the milk of human kindness. Everyone in this room is getting a reprieve. A chance to redeem yourselves. The market got crushed, and I created three billion dollars of fresh capital. Opportunity is knocking hard as a dick on prom night. And we're going to pop some cherries.

"So listen carefully, snowflakes. I expect, *minimum*, twenty-five percent returns by year-end *and* double-digit gains in the first quarter. Every single trade goes to your PM, then to me for review. As always, Compliance makes final approvals. Every single trade *must* be accompanied by a cost-effective hedge. Every single trade has a time horizon of *right fucking now*. I don't want to hear about your 'long-term thesis on medical urbanization in the African subcontinent.' I want *actionable* investments: crushed earnings, massive takeouts, and monster shorts.

"In times like these, opportunity is everywhere. Prove yourselves, and you'll be rewarded handsomely. Fail, and I'll make sure you can't trade stocks in your mama's basement. It's natural selection time. Only the fittest will survive."

Paul tossed the microphone on the floor and disappeared behind the stage's blue curtains. The room remained deathly still for a few moments, then erupted in massive sighs of relief. Bodies shuffled into the aisles, hugging and embracing and agreeing to get "totally fucking lit" over the weekend. Everyone endeavored to make good on their second chances while knowing we were all living on borrowed time. Short-termism was the nature of the beast.

Back at our desks, Karen, Keith, and Dennis gawked at me in silent amazement. VICE had been completely spared and I, the man behind the Icarus bet and the most obvious fall guy of all, had emerged from the meeting inexplicably unharmed. We were the miraculous survivors of a high-speed plane crash, but only I knew our fates had been predetermined by malevolent forces. Under sane circumstances, I would've been thrilled to keep my job, but a darker realization metastasized in my gut. I needed to call Brad's mystery number. I needed to play his sick little game.

# RAW HIDE

The bar was called Demonic Saints. Nestled at the corner of Chestnut and Grant in the North Beach neighborhood, the high-end whiskey joint proved popular with fintech bros who thought paying ninety bucks for a glass of Johnnie Walker Blue validated their existence. At least it was a short walk from my apartment. I'd never been inside before but, after nursing an eye-wateringly expensive Crown Royal, conceded the interior lived up to the hype. The bar shelves were constructed from natural oak and finished with a gorgeous mahogany stain. Steel cabinet hardware added a touch of modern to the otherwise rustic aesthetic, while three crystal chandeliers livened the ambience. Ronnie, a general carpentry contractor and my surrogate father during seventh grade, had trained my eye to such things.

Sunken into my leather barstool, I admired the colorful variety of fresh citric accoutrements—lemon and lime, of course, but also clementine, grapefruit, kiwi, even kumquat—while waiting for Brad.

Or I assumed it would be Brad. A few hours earlier, I'd finally texted the phone number he gave me at the hospital and asked what I was supposed to do. He, or whoever had responded, chastised me for using names over text, then told me to meet here. So here I was. No longer planning to use names. And wondering how I could possibly come up with three hundred million dollars in three months. It was a staggering sum. Star quarterbacks needed ten years to make that much money. Hollywood A-listers fifteen. Minimum-wage workers twenty thousand.

I took out my phone and googled "gun permit San Francisco" as the hostess invited another guest into the bar. I turned and saw Brad. *Womp-womp*. He waved to me like we were best buds and sidled up close on the adjacent stool.

"What're you drinking, Habib?"

"Crown. Neat," I sighed.

"Always slumming it, huh? Do we not pay you enough?"

I shrugged.

Brad yelled to the bartender, "Bring us two Johnnie Blues. And get rid of whatever swill he's drinking."

The barman obliged. Brad sipped first and graciously assured me he'd cover the tab. It was smooth, but not noticeably better than my Crown. I didn't care for whiskey one way or another. Brad gulped down the rest of his libation, then tongued the oversize ice cube like a feral hamster. How in the hell had Paul Kingsley, übermensch, sired this chunky little goblin? He must've fucked Miss Piggy. Genetics were wild.

After a few excruciating moments, Brad said, "You got a game plan, Habib?"

"I'm having a hard time keeping things straight these days, Brad. So why don't you tell me what in the ever-loving fuck we're talking about?"

"Quit playing stupid," he snapped. "Take your phone out, power it off, and set it on the bar."

Déjà vu all over again. I complied, though I should've smashed an empty whiskey tumbler into his porcine face.

Brad leaned in closer. "You think Dad's actually okay with you shitting the bed? The only reason you haven't been shipped back to Abu Dhabi is because he thinks you're good enough to earn back the money. Well, I sure as shit don't. I told him to drop the insider trading charges on your head straightaway. But he wants to wait."

"What insider trading charges? How do I know you're not making this whole thing up?"

He took out his personal phone, tapped WhatsApp, opened a message from a restricted number, scrolled all the way to the top of the thread, and handed me the device. I skimmed through the spartan dialogue and latched on to a few key names: Holloway, Burke, McClane, McNamara. The latter belonged to Dennis.

"This isn't proof of anything," I said. "You could've texted this to yourself."

"You still think this is a game, Habib? I call Dad and tell him you're not playing ball, and you're getting ass-raped at San Quentin tomorrow. You really want to test me?"

I could tell he was serious. Brad wasn't clever enough to make such threats on his own. And even though I knew the criminal justice system—abjectly broken and corrupt as it was—wouldn't immediately send me to prison on unproven charges, I didn't want to explore that thesis. In a political system where money bought influence and influence bought power, Paul was as influential and powerful as they came.

District Attorney Holloway was a golfing buddy. Senator Burke, ostensibly a left-leaning, reform-minded Democrat, was a Stanford classmate. And Governor McClane, an Ayn Rand–humping, technolibertarian "independent," was the happy recipient of a two-million-dollar campaign donation from a Prism-led super PAC. I hadn't just read about these connections in an unflattering *New Yorker* profile. I'd met these people in the flesh. Shaken their limp hands. Seen how they kowtowed to Paul in private like he was their king.

"Let's try this again," Brad said. "Do. You. Have. A. Plan?"

"What—to do the impossible? No, Brad, I don't have a plan for that."

"You're always so negative, Habib," he said, his tone shifting back to dickish. "You really should work on that."

I stared and seethed. The bar was pretty much empty. I could've choked him to death before the bartender pulled me off. Apparently, I was going to prison either way. Murder carried way more street cred than wire fraud, or whatever bullshit charge the Feds would dump on me.

"Here's how it'll work," Brad said. "Dennis is getting shifted to SPACs, and Keith and Karen are taking over the remnants of VICE. You're getting a fresh start. Three hundred mil in a brand-new 'Special Projects' fund. Every trade goes through me, then Dad, then Compliance. All you have to do is double your money."

"In three months?" I scoffed.

"Easy-peasy. Remember: carrots *and* sticks. Make back the cash, and you get your own fund as a full-time PM. Don't? Well, you already know what'll happen if you don't."

"This doesn't make sense. Why would Paul trust me with fresh capital?"

"It's all very straightforward, Habib. You just worry about the task at hand. The VICE reorg happens this weekend. When you log in Monday morning, the money will be waiting for you."

"What happens if I get close but don't make it? Like, what if I make two hundred and eighty mil?"

"Close only counts in horseshoes and hand grenades, Habib. This is a binary deal. All or nothing. To be, or not to be."

"It's impossible," I muttered.

"This is America, Habib—nothing's impossible! That's why you came here, right? To pull yourself up by your bootstraps and make your own way\. To live the American dream." Brad tilted his head and his drink, deposited the remnants of the oversize ice cube into his mouth, then gargled and fellated and chomped until it dissolved.

Everything about this conversation was insane. Everything about this entire week was insane. In the face of such insanity, how was I to respond? I stared through the overpriced amber poison in my glass.

"It's a lot to take in, Habib. But cheer up. I've got another surprise for you." Brad shouted for the hostess and she scurried over. "We're ready to go," he told her.

She shot me an inviting smile and encouraged me to follow them. *The fuck is this?* I reluctantly stood and hobbled over. We walked into the main vestibule, then through a gauche red curtain into a dim hallway. The hostess glided elegantly down the lengthy corridor to the last door on the left.

Brad told me to cover my eyes. I refused, but the hostess gently cupped my face from behind, deftly avoiding my bruises while pressing her pillowy breasts into my back. Brad opened the door and I stumbled inside. The hostess removed her silky-soft hands, Brad flicked the light switch, and the familiar faces of dozens of assholes greeted us with a hearty "SURPRISE!"

$$$

Several hours later, after I'd been plied with an endless stream of top-shelf whiskey, I told everyone in the private VIP bar, including Brad, I loved them. And they were the best family I could ever hope for, and this was the best surprise birthday party *ever*. I seemed to have forgotten I was being held hostage and getting blackmailed for alleged crimes I had nothing to do with. Also, I probably should've avoided binge drinking so soon after suffering a major concussion. Oh well, YOLO.

I ambled into a half circle of Keith, Karen, Jennie, and Preston. *Fucking Preston.* The whole room spun and swayed. I was dozens of drinks past the point of no return. Every burnt slider and bacon-wrapped date I jammed into my mouth made the forthcoming vomit more flavorful. I stretched out my arms and hugged Preston. What could I offer Jennie that he couldn't provide a thousandfold? I desperately wanted her, and she was desperately out of my league. I told Preston I respected him (lie), and he was a better man than me (lie), and I hoped Jennie was happy (truth). He peeled me off, smiled, and said something I couldn't make out, which was surely patronizing. I draped my arm around Keith to avoid collapsing.

"I think maybe you've had enough," Keith said, removing the drink from my hand.

"Actually . . . the problem I see . . . is none of *you* have had enough," I slurred.

Jennie handed me a glass of water. She was the best. I tried to take a sip but poured several ice-cold ounces down my chest. *Refreshing.*

"I still can't believe what happened to Dan and Ben," Keith said. "Paul did them dirty."

"Do you actually feel bad for them? Or are you still sulking about the fifty K you lost?" Karen said.

"You must've known beforehand!" Keith replied.

"Think whatever you want. We bet, fair and square. Will you wire the money to me and Dennis? Or write a personal check?"

"There's like a twenty-dollar fee for wires. Can I Venmo you instead?"

Preston guffawed like a tipsy giraffe. Karen smirked and said they'd work it out later. Keith's head sagged next to mine. I patted his back and told him he shouldn't bet on stupid things. Irony was dead to me. The conversation hit a natural lull. Jennie and Preston drifted from the crowd and readied to leave. Later, they'd make passionate love, and I'd watch porn and masturbate while thinking about them making passionate love. A sort of metaphysical cuckoldom. Karen went searching for the perfect selfie while Keith and I lamented our woes. The cacophony of shouting and shitty alt-rock rang in my ears. I leaned firmly into Keith and was nearly asleep when high-pitched interference jolted me awake like slamming car brakes.

"All right, everybody, settle down. Settle down for a sec," Brad, standing on the red velvet bar, screeched into his handheld microphone. "I hope everyone's enjoying themselves. It's been a helluva week. And I can see you all, like me, needed a stiff drink. Or ten." Assorted chuckles.

"But we're not just here to let off steam, people. We're here to celebrate the man of the hour. Mister Mujahideen himself. Al-Qaeda's in the house, ladies and gentlemen! So let's give him a big round of applause, and wish a happy belated birthday to everyone's favorite sleeper agent!" Rabid cheers all around.

"You know, Al, for a while we weren't sure if you'd pull through. Karen was making prop bets like a Vegas crackhead, and quite frankly, I'm pretty sure she wanted you to die." Scattered boos.

"Fuck you, Brad!" Karen screamed from somewhere behind me.

"Name the time and place!" Brad said. "But seriously, Al, you gave us quite the scare, and we're so thrilled you survived. Dad said without you, not only would we have lost a top analyst and an all-around great guy, we'd have also lost a crucial diversity hire." Uproarious laughter. "So to show you how much you mean to all of us—especially me—we got you an extra-special birthday present."

In my inebriated stupor, I hadn't realized Keith and Dennis had situated me in a dining chair in the middle of the room. The crowd coalesced into a makeshift runway. Struggling to keep my eyes open, I surveyed the scene. Everything spun like a kaleidoscope. The lights dimmed and a red hue enveloped the room. "Hit the music!" Brad shouted into the mic. A sleepy bass line thumped with gentle guitar strums. The crowd erupted. I forced my eyes wide. And held my breath.

Kelly Clarkson's booming voice, in all its Bose-quality bravado, slammed into me like a tsunami. A figure burst through the door and walked straight toward me. Shiny red sequins glistened as she made a beeline down the metaphorical red carpet. I smiled, drunken and drooling. She crouched down in front of me, placed her tiara on my head, and planted a luscious kiss on my cheek. Her perfume drowned my nostrils. I almost gagged. Something wasn't right. The crowd—the best family I could've ever asked for—howled in delight. The stripper turned her back to me, then ripped her dress in half. A red G-string clung to a perfect ass. For an inside linebacker. The body was shaped like a prototypical V. The stripper spun around, revealing Bolo Yeung–caliber pecs, flawless six-pack abs, and an erect penis sheathed in a red harness.

"We heard you like Asians, Al!" Brad shouted into the mic. The crowd was euphoric, gasping for breath between bloodthirsty cheers and hyena-like cackles.

The stripper continued gyrating and thrusting and torquing in front of me, rubbing his hands down my shoulders and his fingers across my lips. He was, objectively, a beautiful physical specimen, but I was, decidedly, not gay. For years I'd tried to convince myself I was, being beyond useless with women and all. And while I wholeheartedly agreed sexuality resided on a spectrum, I lived year-round in Toxic Heteroville. Maybe it was deep-seated insecurity.

Or decades of media stereotyping. Or some combination therein. I just knew my own hairy brown penis—dangling ridiculously off my body like vestigial flesh—repulsed me. And I couldn't countenance some random dude's tethered dong—impressive though it was— flopping around in my face.

I lunged from my seat and pushed the stripper back and shouted apologies at him as I fumbled toward the door. The deafening music disrupted my severely limited echolocation. I exited into the long hallway. Everyone hooted and hollered behind me. Brad muffled something indecipherable into the mic. I shot past the hostess stand. She glanced at me with pitying eyes. That was all I was to everyone. A punch line. A joke.

I barged into the open air, suddenly flushed and boiling hot. Tears welled in my eyes. Across the street I dropped to my hands and knees behind a rectangular hedge and ejected my soul onto the sidewalk. The acidic soup stung my throat and seeped into my sinuses. Johnnie Blue tasted just as awful on the way up as down.

After three evacuation cycles, I thought of the vomit scene from *Team America: World Police* and tried to laugh. Then I realized I was sobbing. Involuntarily. Gasping like a toddler. I kept my eyes closed and held still, trying to stop my head from spinning. Foot-steps worked their way toward me. Probably Brad with his stupid microphone, ready to pile on. "Fuck off, okay," I said, spitting flecks of vomit like sunflower seeds.

A spotless pair of Cole Haans stopped a foot from my face. I squinted into the streetlight above. It was Damon. He grabbed my elbow and helped me to my feet, then handed me a bottle of water and a roll of Mentos.

"Let's get a drink," he said.

# SCENARIO

By some miracle of physics, I wasn't caked in vomit. Damon and I sat silently in a dark booth at a local dive off Columbus. Me nursing what tasted like the new, semen-flavored Gatorade, him a Jack and Coke. Staticky speakers serenaded us with Steely Dan's "Dirty Work." An absolute classic. I felt like death. But Damon looked sharp in his shiny blue suit and crisp white undershirt. He rocked a shaggy beard against a tight fade and had big brown eyes a shade lighter than mine, with smooth brown skin a shade darker.

The two of us had become fast, then best friends during our formative years at NYU. We'd both majored in finance, shared a love of college football, nineties hip-hop, and Marvel comic books, and oft reflected on our experiences of being brown-skinned boys birthed and raised by batshit-crazy White women. We lost touch when I joined Prism and he stayed out east to attend Yale Law, then picked up right where we left off when he moved to San Francisco to take a position in the corporate M&A group at Conrad, Christie, and Cline, a high-powered law firm colloquially known as "Triple C."

Damon glanced back and forth between a college football game on his phone and the Warriors–Blazers game on the TV above the liquor shelf, waiting for me to reanimate.

"Who's winning?" I asked, semicoherent.

"Stanford, by one. Oregon State's about to go for two and the win," he said.

"Lemme see."

He turned the phone around and we watched the final meaningful play of the game. Oregon State, for reasons that will forever remain baffling, tried a fake double-reverse pass on the two-point attempt, which the wide receiver threw into the first row of the quarter-filled stadium.

"Horrible call," Damon said.

"You can't run gimmick plays that close to the end zone. The field's too compressed and there's no room to maneuver," I said didactically.

Damon nodded in agreement. "Feeling better?"

*In what sense?* Physically, yes, I felt better. A decade of public regurgitations had confirmed I couldn't keep down hard liquor. The upshot? I avoided the hangovers and definitively ruled out the idea of drinking myself to death, à la *Leaving Las Vegas*. Did I feel better emotionally? Psychologically? *Spiritually?* The jury was still out.

"Can you drag your sorry ass home by yourself?" Damon prodded.

"Yeah, yeah, for sure. I just need to get my shit together."

"You need to find a new job. The point-one-percenter class is bad for your health." I nodded. He wasn't wrong, and this wasn't the first time he'd suggested I pursue greener pastures. "Seriously, though, Al, *every* person at that bar was straight garbage. Why not bail?"

My lips moved, but I hesitated to speak. Damon was my best,

perhaps my only, friend. Did I really want to implicate him in Paul and Brad's web of insanity? When things went sideways for me—and they invariably would—Damon might also end up in Paul's crosshairs. "It's . . . complicated. I've thought about quitting, but this week I fucked up big-time. Paul's giving me a second chance. I feel like I owe him."

"You don't need some White man's charity," Damon said. "And you don't *owe* him shit. That's exactly what rich guys like Paul want you to think. To feel like you *owe* them so they can act like they *own* you. That way, once they're done fucking you, they'll say they did you a favor."

Damon sipped his drink. "I speak from experience, Al. I threatened to leave Triple C three damn times to get my salary bumped. White boys I graduated with still make twenty percent more than me. And now every time I see my boss, he gives me some bullshit lecture about 'loyalty' and being a 'team player.'"

"All part of the game, right?"

"No doubt. But at least I'm playing. Seems like you're laying down."

That one stung. But maybe he was right. Maybe I'd forgotten how to fight. Maybe I'd gone soft, with my fancy job and six-figure bonuses. Forgotten where I'd come from. Forgotten how hard I'd worked to avoid becoming another faceless statistic. Forgotten what I'd overcome. Teen mom. Absentee dad. Terrorist name. The cards had been stacked against me my whole life, but I kept playing. Kept doubling down on my shitty hands. Kept surviving. Kept *winning*.

"Can we keep it a hundred, Dame?"

"Always."

"Paul's got me over a barrel," I said. "I can't quit because I have to make back the money I lost this week. If I don't, they'll drop the hammer on me."

"Fuck's that mean?"

"It means I'm fucked. I've got *three months* to recover *three hundred million*. Otherwise they're going to pin some dickhead's suspicious trades on me and turn me over to the Feds."

"Paul *said* that?!"

"No, Brad did."

"Brad said that shit, *specifically*? That's fucking textbook blackmail, Al."

"I can't prove it. The only time he said it *explicitly* was before the party. And he made me turn off my phone while we talked."

"White boys always be scheming."

"Paul's not dumb. He won't leave a paper trail. At best, it's my word versus his. You want to represent me in that case?"

"I'm your boy, Al, so I'd have to recuse myself."

"Right."

"How do you know they're not bluffing?" Damon asked. "Or that they won't fuck you even if you make back the money?"

"What choice do I have? It's me versus Wall Street's most notorious decabillionaire. A guy who hangs out with senators and CEOs. It's like you said: I either play the game, or I lay down."

"Damn," Damon said. He then mumbled to himself, "You got no proof. You can't produce any proof—unless you record Paul or Brad incriminating themselves *outside* of California. And even if you *could* produce any proof, there isn't a law firm in the country that'd represent your Muslim-sounding ass against the mighty Prism Capital," before matter-of-factly declaring, "Bruh, you are fucked."

"Thank you for that expert legal analysis."

"Sorry," Damon said. "You know I have your back, Al. What can I do to help?"

"Got a time machine?"

We commiserated quietly for a long while. The Warriors stunned the Blazers in double overtime on a half-court heave by Steph Curry. He made the impossible mundane. I sipped a Sierra Nevada. Damon texted furiously, no doubt targeting his next destination and livelier company. Working West Coast–market hours meant it was well past my bedtime. Damon had no such constraints. He said his friend was hosting a party in Dogpatch and promised "lots of girls" if I wanted to let off some steam. The prospect didn't inspire. I didn't inspire. Cheap hookups weren't my thing. Besides, what lucid person would copulate with me in my current condition?

Damon gathered his things, then removed a business card from his pocket and wrote something on the back. "Listen, Al. You ain't heard this from me, but there's a guy who might be able to help with your . . . predicament. He's a high-net-worth client of ours and—how do I say this?—has been known to traffic in *sensitive* information." He handed me the card. "Dial the number on the back. The call will go straight to voicemail. Leave a message saying you're a prominent hedge fund analyst who's looking for a little 'R and R.' Use that exact phrase: R and R. Leave a phone number but don't provide your real name. I recommend using a burner." I gawked at him, perplexed. "You want to play the game, right? Then you need to get on the winning team, feel me?"

I twiddled the card in my hand and eyed the number.

"Just trust me, Al. You didn't hear this from me either, but take a look at a biotech company called Clockwork Therapeutics. Several interested parties want to acquire it, and I wouldn't be surprised if a deal got announced soon. Maybe even late next week."

# WORD ON THE STREET

*Wednesday, November 18*

M onday and Tuesday delivered unusually light news flow. Markets reeled in the wake of the Icarus crash, with stock prices drifting downward on both panic selling from allegedly sophisticated investors and doomsday prognosticating from clickbait-driven media outlets. It was the perfect time to be greedy. Had I been a legitimate long-term investor instead of a glorified day trader, I would've bought a Vanguard stock index ETF, shut off my computer for the next two years, and doubled my money. Unfortunately, my psychotic boss and his dipshit son had decided time was more valuable than cash.

"Day three, Habib," Brad said, approaching my desk from behind. "Day three and you've produced *zero* investment ideas and *zero* dollars. Need I remind you what's at stake?"

I spun around and glowered at him. He wore a spicy-mustard-yellow blazer with burnt orange elbow patches and brown corduroy pants. Why he insisted on dressing like a decaying boomer had baffled everyone in the office. "I'm working up a solid idea. Should have something by end of day."

"It better be good," he said, then turned to Keith and Karen. "Dad wants a portfolio strategy update ASAP. Send me a mock prospectus and be ready to meet with Dad first thing tomorrow morning, got it?" He skirted away before they could respond.

"This is bullshit," Karen said, loudly, in my general direction. "Al pisses away our entire portfolio and gets a promotion? While we're left to rebuild his house of cards? You got photos of Paul fucking a dead hooker?"

"For Christ's sakes, leave him alone," Keith said. "He almost died last week. And Brad's got his head jammed even farther up Al's ass."

"Whatever," Karen said. She flashed me her entitled death stare and stormed off.

Keith turned to me. "Seriously, Al, *do you* have photos of Paul fucking a dead hooker?"

"I'm managing my own fund, but Paul's got me on a very, *very* short leash. One misstep and I'm finished."

"Seems like that's the case for everyone," Keith said. "What idea are you working on?"

"I'd rather not say."

"C'mon, Al, you think I'll scoop you?"

"No, no. It's just, the diligence is shoddy. I don't love it."

"Want to stress test it?"

"Let me take a walk and think it over," I deflected. "I'll let you know."

Keith frowned, and I felt like a neglectful boyfriend. Before Icarus, it would've been a no-brainer for me, him, and Jennie to analyze an investment thesis together. The three of us were Prism's token minorities, though our respective experiences varied wildly. Jennie was American-born Chinese and fetishized by everyone in the office, myself most pathetically included. Keith was half Japanese and presented as White, which meant he could pass as one of the boys. I was half Pakistani and presented as full Pakistani, which made me the beneficiary of an endless onslaught of racialized abuse, fueled primarily by jealousy at my superior performance. Even Jennie and Keith had fired off a few friendly slurs.

We were more alike than not, however, so we'd stuck together as a tight-knit trio in and outside of Prism's offices, inevitably forming a sexless love triangle with me and Keith vying for Jennie's disinterested affections. When the perfect specimen known as Preston came along—*Fucking Preston*—Jennie jettisoned us half-breeds, and Keith and I were left to pick up the pieces.

I liked Keith. Mostly. Within Prism, he came closest to being a friend. But with Paul and Brad's fun-loving game of blackmail in full swing, I couldn't trust him anymore. What if he took my Clockwork intel and presented the opportunity to Paul and Brad before me? Or what if he shared it with someone else who did the same? If Paul gave another fund the go-ahead, I'd be left with nothing. Worse still, I *knew* my prospective bet—based on Damon's tip—violated every insider trading law on the books. Keith may have been a compulsive gambler and a mediocre stock picker, but he wasn't a bad guy. The least I could do was spare him a conspiracy charge.

The deeper truth was, I couldn't trust *anyone* in the office. Less than a week ago, these savages paid a male stripper to jam his cock into my face, on my birthday, following a traumatic head injury, and thought it was hysterical. They'd watch my back simply to locate the best spot for the knife.

$$$

An hour later I was sitting on a park bench near the Ferry Building feeling mopey and stuffed. I'd gorged myself on a porchetta sandwich and a bucket of sweet potato fries at the pop-up farmers' market. Normally this was a once-per-month affair, but this outing marked the second time in a week. For a few fleeting moments, I considered the possibility of eating myself to death, but then remembered that traumatizing scene from *Se7en* and disabused myself of the notion. The movie came out when I was six years old, but I'd waited until I was ten to see it. I should've had better parents.

I examined the people bustling around me. A skinny brunette wearing a Black Lives Matter T-shirt. A homeless, wizened Black man asleep on the sidewalk. A pudgy guy in a clown suit. A middle-aged dude riding a unicycle (not the clown). A chubby Asian girl in a Hello Kitty onesie. A murder of indistinguishable White dudes, wearing indistinguishable Twitter hoodies, on a bar crawl.

How many of these people had committed crimes? Had they pulled them off? How many of them had contemplated suicide? Of those who had, had they considered it once, in a fit of acute despair? Or had those thoughts progressed into a daily preoccupation? Persistent, intrinsic, and unshakable, no matter how high the SSRI dose—like mine? I theorized that people who didn't think about suicide every day were either total idiots or completely self-absorbed. Perhaps those were the same thing.

I refocused on Damon's tip, turning it over and over in my mind, trying to see all the angles. He'd told me, in no uncertain terms—or at least in no uncertain *Wall Street* terms—a deal was imminent. "Late next week" implied Thursday's market close. Companies rarely announced deals on Fridays because that was when the ultrarich flew to their offshore mansions, typically located in sunny, exotic, low-tax locales, for the weekend. Plus, it was way more fun and extra sadistic to make the junior bankers work through the weekend. Monday morning was by far the most popular time to disclose mergers and acquisitions.

Knowing this, I had two decisions to make. First, would I willingly and knowingly trade on illicit information? And second, if so, how could I produce a justifiable defense of such a trade? I always prided myself on what I'd branded my blue-collar work ethic and white-collar brain. I'd fared well in the intellectual genetic lottery—somehow—but I was also willing to work harder than everyone else. By combining the two, I delivered exceptional returns *and* maintained the intellectual moral high ground.

It was the Batman and Daredevil philosophy: They occupied the gray zones—breaking bones, damaging property, trespassing, impinging on civil liberties, spying, stealing, whatever it took—but they wouldn't kill. Once they crossed that line, they were no better than the villains. The same logic applied at Prism. Surrounded by miscreants, hooligans, scallywags, and loose women, I simply had to grind harder, dig deeper, and be smarter. Then and only then could I declare myself better than them. Which I'd done, time and time and time again.

The flip side of that coin presented the Barry Bonds conundrum. At the midpoint of his career, he was a modern-day Willie Mays, and already one of the greatest baseball players ever. But what did he have to show for it? Nobody cared about stolen bases and defensive prowess. Everyone had turned their attention to Mark McGwire and Sammy Sosa's steroid-soaked home run bonanza.

Pre-juice, McGwire was at least a perennial all-star and likely Hall of Famer. But Sosa? He was replacement-level. When Bonds saw what they could achieve with a little horse testosterone coursing through their veins, he justifiably wondered: *How much better could I be on that shit?* Which got me to wondering: How much better could *I* be on that shit?

$$$

"Clockwork Therapeutics," I announced after barging into Brad's office. He was gnawing on a piece of beef jerky and surfing r/wallstreetbets.

"Vhut thuhfuk iz that."

"It's a small biotech developing a drug for a genetic disorder called Wilson's disease. I want to build a twenty-five-million-dollar long position as quickly as possible. I received an anon—"

"Stop," he said, then painstakingly swallowed the wad of dehydrated cow flesh. "Lift up your shirt and let me see your phone."

"Seriously?"

He walked around his desk and stood in front of me. I handed him my iPhone, which he powered off, then I lifted my shirt, turned around, and raised each of my pants legs. I thought the charade was over, but then Brad cupped my dick with one of his tiny rat claws.

"What the fuck!?" I said, swatting it away.

"You can never be too sure," he said. "Clockwork—why does that name ring a bell?"

"Darren's team invested in the IPO," I said. "They hit a double before cashing out." I loosened my belt and adjusted my manhood and straightened and retucked my shirt. I wasn't fat, but I wasn't skinny, either, and I hated that feeling of errant cloth clinging to my love handles. Better to package everything up neatly and bury it under flattering attire, one of the few lessons I'd learned from my mom.

"Why get back in now?" Brad asked.

*Here goes.* "Clockwork announced positive phase two data for its lead compound a few months ago, which was a significant de-risking event. But the stock didn't pop because it'd already had a huge run. It's plummeted fifteen percent since the Icarus debacle. With data in hand, however, they're well positioned as one of the top takeout candidates in the biotech space, where M and A is currently on fire. Over the past several weeks there's been significant takeout speculation in the *Wall Street Journal* and *Financial Times*. I also conducted two expert calls through GLG with KOLs at the Mayo Clinic and UCSF. Both said the clinical data was pristine, and both had high confidence Clockwork's lead drug would ace a phase three program. Finally, I modeled a risk-adjusted NPV analysis and determined the company was worth at least sixty-two bucks a share. Fully de-risked, it's potentially worth eighty to ninety. Right now, the stock's at forty-seven. It's an event-driven play, but it's thoroughly backed by fundamentals."

Brad rubbed his chin and pretended to look smart. "And you've documented all this?"

"A full investment thesis using our standard template. One other thing: A diligence call with IP lawyers at Triple C confirmed the patent estate's rock-solid."

Brad contemplated my corrupt stock pitch for several long moments. "Let's cut the bullshit, Habib. You do realize if you fuck this up, you're even deeper in the hole, right?"

"If we're cutting the bullshit, let's remember you and Daddy are the ones who imposed an impossible deadline on me. Am I supposed to double the money buying treasury bonds?"

He chuckled dismissively. "Oh, Habib, you see the irony, right? If Dad lets you make this trade and the SEC comes calling, and you can't back it up—"

"This trade is supported by expert fundamental analysis," I asserted with faux confidence. "That said . . . word on the street is, a deal could happen imminently. I only need like two percent of the float, and the stock does monster volume. I should be able to grab a few blocks without disturbing the market."

Brad huffed, then took out his phone and started typing. I waited while his eyes fixated on the screen. A few moments later he looked up. "Dad wants to hear your thesis."

# 1-800-SUICIDE

*Monday, November 23*

Thursday came and went with no deal. So did Friday. On Saturday, I grabbed coffee with Damon and frantically asked WTF was going on. He told me to chill and expect good news on Monday morning. What choice did I have? On Sunday, I watched twenty-four minutes of "in-play" NFL football, three hundred minutes of televised ads, and forty-five minutes of Pornhub. It was two in the morning, technically Monday, and I couldn't sleep. Pre-market press releases normally dropped by 5 a.m. Pacific time. Within a few hours, I'd know exactly how fucked I was.

I grabbed my phone from the flipped-over laundry basket that doubled as my nightstand, opened an incognito tab, and searched for "best ways to commit suicide." The top result implored me to call a 1-800 number and assured me my life was worth living. Sure. Lower down came news stories highlighting recent trends in suicide rates and speculating as to how our latest, ongoing financial crisis would exacerbate the "national tragedy" fueled by so-called "deaths of despair." At the very bottom of the page, a few depraved websites and Reddit forums provided the intel I was after. Unfortunately, as I clicked and scrolled through, I realized I'd read all the links before.

According to the CDC, guns were by far the most efficacious method for committing suicide, and were also the preferred life-terminating choice among men ages twenty-five to thirty-four. They really were flawlessly designed products. As I'd concluded many times, shooting myself in the chest would properly marry effectiveness, efficiency, and elegance, while also keeping my brain intact so researchers could analyze postmortem for CTE or other neurological disorders. Problem was, I didn't own a gun. And despite growing up in Florida, I'd never seen one, held one, or known how to buy one. California's gun laws were far too restrictive—maybe the neo-cons and technolibertarians were onto something—and I was too depressed and lazy to rent a car and drive to Nevada or some other lawless shithole to procure one illegally. I likewise worried that if I did tool up, I'd almost certainly puss out at the critical moment and blow off my left nipple. Even dying was too painful.

I continued scrolling. The *seventh*-best suicide method on an amateurish web page laden with pop-up ads for knockoff Viagra grabbed my attention. *Guillotine.* I read on, intrigued. The author claimed guillotines were exceptionally effective and practically painless, with the added bonus that all the necessary materials were available at Big Box hardware stores. A great DIY for the whole family! The guillotine was such a testament to human ingenuity France had used it for two hundred consecutive years—last seen chopping heads in *1977!*—as its preferred method for capital punishment.

I opened another incognito tab and typed "homemade guillotine." The results astounded. Years earlier, a man in rural Michigan had constructed a mobile contraption—employing a system of pulleys and a swinging machete—and ended his days in a remote part of the wilderness. And just last year, a dude in New York City upped the innovation quotient. He'd tied one end of a chain around a telephone pole, wrapped the other around his neck, got into his car, and floored the accelerator. The *New York Post* documented the incident with its typical care and finesse.

*The courage of those men.* I always resented arguments about how people who took their own lives were cowardly or weak. It was just the opposite. A person required immense strength and tenacity to *knowingly* put their head in a *homemade fucking guillotine*. And then go through with it. I considered such feats the ultimate form of bravery. The ultimate representation of agency. A declaration that one's existence was invalid and nonsensical, and a dignified rejection of its absurd premise. *If only I had a fraction of that strength within me.* I put my phone on airplane mode, rolled over, and placed a pillow over my head. Maybe I'd get lucky and suffocate.

$$$

Four hours later I was, regrettably, alive. I glanced at my phone, then shot out of bed. *Fuck, fuck, fuck!* I tapped off airplane mode and stared at the phone's screen like it was a ticking time bomb. The dreadful number in the dreadful red circle in the corner of my email app shot from 22 to 502. Over twenty voicemails and two hundred texts followed. My heart raced with anticipation. This much panic on the screen usually meant a CEO had been crucified, though I considered the possibility of good news.

I started with the texts. Brad. Damon. Keith. Karen. Dennis. *Jennie?!* Her message said: *Everyone's looking for you. Are you ok?* That didn't inspire confidence.

Damon next: $, 🐢, $, 🦙, $. A much better sign!

What did Brad have to say? Twenty-odd messages in some variation of: *[Where the/what the] [fuck/hell] [are you/are you doing], [Racist Caricature]?*

I dialed his work phone. While the call connected, a blinking red light caught my eye. It was the LED indicator on the burner. I opened it and found dozens more texts from (I assumed) Brad inquiring about my whereabouts.

"Where the fuck are you!"

"I couldn't sleep, then I must've overslept. What's up?"

"What's up is your stock is blowing the fuck up! Novartis announced a three-billion-dollar deal for Clockwork two fucking hours ago!"

*Sonofabitch.* Alone in the dark, my grin stretched from ear to ear. "What's the premium?"

"How the fuck should I know?"

"I'm going to sell everything ASAP—is that okay?"

"Yes, you fucking moron! I was about to have Robbie pull the trigger. It'd be a lot easier if you did your own fucking job!"

"On it."

"Don't do anything else until you've unloaded every single share. And text me when you're done," Brad said, then hung up.

I logged in and got to work. I—or rather, Prism—was the beneficial owner of stock, options, and other esoteric derivatives equating to over six hundred thousand common shares of Clockwork Therapeutics. The delayed deal announcement had proved quite fortuitous. After Paul gave me the go-ahead and Compliance approved my trades, I'd snagged a little over three hundred thousand shares by Thursday afternoon. Since I originally anticipated an announcement at market close, I'd aggressively supplemented my position with call options. But then no deal came through.

On Friday morning, our Jefferies account manager told me she'd found another two hundred thousand shares at the unlikeliest of places: the "development fund" for the Church of Jesus Christ of Latter-day Saints. They had a legacy position in Clockwork because one of its pipeline compounds originated at BYU. I was pot committed by then, so figured why the hell not and pushed all in. The Mormons had been content with their $5 million return, and their prudence became my providence. At Novartis's announced all-cash acquisition price of $85.54 per share, my nascent fund held $51 million of equity value and had generated a $24 million return.

When the dust settled and our brokers had offloaded our shares to a bunch of dipshit merger arbs and other event-driven donkeys, I breathed an indulgent sigh of relief. In one single trade, I'd put a massive dent in my three-hundred-million-dollar hole. *Maybe, just maybe, I can pull this off.*

I informed Brad, inhaled a trough of Grape-Nuts, Greek yogurt, and frozen strawberries, guzzled a second carafe of coffee, and clogged my undersize toilet with an unholy deposit. After resolving that problem, I enjoyed a celebratory wank, took a steaming-hot shower, threw on my favorite navy suit, and levitated to the office.

Walking toward my cube, I received a conquering hero's welcome. Hugs and high fives and "Death to the infidels!" greeted me throughout the hall. Keith enveloped me in a bear hug. Dennis slipped an edible I wouldn't eat into my hand. Even Karen, who'd been forced to hype my trade on Prism's official Twitter account, bestowed a reluctant "Nice work, Al." That must've hurt. The celebration could've lasted for a glorious eternity, but Paul's booming baritone smothered the brewing bonhomie like a chloroform-soaked rag.

"Nice of you to join us this morning," he said to me. The small but growing crowd went still. Brad lingered at Paul's side like a demented bridge troll. "Quite the play you pulled off. Good to see you haven't lost your edge."

"The sun shines on a blind squirrel's ass once in a while. Or whatever," I said.

"Twenty-four million's quite a nut," Paul said. "Let's discuss what you've got planned for an encore."

A tense silence consumed the crowd, like I'd been summoned to the principal's office in a high school dramedy. Everyone dispersed and I followed Paul and Brad to the lion's den.

After the surrendering-phones-and-checking-for-wires dance—Brad didn't fondle my manhood this time—we sat in the dreaded leadership center. They sipped cappuccinos from Peet's but didn't offer me anything.

"How'd you know about the Clockwork deal?" Paul asked.

*"Know?"*

"Dad didn't stutter, Habib," Brad said. "Answer the question."

"Well, I didn't *know* anything. Like I said, I got the initial idea from a sell-side note. JPM's been humping them as a takeout play, so I took a closer look and liked what I saw. Given my, um, circumstances, I was trying to think a little outside the box. Get more aggressive."

"That's all well and good," Paul said. "But my question remains: How did you know about the Clockwork deal?"

"Look, Paul, I'm being completely honest with you here. I didn't—"

"Shut the fuck up. I know you got an insider tip. And I want to know who told you."

I didn't know what to say. I couldn't rat out Damon. I'd told him Paul was holding me hostage and he was only trying to help. He certainly hadn't signed up to be a coconspirator in my inevitable downfall. I sat motionless and, as instructed, shut the fuck up. Maybe I'd pass out again from the stress.

"The foundation of any good relationship is trust, Al," Paul said, shifting his tone. "I trusted you with a fresh pot of capital—despite Bradley's vocal protestations—and I trusted you on Clockwork. And so far, my trust has been rewarded. But now we need to trust each other on a deeper level. On a fundamental level. If you're going to manage your own portfolio for me—after you've reconciled your debts, of course—I need to know everything you know. If there's any doubt in a relationship, any bit of distrust, no matter how small, the relationship becomes brittle. And eventually breaks. Broken relationships never quite recover. Do you understand what I'm saying, Al?"

*That I'm a fucking hostage?! YES!* The sublime solipsism of the 0.0000001% defied comprehension. "Paul, I told you everything. I swear." He gazed at me quizzically for a solid ten seconds. I would've rather stared at Medusa.

"Fine," he relented. "What's next, then? You're off to a strong start, but we're still in the first inning. Your—how did you describe it?—'circumstances' haven't changed. But I have faith in you, Al. I'm rooting for you. But I'm not sure I'm betting on you just yet—if you know what I mean."

"I don't have a clear strategy," I stammered. "Clockwork came to me on a whim. I'm not sure which sector to play in next. Obviously, I'm not long-term oriented—"

"Obviously," Paul quipped.

"—so I haven't had time to develop a new thematic approach. For now, I'm looking for binary events with massive asymmetric upside."

Paul smirked and reclined into the sofa, stretching his arms wide across the backrest.

Brad gulped down the remainder of his cappuccino. "We need three ideas by Wednesday morning," he said. "Otherwise, you should get used to the idea of having a Black boyfriend."

"Is that all?" I stood to leave, fantasizing about lodging an ice pick in Brad's forehead.

"One more thing," Paul said. He leaped from the couch, jogged a diagonal across the room, disappeared into the humidor, and emerged a few seconds later with a wooden box containing a dozen Cuban cigars. "Take these and celebrate with the team," he said affably. Then his face tightened and his eyes narrowed. "And then you better dream up another killer fucking trade idea—with 'massive asymmetric upside.'" With that, he shoved the box of cigars into my gut and nudged me toward the door.

"Good luck!" Brad gloated.

# STAKES IS HIGH

U S markets closed higher on "renewed M&A enthusiasm," but were still firmly in bear territory. My stomach cried out for nourishment around two, but my brain had gone numb. Idling at my desk, I clicked back and forth between Bloomberg, FactSet, Outlook, and ESPN.com. Every now and then I looked at my portfolio balance. Tradeable funds: $324 million. I'd had a monster day, but it didn't feel that way. I still owed the house $276 million and, worse still, had no discernible path forward. *What the fuck am I going to do now?* That was life's only relevant question. I never had any answers.

Paul and Brad wanted *ideas*, which meant trading tactics, which meant get-rich-quick schemes. But that wasn't how my brain worked. I was—at the risk of sounding like the douchiest McKinsey-humping corporatist cuck on God's green earth—a *strategy* guy. I liked big themes and big topics: new technological innovations, scientific breakthroughs, emerging economies, burgeoning markets, and the cultural zeitgeist. When I studied those types of concepts, I could synthesize a worldview and identify how our society might change, evolve, or adapt.

Take the iPhone. When the device debuted, everyone knew it would be a monster hit. The obvious play was to buy Apple stock. The less obvious but even more profitable strategy was to also buy securities in the iPhone's chip developer, and its touch screen manufacturer, and the mining company that dug up the molybdenum and other rare earth elements required to make the damn things. On the flip side, if you had the stones, you'd short the shit out of BlackBerry and Nokia, too.

Everybody saw this strategy in hindsight. The true goal—the way to become a legitimate Master of the Universe—was to identify the strategy beforehand. I fancied myself one of the rare few with the talent to do so, and I'd delivered proof of concept during my introductory finance course at NYU. My professor liked my iPhone investment thesis so much, he put me in contact with the head of the university's endowment fund, who handed me an internship and let me put my aforementioned plan to work with *real* money. NYU generated $150 million over the next four years. I got twelve credit hours.

I used the same methodology to break into Prism and centered my investment thesis on US opioid manufacturers. Americans hated vaccines—the most-studied medical technology in human history—but couldn't shove pills into their diabetic mouths fast enough. Especially if they dulled the pain of neoliberalism's false promises. I used that spark of intuition to rock my interviews with Paul and his then healthcare portfolio manager, Clyde, now deceased (overdose).

When I came on board, Clyde and I built concentrated positions in über heroin manufacturers Insys, Mallinckrodt, and Endo as well as two companies, Lannett and Akorn, which were market-leading producers of naloxone—the drug people took to *reverse* the effects of an opioid overdose (#bothsides). Thirty million dollars turned into a hundred. Clyde cashed out—and checked out—and I became a rising hedge fund star destined for great things.

Paul shuffled me from team to team—agnostic of sector—and let me work my magic. I was practically unbeatable, generating monster returns for Prism year after year after year. The apotheosis of my preternatural "talent" led to the creation of the VICE fund. Paul had ordered me to create an investment approach that could support 20 percent annual returns over one-, three-, five-, and ten-year time horizons. There were some sector-specific strategies that could've achieved those lofty growth objectives. Social media, for example. Or gene therapy. But those bored me. I liked to see how all the puzzle pieces fit together across the entire spectrum of humanity. Not just in one small corner. So I dreamed up VICE. What technological, financial, or sociopolitical phenomena could ensure perpetual gains in the stock market? Human nature. Vicious. Venal. Vapid. Vacuous. The straightest possible line to enormous profits.

I pitched Paul the ultimate portfolio, which ran the gauntlet of man-made depravity. VICE would invest in payday lenders, opioid manufacturers, gunmakers, mining companies, for-profit education, you name it. If it was a blight on our species, it was a surefire moneymaker. Paul green-lighted the plan and rolled me, Keith, Karen, and Dennis under Brad—ensuring his twenty-six-year-old failson would oversee a winning fund—and it took off like a rocket. A rocket that reached escape velocity and promptly crashed into the surface of the moon.

My obvious sure-thing was all but dead. In the wake of the Icarus disaster, politicians had thrown out detestable, reprehensible, positively Orwellian terms like "regulation" and "oversight" and "accountability." And they'd threatened to do the unthinkable: increase corporate taxes, pay restitution to the "alleged" victims of so-called vulture capitalism, and—*my pearls!*—redistribute wealth to the underprivileged. An elite cabal of oligopolists, corporatists, kleptocrats, and neoliberalist cucks might've funded political campaigns, but they didn't hire private mercenaries or buy bunkers in New Zealand. When the mobs came calling—with metaphorical pitchforks and actual AR15s—they'd come for their "representatives." Devoid of any principle beyond survival, and elected through iterative rounds of adverse selection, Congress had pivoted faster than LeBron James.

These thoughts ran through my head as I contemplated that nagging question: *What the fuck am I going to do now?* The world as I knew it, or believed I knew it, had unraveled. Suddenly, I couldn't see all the angles. Couldn't decipher all the data. Couldn't come up with a game plan. The more I thought about it, the more a depressing truth crystallized: *I'm not as smart as I thought.* I'd just been lucky. No different from all the other superrich assholes whipping millions and billions of dollars around with the click of a mouse or a tap on a smartphone.

To win on Wall Street, you cheated, or you got lucky. I'd deluded myself into thinking I was *better*. Reality didn't square with my Batman shtick. Worst of all, luck—like all facets of existence—adhered to a normal distribution. I'd exhausted mine, which meant I'd regress toward the mean, which meant I had nowhere to go but down.

None of this self-indulgent wallowing solved the massive, intractable problem in front of me, of course. I was a so-called strategy guy who'd been reduced to tactics, and the limited tactics available to me reinforced the hopelessness of my predicament. I could continue to play the M&A game and try to defeat the laws of mathematics, like a decomposing chain-smoker at a Reno slot machine. I could short the currency of an alleged Western democracy descending into chaos and fascism. The Hungarian forint, anyone? But that'd be no different from picking red or black at a roulette wheel. And the most obvious currency to bet against—the good ol' greenback, backed by the bad faith and deteriorating credit of the U S of A—was a guaranteed loser. The stock market may have been *efficient*, but what everyone misunderstood was efficient allowed for *dumb as fuck*.

Trades like those amounted to little more than gambling. To play Paul's game—to beat the house—I needed something foolproof. Another Clockwork. And even though I hated myself for exploiting Damon's intel—and Batman and Daredevil were disappointed with me—who could argue with the results?

That was why another nagging thought in the back of my mind kept bubbling to the surface. Concerning the card Damon had handed me after my birthday party debacle. The cagey one. With no names. And the number I was supposed to call with a burner. About "R and R." I'd already opened Pandora's box. Why not see what other horrors streamed out?

$$$

Hours later, lying in bed, I tried to distract myself with the *New York Times* daily crossword puzzle. *Why haven't they called?* I'd followed all the steps. The burner rested, lifeless, on my lap. They'd said eight, and it was quarter past. I set down my iPhone, grabbed the old-school flip device, and scrolled through the text exchange for the dozenth time. There was one message, from a blocked number, and all it said was *8PM*. I looked at it over and over and over again, expecting it to magically change. *8PM.* They hadn't even included a time zone. WTF.

I went back to the crossword and fixated on one of those stupid clues that was a piss-poor double entendre whose answer was a nonstandard abbreviation. And the media wondered why nobody trusted the media anymore. Two more inscrutable hints had my blood near boiling when a call from my mom popped up.

"You're awake?!" she said, sounding drunk.

It was after eleven in Miami, which meant her man of the hour had deposited his life force inside her and skedaddled. With her slim frame, Atlantic blue eyes, and tacky blond highlights, she must've imagined herself as the lead character in an animated Disney movie: If she just screwed enough randos, eventually she'd meet Prince Drug Trafficker and he'd whisk her away to a compound in Colombia. Unfortunately, and predictably, her suitors always had to work early the next morning.

"Obviously I'm still awake," I said. "What are you up to?"

"Oh, nothing. Just, you know, trying to figure it all out."

"How's that working out for you?"

"Not well," she sighed. "When are you going to find a nice girl for yourself?"

*For the love of Christ.* "I don't have time for this. I'm expecting an urgent work call any minute. Do you need something? Or were you just saying hi?"

"I'm worried about you, sweetie. This is the fourth year in a row you won't be home for Thanksgiving. You should quit that awful job of yours and come back to Miami. All the girls at the salon are *dying* to meet you. They see your picture at my station, and they all say you're so dreamy. I could play matchmaker!"

"Are you at home?"

"I don't need you checking up on me, Al. I'm your mother. I'm a grown-ass woman. I can do whatever I want, with whoever I want, wherever I damn well please." After an excruciating silence, she said, "Yes, I'm at home."

"Is the power back to normal?"

"Yes."

"Any issues with the house?"

"No."

For once, some good news. That house was my mom's only asset, and when I was little, refinancing it into perpetuity had kept clothes on our backs and food in our bellies. After I received my first performance bonus from Prism, I'd paid off the ever-expanding mortgage in one fell swoop, and my mom's net worth turned positive for the first time in her sad, regrettable life. I'd been sending her five thousand dollars per month for upkeep and living expenses ever since, which she promptly wasted on scoundrels and unsavory men.

"Anybody staying with you these days?" I asked.

No answer.

Like so many of our conversations, it had taken less than two minutes to grind our respective humanity to dust. I had nothing meaningful to say to this woman. Unless she wanted to stroll down memory lane and reminisce about the countless times I'd caught her screwing a stranger in our Florida room. Or fondly recall how she'd frequently forgotten to pick me up from freshman-year football practice, then awkwardly flirted with my married coach. Or maybe she finally wanted to apologize for laughing *every single time* Jesse, her six-month fling when I was in fourth grade, called me a "camel jockey."

Each pitiful recollection made me more resentful, and each passing second my background panic reached a new octave. *Why the fuck haven't they called?!* I was about to go thermonuclear on my mom, to vent, when the burner chimed. I flipped it open and saw two sparse text messages. The first included a new phone number and the second a single word: *Signal*. I couldn't use the encrypted smartphone app on my burner. *Shit.*

"Gotta go. Urgent work business."

My mom huffed into the phone like a pouty teenager.

"I'll call you later," I lied, then hung up.

I opened the Signal app on my iPhone. I used it regularly to communicate with industry execs, journalists, sell-siders, and fellow hedgies who wanted to stay as far off the grid as possible. But something about this didn't feel right. I didn't want to dial that number. I didn't want to go to prison, either.

On the second ring, a man with an unplaceable European accent answered: "With whom do I have the pleasure of speaking?"

I paused. "Uh, Mike. Mike Johnson."

Awaiting his reply, the call ended. Panic surged into my brain. *Did we get disconnected? Did he hang up on me? What did I do wrong?!* I redialed. On the second ring, the same voice asked the same question. This time, I hesitated, then said, "Ali Jafar. I go by Al."

"Pleasure to meet you, Mister Ali. Please call me Simon. I understand you're interested in a little R *und* R, is that correct?"

"Uh, yeah, I think so."

"And may I ask who recommended you to us?"

"A lawyer I know at Triple C. They said you were a client and might be able to help me out with some, uh, R and R." *What the fuck am I doing?*

Simon chuckled. "And what firm are you with, Mister Ali?"

"Prism Capital. I assume you've heard of it."

"Of course, of course. We service all the major investment houses, though we haven't yet had the privilege of working with anyone at your esteemed firm. Can you meet in New York City this Friday?"

"Two days from now, Friday?"

"Correct."

"For what?"

"For your R *und* R orientation. We require all new clients to complete their introductory session in person. We prefer to establish a professional rapport from the outset. Of course, we ensure the utmost privacy and security."

I'd winged it to this point. What else could go wrong? "Where and when do I meet you?"

"We'll be in touch."

The call ended.

# SIMON SAYS

*Thursday, November 26*

I flew to Newark on Thanksgiving Day without telling Paul and Brad. They'd be apoplectic. They could also go fuck themselves. Thanks to Icarus, Paul's propitiously timed bet against the US bond market had made billions for his firm. I'd generated a nifty twenty-four million on Clockwork in three days' time, too. Prism wasn't exactly strapped for cash, so the three "ideas" he and Brad wanted could wait. Plus, if this R-and-R thing—whatever the fuck it stood for—turned out to be legit, I'd have a helluva lot more to work with than three random rolls of the dice.

And what would Paul do if R and R didn't work out? Fire me? I was beginning to realize being a hostage-cum-corpse conferred some strange, unexpected superpowers. Their threats only mattered if I failed to achieve my objective *and* I intended to remain alive after said failure. We all knew the inevitable outcome of this farce, so I could pretty much do whatever I wanted during my lame-duck period.

I spent Thanksgiving traversing the thinned-out streets of Manhattan, dipping into a random Starbucks every mile or so to warm up and avoiding the parade like the plague. The city was always at its best when everyone was gone, though you could say that about most places. The problem with humanity, after all, was the humans. I celebrated the Native American genocide in a tiny, moldy room at a downtrodden hotel that didn't require a credit card for incidentals. I listened to Ras Kass's "Nature of the Threat" on repeat, watched the Egg Bowl, and feasted in solitude on a makeshift holiday spread from the Whole Foods hot bar.

If I'd planned better, and was less prudish, I could've booked a high-end escort for the evening. I contemplated the idea for two whole seconds before realizing I couldn't fathom a more depressing scenario. Plus, having internalized all the lessons from all the ridiculous action movies and sensationalized spy shows I'd seen, my objective was to stay as under the radar as possible. I'd turned off location services on my personal phone, left the burner in San Francisco, paid cash for the black car I took from EWR into Manhattan, and had done likewise for the moribund hotel. I wore hats and thick scarves everywhere and hadn't shaved. That was to throw off the facial recognition technology that had popped up in big cities all over the country, and was modeled after the Chinese government's crackdown on the Uighur population in Xinjiang. I'd read about said horror show in *The Economist* and knew, as totalitarians went, so did the world's (alleged) greatest democracy. After putting in all that tradecraft, there was no way in hell I was gonna let myself get caught by a $3,000 credit card charge to the Pussy Cat Lounge.

Around midnight, engrossed in a MFFFMFMF mixed-race orgy on Pornhub, a Signal notification from Simon popped up on my phone. It read: *79 Jane St, 10AM.* I wiped the chalky hotel lotion on my underwear and my member went semiflaccid as I opened the message. I didn't know how to respond. *OK! See you there!* 👍? I wanted to acknowledge receipt without seeming like a total amateur. I settled on *Roger* and instantly sounded like a total amateur. Whatever. I purged the baby batter, showered, and fell into a restless sleep.

$$$

The address was located in an unremarkable part of the city, sandwiched between the Meatpacking District and the Village. Shabby row houses, run-down high-rises, and cheap take-out places littered the surrounding streets. As I wrangled my paper map on the way down Hudson Street, making myself quite an attractive target for pickpockets and other undesirables, I wondered if this was another elaborate prank. Maybe "Simon" was in cahoots with Brad—*and Damon?!*—and they all thought it'd be hilarious to have me fly to New York and meet with the head of a secretive organization that provided clandestine services to down-on-their-luck white-collar cucks. The more I thought about it, the funnier it became. If it was all a ruse, I'd have to hand it to them.

The building at 79 Jane Street looked condemned. A rotting brick facade and the burned-out windows on the second floor suggested I should write off this entire episode. Then something incongruous caught my eye: a basement-level entryway outfitted with opaque, state-of-the-art sliding glass doors and a shiny metallic keypad. I descended the stairway and approached the entrance. Mounted security cameras appeared on both flanks. The keypad had a fingerprint scanner and a large doorbell, which I rang.

After a few seconds, the sliding doors opened, and two heavies in matte blue suits emerged. The one with the thick black goatee and curly shoulder-length brown hair told me to raise my arms, then administered a comprehensive pat-down. The other, devoid of any hair whatsoever, scanned me with some kind of flashing wand. After I passed inspection, the goateed one told me to empty my pockets—including my cell phone—into the small plastic bag he'd pulled from his jacket.

"I'll need my ID back," I said.

"No personal effects allowed beyond the security checkpoint," the bald one said. "Protocol."

*Shit just got real.* I wasn't in a position to argue, but at least I was certain this Simon scammer was legit. The security guards directed me to a waiting room with plush black leather furniture. I took a seat on the sofa and immediately recognized I had no idea how to entertain myself without my phone. I rehearsed the talking points I'd scripted. *I'm an analyst at Prism Capital. I understand your firm offers exclusive consulting services, including access to premier expert networks and bespoke investment research. I'd like to engage your firm to help construct my new portfolio.* I'd carefully planned each of those words. That way, if this ended up being some kind of overelaborate FBI pinch, all my coded language would keep me out of trouble. I was just an ambitious hedge funder looking for an edge. That wasn't illegal. It was downright patriotic.

I was literally twiddling my thumbs when Simon entered the waiting room. He was tall and lanky with jet-black hair, baggy hazel eyes, and fair skin. He wore a gunmetal-gray suit with silver pinstripes and a classic white dress shirt with no tie.

"Mister Ali, I presume?"

"That's me," I said, pegging him as Dutch. Or maybe Belgian. He was definitely from somewhere in Western Europe where it rained constantly and everyone was super tall and rode a bicycle to work.

He led me to a private, windowless conference room with bright white walls and a large glass table with comfortable office chairs. After I declined a hot tea, Simon steeped one for himself and finally broke what felt like a week of silence.

"You must forgive all this theatricality, Mister Ali. But, as I'm sure you can appreciate, one cannot be too cautious these days."

"It's a jungle out there," I agreed. "You can call me Al."

"Very well, Mister Al. I'm aware your time is extremely valuable—time is money, after all—so let's begin. Do you wish to convey your specific needs as a potential client? Or would you like a brief overview of our services first?"

"I'll take the overview. But could you tell me—specifically—what R and R is?"

"Ah, the most pertinent question," Simon said with a smile. "Reformation and rehabilitation. R *und* R. It's not a specific service, per se, but a philosophical platform from which we offer many possibilities, depending, of course, on a client's circumstances. Allow me to indulge in a few illustrative examples.

"First, imagine a client who is, much like yourself, a sophisticated financier. But a sophisticated financier who has been unjustly persecuted by oppressive government authorities. Perhaps they've incurred financial penalties. Lost their job. Served prison time, even. R *und* R for such a client might include, among other things, legal consultations, personal loans, networking opportunities, and access to emotional support groups comprised of like-minded peers. Our firm provides opportunities for such clients to get back on their feet. And back in the game, as you Americans might say.

"On the other end of the spectrum, we might have a client who's doing well—thriving, even—but who feels stuck. Someone who's ambitious and hardworking, but not realizing the career growth commensurate with their underlying capabilities. In this case, R *und* R might include expert coaching, access to proprietary research, entrepreneurship opportunities, and exposure to deep-pocketed investors.

"In essence, we provide the tools our clients need to reach the next level. Or, as our firm's mantra states: 'We provide the world's best talent with the world's best resources.'"

"I see." Clearly I'd stumbled into some Goop-for-crusty-old-White-dudes shit.

"Skeptical, Mister Al? I should hope so. Our clients are among the most successful executives, politicians, and financiers in the world. They would not be in their positions if they were idiots. But I can assure you: Our results speak for themselves."

"The secrecy, the security guards—I don't doubt it. But I'm not sure R and R is the right answer to my specific, uh, problem."

"Intriguing. Please, Mister Al, enlighten me."

"Well, frankly, I need to make a *fuckload* of money. *Fast.*"

"A gambling debt?"

"Sort of. But not an eighty-thousand-dollars-to-the-local-bookie kind of thing. That I could handle on my own. It's more like a three-hundred-million-dollars-to-keep-my-job-and-save-my-neck kind of thing. And if I don't deliver, I'll need that ex-con-getting-back-on-his-feet thing you mentioned."

"Sounds like you find yourself in a very interesting predicament, Mister Al," Simon said, downplaying the obvious. "Given your position at Prism, I assume you have access to capital? And can move significant sums of money on short notice?"

"Yeah, sure."

"And you have the financial acumen and technical skills required to transfer money between domestic and offshore accounts? Without drawing undue attention?"

"I'm a fast learner."

"Then let's say we could offer you preferential access to CEOs, CFOs, board members, and other corporate executives. People who could provide you with a significant *edge* in the marketplace. Would that be something that interests you?"

"You're talking about inside information."

"Such a reductive and misleading term," Simon scoffed. "I'm talking about *competitive advantage*, Mister Al. Which all businesses and entrepreneurs seek and, in fact, require to succeed."

That was some next-level doublespeak. "Can you guarantee this so-called 'competitive advantage'?"

"There are no guarantees in life, Mister Al. Let's just say we can provide an exceedingly high degree of certainty."

"How much would that kind of certainty cost?"

"It depends. Bespoke research rates vary. If we execute transactions on your behalf, we require a twenty percent service fee. If we also provide the capital, the service fee increases to fifty percent."

"That's pretty hefty," I said, doubting both the veracity and the viability of this operation.

"You get what you pay for, Mister Al. But at R *und* R, our incentives are aligned. We succeed when you succeed."

"This is all very, uh, intriguing. But how do I know it's legit? This is a super-high-tech setup, and you don't seem like the kind of dude who fucks around. But I'd like to see the service in action. Is there, like, a free trial or something?"

"You will surely be an excellent client, Mister Al," Simon chuckled. He produced a business card from inside the breast pocket of his jacket and started scribbling. After a moment he extended the card to me. "Several of our top clients are having a special celebration tonight. Give this to security when you arrive and tell them Simon sent you. Once you see what we have to offer, you will have no more doubts."

I glanced at the small, rectangular piece of paper. It was all white. The only type—black, bold, all caps—read **SIMON SAYS**. On the back, he'd written an address in Stamford, Connecticut.

# ABOVE THE CLOUDS

The drive to Stamford seemed endless. On Simon's recommendation, I booked a $300 private Escalade, and had less than a thousand bucks of cash left. Pretty soon I'd be forced to originate a digital paper trail. Given the elite-globalist-cabal shit I was diving into headfirst, that could certainly become a problem down the line. I focused on the present. On the herculean task at hand. Simon had pitched me a nice story with his bullshit Euro-sophisticate charm, but "R and R" was thin at best, fraudulent at worst. Much of my day job involved telling people who were trying to sell me shit I didn't want to buy—covetous investment bankers, clingy sell-side analysts, and sycophantic CEOs, to name a few—to fuck off. The proof, as they say, would be in the pudding. If this high-class soiree generated some actionable intel, I might start warming up to the scam.

When we crossed the state border into Connecticut, my driver, who smelled awful but had remained delightfully silent, said, "Ritzy neighborhood you'ze heading to. Come around here often?"

"A few times. But only for meetings in Greenwich. What am I in for?"

"Pffft. The address you gave me. We're talking about the one percent of the one percent, my friend. This neighborhood makes the Upper East Side look like Camden." I wasn't surprised, so I didn't respond. "Lot of crazy stuff happens up here. Wild sex parties and whatnot. Just rumors, ya know, but you shoulda seen some of the broads I've driven up here. Magnificent pieces of ass."

His lecherous eyes, beady and sunken into his chubby face, peered at me in the rearview mirror. He seemed a cheerful fellow, probably harmless, who was just looking to make small talk before we said goodbye for the rest of our lives.

"You ever get lucky? Pick up any table scraps?" I asked, playing along.

"Ha! I wish. These girls are handpicked for the bigwigs. High-class call girls, escorts, wannabe actresses. They know better than to waste their time on a bum like me."

"Well, if I happen to find myself at an underground orgy, I'm sure they won't bother with me either," I said.

"You got square shoulders and a solid jaw, kid. Don't sell yourself short."

"Which bigwigs party up here? Anyone I'd know?"

"Driver's code is to always respect the client's privacy. But I'll tell ya this: Half of Congress and most of the Fortune 500 CEOs would have a lot of explaining to do if their wives found out where they'd been."

Funny line, and I chuckled, but it was definitely exaggeration. *Right?* "You ever drive a guy named Simon up here? I know you don't name-drop your clients, but he's the guy who gave me this address."

"He got a last name?"

"I'm sure he does. He's real tall. With a German-sounding accent."

"Hmm. Doesn't ring a bell. But I'll tell ya, if he's hosting one of these shindigs, he wasn't sitting in traffic with us. Probably took a private helicopter."

The more he said, the more I rued not probing him for intel the entire ride. I was supposed to be an information trafficker, FFS. "What's your name, sir?"

"Richie. Richie Delicato."

"Nice to meet you, Richie," I said. "Hey, listen. It sounds like you know this neck of the woods a lot better than me. To be honest, I have no idea what I'm getting into. So I want to ask you for a favor: After you drop me off, can you hang around the area until I call for a pickup? I don't know how long I'll be tied up, but I do know I'll need a ride to Newark airport once the party ends."

He'd listened, intrigued, and arched his eyebrows in the rearview mirror.

"Richie, if you hook me up, there's seven hundred and fifty dollars in cash with your name on it. Give whatever you need to your bosses and keep the rest. Deal?"

He smiled. "I think I can arrange that."

$$$

As we drove through the deserted streets, the houses grew larger and more secluded. My destination appeared to be the sole property nestled deep inside a tree-filled cul-de-sac. Richie joined a short queue of cars that had formed at the cartoonishly high metal security gate. Escalade limo. Navigator limo. Lotus. Benz. He wasn't lying about the crowd.

At the front of the line, I told Richie I was leaving my suitcase in the car and handed him half the cash. I hopped out, straightened my jacket, and walked to the security checkpoint. The guard eyed me suspiciously at first, then waved me through without incident after I produced Simon's card.

It seemed like a mile-long walk to the actual house. Or, more accurately, fortress. I'd been to Paul's place several times for Christmas parties and BBQs and the like, but considering his wealth, his home was remarkably modest, physically constrained by its Pac Heights topography. Whoever owned this joint, be it Simon or otherwise, had the perfect blend of insecurity, entitlement, and tackiness to *go for it*. It teemed with chandeliers, sculptures, and gargoyles—each more gauche than the last—that all looked oddly familiar, as if I'd seen them in tone-deaf tweets from the *FT*'s "How to Spend It" column. Surely there was an Olympic-size swimming pool in the back, a bowling alley in the basement, and a helipad over the twenty-car garage.

I grabbed a flute of Champagne from a metal tray—I thought people only did this shit in movies—and lingered awkwardly between an impressionist painting and a marble bust of some whitewashed Greek god. They were almost certainly phonies. I'd learned from Paul that proper collectors stored their status symbols in climate-controlled vaults, which protected their ostentatious investments from the prying hands of proles and pretenders.

Scanning the crowd of several dozen—mostly nondescript White dudes in their fifties with a few Eastern European supermodels scattered throughout—I couldn't find Simon and recognized nobody else. I felt overwhelmed by the scene. Sweat formed on my brow. My custom fit three-button from Suitsupply highlighted just how far out of my league I was. I wasn't wearing the twenty-thousand-dollar bespoke suit that screamed I was made of money, nor the ironic Pink

Floyd T-shirt and Levi's jeans that proved I was so fucking obscenely rich I didn't have to care. I hoped, in vain, nobody would notice.

I'd always wanted to be a spy when I was little, like my hero James Bond, until I realized I wasn't tall and blue-eyed enough. As I got older, I thought I'd at least make a cool Bond villain: short, stocky, ethnically ambiguous, and always threatening a trace of controlled menace. After a few moments of mingling with the world's legitimate high rollers, I doubted I was debonair enough to park the cars.

I spotted the token Black dude walking in a few minutes later and decided to make my move. He was pushing six-six with a shiny bald head, gold-rimmed glasses, and a gorgeous black two-button, and like me, he stood alone and read the room. I moseyed over, forced eye contact, and gave the nod—a little gesture Browns and Blacks used to show solidarity in mad White spaces. He arched his brow.

"Interesting crowd, huh?" I said.

"First time?" he asked, towering over me.

"That obvious?"

"Yes. But don't worry. The people in this room may be worth billions, but everyone's very friendly."

I couldn't tell if that was supposed to be a joke. His accent was strange, and his face remained expressionless. "What line of business are you in?" I asked.

"Mining. You?"

"I'm with a prominent hedge fund."

"Dirty business," he said, and laughed. "Who invited you?"

"Simon," I said. "I'm a prospective client, taking a little test-drive." I shouldn't have said that last part. The less people revealed, the smarter they seemed. When I was nervous, I was a total clown show.

"An invite from the man himself. You must've made quite the impression."

Before I could say another stupid thing, a hefty man wearing a bolo tie and a cowboy hat interjected.

"Nigel, my man!" he said, jerking the tall mining executive's hand. "How the hell are you!?"

"Very well, Ted," Nigel replied dutifully. "How's business?"

"Frackin' great!" Ted replied, a joke he'd undoubtedly used thousands of times. "Say, when're you gonna let me set up a few rigs in your neck of the woods? I guarantee there's a lot more than precious gems in those fertile lands of yours."

"The situation back home is . . . politically sensitive. Foreign oilmen make for bad optics. We have enough problems with the Chinese."

"Don't we all!" Ted howled. "Well, keep us in mind. A whole lotta liquid gold's just itchin' to be freed." Nigel forced a smile, and Ted asked, "Say, who's your friend?"

"A high financier," he said, then turned toward me and added, "though I didn't catch your name."

"Al," I said. Ted yanked my arm forward and slathered my hand with his clammy paw.

"You're on Wall Street, Al? Well, if you're lookin' fer a sure bet, let me tell you about our domestic fracking operation. Based outta Oklahoma City, it's one hundred percent owned, operated, and managed in the U S of A. We're expanding rapidly and preparing to raise a boatload of capital. Say, you're the expert, what would you recommend in this crazy market? Junk bonds? Convertibles?"

Nigel wisely drifted toward the supermodels, saddling me with Ted. His questions and comments gave lie to the idea of America being a meritocracy. A quick Google search would certainly reveal Yosemite Sam was another failson living off great-grandpa's genocidal glory. Standing next to this redneck proved I wasn't the lamest person in the room, at least, and boosted my confidence. I'd been admitted to an asylum full of batshit-crazy rich people, so why shouldn't I act like a batshit-crazy rich person, too?

After entertaining Ted for seven of the longest minutes of my life, I finally saw Simon out of the corner of my eye. He must've just arrived. People gravitated in his general direction like he was a politician on the campaign trail. I did my best to steer Ted along a productive vector, hoping to God Simon's promised intel wasn't related to this dunce cap's fracking operation. When I got within earshot, Simon treated me like the belle of this corrupt-AF ball.

"Mister Al!" He shoved toward me with a million-dollar smile and shook my hand vigorously. "Are you enjoying the party? Making any interesting acquaintances?"

"Ted and I are new besties," I said. Simon laughed, then put his hand between my shoulder blades and directed me to a quiet spot behind an enormous tropical plant.

"Ted's an incompetent buffoon. Did you meet anyone useful?"

"A tall guy named Nigel?" I said, uncertain.

"Ah, a most interesting fellow. But his specific expertise lies in the geopolitical sphere, not the public markets." He looked up and took stock of the room. "Follow me." Simon glided into the center of the ballroom and invaded a tight circle of well-dressed middle-aged men. He tapped his wrist like he was asking for the time, and our small group retreated to a private study adjacent to the kitchen.

"I'd like to introduce everyone to Mister Al. He's a portfolio manager with Prism Capital—a firm that requires no introduction," Simon said. "Mister Al is a prospective client, and like any good businessman, he's conducting due diligence on our organization. I promised him a—how did you say it again, Mister Al?—ah yes, a *free trial.*"

"You did indeed, Simon," I interjected. "I had the great fortune of meeting our esteemed host just last week and I'm *extremely* impressed with the organization he's building. Recently, I became the youngest-ever portfolio manager at Prism Capital, and I'm currently sitting on over three hundred million dollars of dry powder. My boss, Paul Kingsley, challenged me to best my already industry-leading returns, and as you gentlemen might imagine, I'm looking to make a series of *aggressive* investments, of *considerable* magnitude. After my introductory session with Simon, I knew R and R was the perfect place to scour for new opportunities." My spur-of-the-moment bullshitting abilities shocked even me.

"As you can see, Mister Al has access to tremendous resources, and will be an invaluable addition to our R-*und*-R family," Simon said, beaming. "Would you gentlemen kindly introduce yourselves?"

Rotating clockwise, the men were Peter Starling, CEO of some type of software analytics and data-mining company; Benjamin Roth, CFO of a biotech company called Powerhouse Therapeutics; and Hugo Sorensen, a semiretired investment banker who sat on the corporate boards of logistics powerhouse DHL, industrial conglomerate GE, and defense contractor Lockheed Martin. All these venerable captains of industry were so pleased to meet me. Then I remembered why I recognized Roth's face.

"Benjamin, did you used to be with Jackknife Bio?" I asked.

"Yeah—I thought you looked familiar!" he said. "You worked for Clyde, right?"

"I did." We both paused to remember how Clyde had injected a lethal dose of fentanyl into his veins. "Jackknife was one of our all-time-great bets," I said. "I got quite the Christmas bonus that year."

"A most fortuitous reunion!" Simon said. "Which brings us to our next piece of business. As our young friend indicated, he's looking to make a big splash with his new portfolio, and therefore requires business intelligence of the highest quality. You gentlemen are among our most reliable patrons, which is why I asked you to step away from the festivities. Any suitable suggestions for our honored guest?"

"We printed monster numbers and did a sizable deal last month, so I don't have anything certain," Starling said. "There's a lot of rumors about how Microsoft's looking to scoop up any- and everybody in artificial intelligence, but that's still guesswork."

"Similar boat," Sorensen said. "Most large companies just wrapped up earnings, and deal flow dries up around the holidays. I can tell you one of my companies is planning to make several large acquisitions next year. But until I have more visibility, I don't feel comfortable providing names. I wouldn't want to lead you astray. Of course, I'm more than happy to provide actionable information in the future."

"Unfortunate, but not atypical this time of year," Simon said.

"I've got something," Roth blurted out. "Something big. Something *really* big."

"Well, spit it out, Ben," Starling said.

"Powerhouse is . . . Powerhouse is done. We're *done*," Roth said, stilted. I remembered this guy being squirrelly even when we weren't conducting aggressively illegal business.

"What do you mean?" I asked.

"Our phase three trial—it's a bust. We got the data last week and the drug completely whiffed. The medical guys are crunching the numbers one last time, but the primary investigators determined it didn't work. *At all.* I've been in nonstop meetings trying to figure out when to disclose the data. It won't be a press release. More like an autopsy report."

"That must be hugely disappointing," I said, feigning concern. Few things on Wall Street were more satisfying than a bogus clinical trial imploding, and suppressing my ebullience took superman resolve. "What was the indication?"

"PDN. It's, uh, peripheral nerve pain associated with diabetes."

*Always treat the symptoms, never the cause*, I thought. "Biotech's a boom-or-bust business. Clyde and I took many a beating during our days together," I said, bending the truth and hoping to soften him up. "Do you guys have any protection built into your pipeline?"

"We're a one-trick pony," Roth said. "Our stock's going to get killed."

That last sentence was something no CFO would dream of uttering in the public domain. He'd all but told the group he was about to lose a personal fortune, and the rest of us should short as much of his bullshit company's stock as we could find.

"Well, if it's any consolation, I lost a hundred million on Icarus," I said, unprompted. Simon perked up, and I kicked myself for not keeping my cards closer to my chest. Lying—both outright and via omission—came unnaturally to me, which was why I ultimately failed as a hedge fund scumbag. "How and when will you disclose the data? I assume you're willing to share that information?"

Roth looked cautiously at Simon, who said, "I will be delighted to broker an exchange as expeditiously as possible. Mister Benjamin, please use our normal channels. I will personally oversee delivery to Mister Al."

The group nodded in satisfied agreement. Another shady deal done. The ultrarich would get richer. The plebes would be none the wiser. Simon's firm would take a gargantuan cut. It was almost admirable. These amoral shitheads pulled the strings and turned the screws and did, in Lloyd Blankfein's immortal words, *God's work*.

With our conspiracy concluded, Simon said, "Now, gentlemen, for the real excitement!" The three executives filed out of the room.

I hung back. I wanted to ask Simon what to expect next. How he'd coordinate the file handoff. How, if I joined his illicit club, I'd pay his illicit fees. And, most obviously, why I should trust him. Or, for that matter, anyone at this Illuminati shindig. He could sense my onslaught of questions and put his lanky arm around my shoulders like a placating uncle.

"You must learn to relax, Mister Al. This is the beginning of a beautiful friendship."

# PROTECT YA NECK

## *Sunday, November 29*

Monday-morning panic began a day early. Reality was striking back. *Hard.* In less than twenty-four hours, I'd have to stare down Paul and Brad, come up with a plausible reason why I flew to New York City on a whim, and conjure up a believable thesis for why my next big bet should be against Powerhouse Therapeutics, a company I only found out existed two days ago. In spite of all this head-spinning agita, my member throbbed like I was thirteen again, in gym class, catching a glance of my first IRL boob. I mass-murdered trillions of viable souls but couldn't shake Amira from my thoughts.

Amira was the forty-two-year-old Lebanese trophy wife I'd been *thisclose* to penetrating in a spare bedroom at Simon's party, before she withdrew, fearing we'd get caught, I'd get beaten to within an inch of my life by her husband's henchmen, and she'd get exchanged for two twenty-one-year-old replacements. I could still feel her silky-smooth skin. Smell her perfume. Taste her lipstick.

I didn't know which of the White devils was her husband. Or why she'd been invited to the party in the first place. I'd pleaded desperately for her to stay with me, and tried to convince her I'd happily be murdered to consummate our love, to no avail. I was lost in reverie when my iPhone buzzed with a text from my mom. She wanted to know how I was doing, which was really an excuse for her to call and tell me how *she* was doing. I then realized Amira, my latest obsession, was just a year younger than my mother, and the Oedipal implications pushed the weekend's surrealism from my mind.

Routine took hold. Coffee. Grape-Nuts. Suicidal ideation. Evacuation. By sunrise I felt focused and refreshed. I logged into my laptop, dragged my entire inbox into my "read later" folder, and set to work on why I hated Powerhouse Therapeutics. This insider trading thing had some real merit. Picking stocks when you knew what would happen was *by far* the best investment approach I'd found. *Why are we suddenly interested in Powerhouse stock?* A just-published sell-side report from Morgan Stanley, which highlighted the "binary" aspect of the imminent clinical readout and presented a variety of upside and downside scenarios, sparked my interest. *Why should we bet against the trial?* A KOL consultation—which I would actually conduct two days from now—suggested there was plenty of healthy skepticism surrounding the drug's purported mechanism of action. *How do we justify the scale of our bet?* Based on my comprehensive and thorough research, I felt extremely confident in my investment thesis. At this rate, I could all but book my next twenty-five million before the Steelers got pantsed by the Patriots.

Around midmorning, my doorbell rang. There were only a few people who knew where I lived, and I didn't want to see any of them. Maybe it was an accident and they'd leave. The bell rang again. I threw on a hoodie and went to my shitty front door with no peep-hole. I listened for a second. Another ring. I thrust the door open and found Brad decked out in a blue-and-red flannel shirt and tan cordu-roy pants. I couldn't believe Daddy let him go out in public like that.

He barged past me into the tiny living room and plopped down on my IKEA futon. I shut the door, closed my exposed laptop, and stood in front of the TV.

"What in the flying fuck do you think you're doing?" he asked, enunciating every syllable.

"Good to see you, too, buddy!"

"I don't know how many times I have to tell you this, Habib, but this isn't a fucking game!"

"Oh, but it is, Bradley. It's a game Daddy dreamt up. And now we're both playing along. The biggest difference is: I'm getting re-sults."

"Results?" he scoffed. "You've only made *one* trade. You're not even close to your target."

"Just watch," I said, more confident than I had any right to be.

"Take out your phone and turn—you know the drill. And where the fuck's your burner? I tried calling it a million fucking times."

"It's right there," I said, pointing to the kitchen counter. "I left it here while I was traveling."

"That wasn't part of the arrangement! I need to be able to reach you—securely—at all times."

"Yeah, well, sorry to inform you, Bradley, but your arrange-ment's bullshit. *The Wire*—which is where I assume you got this ri-diculous idea—may be an all-time great show. But it's aged poorly."

"This is— You're fucking unbelievable, Habib. I'm going to call Dad and tell him about this."

"Go for it."

"I'm serious! You think I won't?"

I shrugged, then sauntered into the kitchen and refilled the electric kettle. I flipped it to boil and rinsed out my French press while Brad skittered back and forth, waiting impatiently for Daddy to answer his call. He didn't. Brad screamed "Fuck!" at the voicemail lady, hung up, and dialed another number. An answer after the first ring, which meant he'd called Marvin, Paul's personal chauffeur. If someone really needed to get ahold of Paul, they went to Brad. If Brad really needed to get ahold of Paul, he went to Marvin. That was the order of operations. Their call ended quickly and Brad glowered at me, like one of those yappie dogs who barked and yelped and lunged and threatened a fight because they knew their master would protect them. WhatsApp rang on Brad's phone.

"Why are we having this call?" Paul asked, on speaker.

"Our mutual acquaintance isn't playing ball. He's not taking his task seriously. And he's not treating me—or you—with the proper respect," Brad said.

"Is that right, Al?"

"Dad!" Brad interjected. "Names!"

"Save your gay little Mission: Impossible nonsense for the movies, Bradley. This call is end-to-end encrypted. And if I were so inclined, I could call Mark and have him scrub the entire fucking server. So—Al? What seems to be the problem? You've been acting real cagey lately, and your clock's ticking fast. I shouldn't have to remind you what's at stake. Or that I'm a man of my word."

"Listen, Paul—*with all due respect*—I'm about to go on a fucking heater. I'm talking thermo-fucking-nuclear. I'm developing sources. Chasing down proprietary leads. Doing the fieldwork—the hardcore due diligence. Generally speaking, I'm getting shit done. I've got several *monster* ideas on tap. Total fucking monsters. But I have to tell you, Paul, my biggest challenge is having you and Brad breathing down my neck. So the real question *you* have to ask yourself is this:

Do you want me to bag that three hundred million? Or do you want to keep getting in my fucking way?"

The line sat silent. Brad's mouth hung agape while he waited for his old man to bring down the hammer. The electric kettle reached its roiling crescendo. Finally, in a flat tone, Paul said, "Leave him be, Bradley. He's made his point, and he still has plenty of work to do." Brad stood petrified and stunned. Paul raised his voice and said, "All your ideas go through me, and all approvals go through Compliance. *No* exceptions. Understood?"

"Loud and clear," I said.

The phone went dead. Blood drained from Brad's face. It was possible he'd never seen *anyone* stand up to his father, let alone a young, short, cocky, dark-skinned, weird-named, *who-the-fuck-does-he-think-he-is?* token minority.

"Thanks again for dropping by, Bradley," I said. "Now, if you don't mind, I have important work to do for your daddy."

$$$

The ensuing days melded into one continuous blur. First and foremost, I needed to verify the Powerhouse tip was legit. My gut feeling said it was, and I didn't want to miss out on the action, so I asked Paul to sign off on a modest five million dollars short, which Compliance approved. Compliance wasn't a real department at Prism, nor was it staffed by real people. It was a throwaway term Paul inserted into every trading discussion to indemnify himself against bets gone criminal. This way, no matter how brazenly illegal a trade might end up, he was always protected.

Knowing this, I bumped the Powerhouse play to nine million dollars and executed it in three tranches: two, two, and five million. Better to ask Paul for forgiveness rather than permission, right? Besides, Compliance approved my trades.

Creating the positions was easy, but *every single time* I shorted a stock, I reflected on the transaction's nonsensical mechanics. It was a stepwise procedure requiring both a detached middleman and, more important, a sucker standing at the ready. The best layperson explanation I'd ever heard, which I'd tried to convey to my mom *countless* times, with *fruitless* results, came from the NPR comedy show *Wait Wait . . . Don't Tell Me*. Their analogy involved a retail store, a fancy dress, and an unwitting friend.

Inspired by public radio's cleverness, and pleased with the return on my tax dollars, the modified scenario I'd tried to describe to my mom went like this: Imagine one of your wealthy clients, who's an idiot, buys a fancy cocktail dress at Macy's for $1,000. You, by virtue of being dirt poor and destitute, are much savvier with money, and know that exact same dress is about to go on sale for, say, $800. You ask to borrow the fancy dress from your wealthy client, who's an idiot, so you can wear it on a hot date with your latest paramour. She agrees, because she's an idiot, and gives you the dress, which you immediately return to Macy's for $1,000 in cash. Later, when your intuition pays off and the expected sale begins, you go back to Macy's and buy a *brand-new* version of that exact same fancy dress at the new, lower price of $800. Finally, you give the brand-new fancy dress back to your wealthy client, who's an idiot, and pocket the $200 difference for yourself.

My mom, bless her little heart, could never get past the obvious question: Even if she's an idiot, why would I want to rip off my wealthy client? And that's why she didn't work on Wall Street.

With respect to my Powerhouse play, the process would unfold in similar fashion. For a smallish fee, I "borrowed" nine million dollars' worth of common stock from a too-big-to-fail broker-dealer, then immediately sold said common stock to unwitting idiots in the open market. Those transactions delivered nine million dollars of cash to my account, which I was free to spend however I pleased. In a few days, after Powerhouse's clinical trial flopped and its share price tumbled, I'd buy back the equivalent number of shares from a (presumably) different batch of unwitting idiots in the open market, then return those shares to the original too-big-to-fail broker-dealer where I'd borrowed them. When it was all said and done, I anticipated booking a net profit of up to eight million dollars.

Did this circuitous sequence serve any useful societal purpose? Did it house the homeless? Feed the poor? Cure cystic fibrosis? Or remove greenhouse gases from the atmosphere? No, obviously not. But it matched short-term buyers with shorter-term sellers, increased liquidity, and enriched middlemen, and countless punters across the Street did it countless times per day. The Founders would've been impressed.

Market insanity notwithstanding, executing my trades in three buckets carried additional benefits. The progression allowed for a slower buildup in my position, which helped me avoid drawing too much attention from other market participants. If anyone got wind I—or more specifically, Prism—had taken a hefty short position in a stock, a lot of shit could hit the fan. Playing in a "well-functioning market" was essential. Another reason to ramp up slowly? Plausible deniability in case my bets attracted unwanted attention from nosy regulators. My strategy was all very straightforward: I positioned myself short ahead of a major market catalyst, then continued to conduct due diligence with the KOL call, which in turn increased my conviction level, which enticed me to accumulate an even larger short position. Situation normal. Nothing to see here.

On the first sleepy Friday of December, Powerhouse Therapeutics issued a press release confirming its clinical trial had shit the bed. It was a carbon copy of the draft soon-to-be-former CFO Benjamin Roth had sent to Simon (by unknown means), which Simon subsequently forwarded to me (via Signal). When the market opened, the company's stock was *decimated*. Closing the short was easier than hailing an Uber. By lunchtime, I was over 10 percent of the way toward repaying my ransom. The R-and-R free trial had proved a resounding success, and I was itching to become a full-time subscriber.

# TIC TOC

*Saturday, December 5*

Damon and I met at a rowdy sports bar in the Mission. A Columbus native, his beloved Ohio State Buckeyes were fresh off another demolition of Michigan and ready to hang half-a-hundred on lowly Northwestern in the Big Ten title game, before themselves getting routed by Alabama in the playoff semifinal. I'd seen this script before and was bored with it, but Damon's fandom was far from rational. Growing up in Miami, I respected—though despised—"the U." This let me occupy a happy middle ground: I enjoyed human meat grinding without suffering from its tribal-induced brain damage and other associated negative externalities. The current contest took a back seat to a much more pressing reason as well. I needed info on Simon and R and R.

On game days, the bar's billiards room converted into a small amphitheater, replete with a large-screen projector and surround sound. Damon and I snuggled in tight with two hundred of our closest associates, a scene that would've given the fabled fire marshal fits. The environs were loud, humid, saturated with scarlet and gray, and—despite teeming with computer programmers, biochemists, and brand managers—the crowd could've been mistaken for a Mercer County antiabortion rally packed with conspiracy theorists, opioid peddlers, and off-duty cops in Proud Boys attire. With three minutes left in the first half, the Buckeyes held a slimmer-than-expected lead, and everyone was on edge.

"That R-and-R hookup was legit," I yelled into Damon's ear over a deafening KIA Sorrento ad. He nodded and fist-bumped me. "But I need another favor," I shouted. "A big one." His brows arched and his lips pursed. We both knew he wouldn't like what I had to say.

At halftime we exited the bar and ducked onto a side street. I'd mistakenly worn my purple NYU hoodie, which the marauding Buckeyes faithful had mistakenly assumed to be Northwestern gear, and I'd been enjoying a steady stream of unsavory invective for my oversight. After a morbidly obese White woman wearing a garland of fake plastic tree seeds flipped me off and told me to "Go back to Mexico," Damon said, "So, what's up, Al?"

"You know I hate asking for favors. But given this shitshow with Paul, I need one. A big one."

"How big?" he sighed.

"I need everything you have on this R-and-R firm and the Simon guy who runs it—though I sincerely doubt that's his real name."

"*Damn*, Al," he said, throwing his arms above his head. "That's a *big* ask. That kind of information—those kinds of files—are confidential. Even if I *could* get access, I could get disbarred for passing them along."

"I know, I know. I don't want to jam you up, especially after you hooked me up. But hear me out. After I called the number you gave me and talked to Simon, I flew to New York and ended up at this wild Illuminati bash at a fucking castle in Connecticut. The shit was bonkers. A bunch of old dudes pretending to be supervillains."

"For real?" he asked, skeptical.

"Bruh, you don't know the half," I said. "These people were real-deal power broker types. Corporate execs, foreign leaders, Hollywood stars—I'm pretty sure I saw Matthew McConaughey. Anyway, Simon introduced me to a few people and told them I was looking to make some moves in the market. One of the guys gave me a trade idea and it paid off beautifully. Now I'm supposed to go back for more info, but this time I have to pay for it. Simon's operation is legit, but it's shady as fuck. Before I get in too deep, I need to know more about him, his company, and what kind of people I'm dealing with. The last thing I need is to do business with Simon, find out he's a Russian oligarch, and get disappeared." I wondered if I really meant that last part. Crossing the Russian mob would quickly—though not painlessly—solve all my problems.

"So you want *me* to dig around, and stick *my* neck out for *you? Again?*"

"When you say it like that, it makes me sound like a real asshole."

"You *are* a real asshole. Plus, I'm about to miss the second half." I was an asshole. But I was a desperate asshole who needed help from a friend, so I moped silently and pathetically. "What do you actually *need?*" he asked after a brief pause.

"Whatever you can find without raising eyebrows. How about Simon's real name and where he's from? And the real name of his company? And its articles of incorporation? After that, a list of the company's officers, its legal domicile, and its tax jurisdiction would be good. I don't know shit about the people I'm dealing with, so I'll take whatever you can get."

"You got a time frame?"

"Next week."

Damon shook his head and took a long, deep breath through his nose. "You owe me, Al. Big time."

"Bruh, if I survive the next few months without ending up in prison, I'll buy you a brand-new Ferrari."

We dapped and shoulder-hugged. Damon made his way back inside the bar, but I couldn't stomach any more of the sights, sounds, and smells of the Buckeye State's shittiest exports.

My apartment was three and a half miles away, though I wasn't in the mood for another interrogation by another melanin-rich Uber driver concerning the little-known origins of my race, ethnicity, or culture. Or interested in explaining why I went by Al instead of Ali. I popped in my headphones, cued up *Only Built 4 Cuban Linx . . .*, pressed play, and started walking.

$$$

Considering my literal freedom was on the line, the ensuing week proved quite uneventful. My second call with Simon ended after a few seconds. He insisted on another in-person meeting, which sent me scrambling yet again to Orbitz in search of flights to New York City. I was originally slated to leave around three on Friday afternoon, but on Thursday morning at 4:10 the requisite plot twist occurred: Paul had scheduled another all-hands meeting for Friday at market close. It was our obligatory—yet never announced in advance—year-end review and portfolio update. Obviously, it derailed my plans to do financial crimes. I weighed the risk-benefit ratio of skipping altogether and decided against it. I'd brushed off Paul once and just last weekend shat all over his only son. I was a wild card, but there were limits, so I booked the dreaded red-eye into JFK.

With no word from Damon, life bungled on as usual. I dodged several calls from my mom, Jennie had Preston, Dennis had jokes, Keith had hard feelings, and Karen had shade. Same old, same old, save one exception: I'd disintermediated the middle troll. I hadn't seen Brad's fat, miserable face once, let alone suffered his casual racism or incessant bullying. The conditions were perfect for getting real work done, which was ironic, because I'd given up on developing investment theses of my own.

Not that there weren't some pretty good ideas out there. Financial crises were precipitated by fear, and when Americans felt uneasy, nothing calmed their nerves like cold, hard steel. Stocks of blue-chip gunmakers had surged 15 percent and had a lot more room to run. The so-called deaths of despair—drug overdoses, suicides, and the like—would concomitantly spike over the next several quarters, which meant funeral and cemetery service providers would see a strong uptick in business. But those approaches, macabre as they were, took time to bear fruit. As it stood, I was preposterously short of my goal and had placed all my metaphorical eggs in Simon's mercurial basket. Slippery slopes and moral hazard and yeah, yeah, yeah, fuck off.

$$\$\$\$$$

The show started promptly at 1 p.m. PT. Electronic devices were once again confiscated and Paul once again wore his executioner's attire. But unlike the last all-hands meeting, when we all knew we were screwed and a chummy gallows humor had taken hold, this time the fear was much more acute. Paul had made it clear nobody was getting canned. In fact, he'd thrown us all for a loop by doubling down on (almost) the entire organization (RIP, Dan and Ben). He expected results, and there would be *real* repercussions for those who didn't deliver. The latent relief afforded by permanent dismissal was off the table. Succeed, or Paul would torment you in the cruelest possible fashion. Exhibit A: Jafar, Ali.

"The word that comes to mind is *disappointment*," Paul's sermon began. His tone was somber. Reserved. It wouldn't last. "Disappointment. It's worse than anger. Worse than heartache. Worse, even, than betrayal. Because it means you've been let down. Let down by the people you believed in. By the people you *know* could've—and should've—done better.

"Disappointment. The thing that makes disappointment so hard to stomach is you're left wondering: *Why?* Why do I feel disappointed? Am I disappointed in you, because I know you could've—and should've—done better? Or am I disappointed in myself, for believing you could've—and should've—done better? Maybe I'm disappointed because my standards are too high? Or maybe I'm disappointed because you little snowflakes—beautiful and unique and special as you are—have fallen prisoner to the cult of low expectations.

"Disappointment. Expectations. You can't have one without the other. Let me show you what disappointment looks like."

Paul flipped on the projector and revealed the state of Prism's portfolio. As of yesterday's close, in the month since the Icarus crash, we'd lost seven hundred million dollars—a return of –3 percent—only this time, Paul hadn't bailed out the entire firm with one of his legendary hedges. The room fell still as a Siberian winter. I studied the table and a grim sense of satisfaction washed over me. The last column, called "Special Projects," was my portfolio. I was up 10 percent. Everyone else was in the red.

"I could've bought T-bills for the past month," Paul said, "and saved myself *SEVEN HUNDRED MILLION FUCKING DOL-LARS!*" I'd never heard him shout so loud. He slammed his headset to the ground and roundhouse-kicked the podium off the stage. It collapsed into pieces with a hearty *thud*. Paul adjusted his jacket, then rubbed both his hands through his hair. "If this was a civilized country, I'd have everyone in this room. Fucking. Executed." Paul had whispered the final two words, sans mic, with disconcerting calm, and somehow seemed more insane. "Well, almost everyone," he said, his voice suddenly back to normal. "But I'm getting to that."

A security guard brought him a handheld microphone. He tapped it twice. "Karen, explain to me why VICE is down two percent?"

My loins immediately went hot and my dick actually got hard. Karen had *never* been called out before. Shocked, she rose slowly.

"Um, well, you know, the sector has been really volatile since the Icarus thing and—"

"Volatility is your best fucking friend, you stuck-up cunt!" Paul boomed. Her face crumpled. Another volley and she'd burst into tears. I *almost* felt bad for her. "Maybe if you spent less time showing off your tits, and more time doing research, you'd make some goddamned money. Fix it. Or you're finished. Now sit the fuck down." Poor Karen. She may have been an icy bitch, but she was whip-smart and produced steady, if unremarkable, returns.

"Doug. What's going on with REITs?" Paul inquired. This guy, on the other hand . . .

Seated in the back of the auditorium, Doug said, "Yeah, Paul, uh, honestly, I got nothing. It's been—"

"Stand up, Doug. I can't hear you."

"It's been a really tough environment," Doug said, erect and shouting. "Nobody knows what to expect from the Fed. You know, what they'll do with rates. And you know, how that might affect, uh, capital investments. Valuations. And stuff."

"Jesus H. Christ," Paul said. "Bradley, what are long-term interest rates right now?"

Brad, sitting in the front row by himself and obviously caught off guard, said, "Zero percent?"

"Zero percent. And what happens to rates when the economy is fucked?"

"They go . . . down?"

"They go down," Paul confirmed. "Is there a number lower than zero?"

"You mean, like, a negative number?" Brad asked. Grimaces abounded. Betty started crying.

"Listen closely, Doug," Paul said. "Rates are zero. Rates have been zero. Rates will stay zero. So there's only one way to explain how you lost three hundred and twenty-five million dollars in a month: You're a fucking moron. I'm cutting your pay by half. Hopefully that concept's not too hard for you to understand."

Paul had hired Doug, whose dad was the president of MIT, in exchange for preferential access to the *actual* talent coming out of the university's quant-heavy finance program. Doug thoroughly deserved this excoriation, and I laughed under my breath. Before I could revel in the carnage, I realized which group was next. *Biotech.* They were the second-worst-performing sector after REITs, down 6 percent, or just under two hundred million. I hoped Paul wouldn't pick on poor, sweet, kind, beautiful Jennie. She was a rock star in the making. It wasn't her fault Chuck was on a losing streak.

"Chuck," Paul said. *Thank God.* "Chuck, Chuck, Chuck. I'll make this one quick: You're fired." Reflexive gasps from the traumatized audience. "Jennie, imagine you're the new head of Biotech. What's your best idea?"

*Please don't blow it, please don't blow it, please don't blow it.* "Tachyon Bio," Jennie said. "They've got a phase three CAR T asset for AML and multiple follow-on programs in B-cell lymphoma." *She blew it.*

"Peak sales?" Paul asked.

"Two billion."

"Expected stock appreciation?"

"Risk-adjusted, at least fifty percent."

"Thank you, Jennie. Oh, one last question: How is it that you and Chuck can't generate a single moneymaking idea, but Al—who has nothing to do with Biotech—made thirty million on Clockwork and Powerhouse in two weeks?"

Jennie's shoulders slumped. I couldn't stomach what he'd say next, but apparently neither could Chuck, who projectile vomited onto the floor between his feet. The sound of retching and splattering chunks echoed throughout the amphitheater.

"Oh Jesus fucking Christ, die with some fucking dignity!" Paul shouted. "Security, get a mop in here. This is why I have you people removed immediately."

Jennie rubbed Chuck's back and tried not to gag. Her Uggs were unsalvageable. She kept her head down, hoping Paul would move on. I knew the feeling all too well.

"You should thank Chuck for bailing you out," Paul said to Jennie. "You know, maybe I should make Al your boss. Spice things up a little." Dennis, Brad, and their ilk laughed aloud. My eyes welled with rage. That was the final straw. I'd had enough of Paul and Brad's bullying bullshit. I'd walk onto the stage and punch that arrogant prick in his mouth. "Speaking of whom, where's Al?" He quickly spotted me, the lone tanned face in the crowd. "Al, come on over here!"

Feeling equal parts shock, dread, and pride, I walked down the aisle, past the departed podium, and up the steps. Paul shook my hand heartily. I should've followed with an uppercut but was too disoriented.

"I want you people to take a long, hard look at this man," Paul said. "This is what a winner looks like. Thirty million in two weeks. Ten percent absolute return. *That* is what we do at Prism." I wobbled and smiled sheepishly at the crowd. Paul had never singled out anyone for anything except abuse. My body tensed, waiting for the swerve.

"Performance comes with consequences, good and bad. Since Al's the only person capable of making money, I'm personally awarding him a five-hundred-thousand-dollar bonus. Congratulations, buddy. You can pay rent for the next six months." He put his arm around my shoulders. It was a strange sensation. Did my tormenter actually care about me? "For the rest of you, there'll be no bonuses this year," Paul said. The room filled with expletives and flailing appendages. "Our shareholders demand better, and so do I." Paul dropped the mic and told me to follow him offstage.

We walked briskly down the winding corridors to his humongous office. What misery awaited? There was simply no way something horrible wasn't about to happen. The universe had to remain in balance. Passing through the glass doors, my pockets emptied, Paul made a beeline for the smoking quadrant and asked what I was drinking. I declined. He implored me to sit in his favorite chair and handed me a generous helping of brandy.

"What are you up to, Al?" he asked, inspecting me.

"What do you mean?"

"Bradley's the one who thinks he's James Bond. I, on the other hand, like to cut to the chase. It's why I'm one of the richest men on the planet." He paused to admire himself. "Your recent behavior has been very uncharacteristic. And highly unpredictable. Insubordination. Absenteeism. *Tardiness.* Normally that kind of stuff would worry me. But in your case, I find myself intrigued. You're a wounded animal, and I've backed you into a corner. That makes you dangerous. But how that danger manifests isn't always clear. Are you dangerous, Al? Or rather, *how* are you dangerous?"

"Paul, I can assure you, dangerous is the last word anybody

would use to describe me. I'm simply executing my normal research process, but at a much more accelerated pace. Because I don't want to go to jail."

"You're a funny guy, Al. Humor is a great weapon. It can defuse volatile situations. Throw people off-balance. Keep the peace. How's your drink, by the way?"

I took a sip. "Strong."

"At five thousand bucks per bottle, it better be." Paul sat down on an errant ottoman opposite my chair and loosened his black tie. With his slicked-back hair and all-black getup, cradling his drink, he looked like Death himself, preparing to end another meaningless existence.

"I know you've been getting into some shady shit, Al. Can't say I blame you. It's not like this place is crawling with saints. Everyone crosses the line in this business eventually. And to be fair, it's not like you have much choice. I gave you an impossible task, and you're doing whatever it takes to get the job done. It's what I admire most about you people. The work ethic. It's just incredible." He took a swig of brandy and swallowed the burn. "You keep bringing me those juicy trades, Compliance will keep approving them, and I'll make sure everyone, including Bradley, stays off your back. Deal?"

"Uh, sure. Deal."

"But I want to make something very clear, Al. Whatever you're doing, sooner or later, I'm going to figure it out. And when I do, if I find out you're trying to fuck me, I'll make you wish you'd never been born. Understood?"

Considering I already wished I'd never been born, the threat didn't land. But I got his gist. "You've got nothing to worry about," I said.

Paul smiled. "Now, if you'll excuse me, I'm hosting an important charity gala this evening for UNICEF. I'll have Bradley wire your bonus."

I exited the office and was greeted by Marvin, who handed me my iPhone. "I like your style, youngblood," he said. "You got some fight in you." I nodded, perplexed, and walked away. Six hours until flight time.

$$$

I sipped a Starbucks at the sparsely occupied gate to JFK. *What am I doing?* Only the saddest, most desperate people took a red-eye on United. A haggard, middle-aged man heading to see his mom—who was probably dying of cancer—one last time. An elderly Chinese couple, devoid of retirement savings or a social safety net, traveling to see their grandkids on the cheap. A scattering of management consultants, billing their clients for weekend reroutes to exotic locales, pretending they'd found meaning in their meaningless jobs.

Maybe it was time I went to the authorities and told them everything. It'd be my word versus Paul's. I'd be a huge underdog, but I'd been a huge underdog all my life, and look at me now. Young and ambitious and successful. My thoughts turned darker. On the other hand, maybe it was time I got serious about the "final solution." I'd been all talk and no action. And to what end? Even if I repaid my illicit "debt," my reward would be more work, more stress, and more face time with Paul. I had nothing to look forward to. Nothing worth living for.

My cell phone vibrated and disrupted my despair. *Damon!*

"Cutting it close, huh? I'm about to board my flight."

"*Woooooow,*" Damon said. "How about you start over, like, 'Hey, Damon, thank you so, *so* much for putting your career on the line to get me the information I requested. You're the man! And so handsome. How will I ever repay you?'"

"You got it?! You *are* the man!"

"I know. And so handsome."

"So what's the deal?" I asked impatiently.

"Your boy Simon seems legit. The whole R-and-R thing's a branding gimmick, though. His company's real name is Silverlake Holdings LLC. It was incorporated in the UK in nineteen ninety-eight and it's headquartered in Birmingham. They even pay a few million in taxes to the Queen every year."

"What industry do they list?"

"The filings say 'logistics and business services,' but it's a classic holding company. I dug around a little bit and Silverlake is the beneficial owner of a shitload—I'm talking hundreds—of other British shell companies, which are the beneficial owners of even more British shell companies. These things are built like Russian nesting dolls," Damon explained coolly, as if he'd conducted this type of investigation thousands of times.

"And Simon's real name?"

"Simon, supposedly. Simon Hellstrom. He's the managing director listed on the company's most recent filings. The other two are Trevor Belmont and Samus Aran."

"Wait, what? I thought you said this company was legitimate."

"It is."

"Constructed like a maze? And run by Nintendo characters? That doesn't make any sense."

"Actually, it does. All this information is available online, but nobody checks it. There's *zero* enforcement in the UK. What matters is this: Whoever took the time to set this operation up knew exactly what they were doing. The paperwork is airtight. The filings are completed on time. The taxes are paid. Most important, the holding structure is a complete goddamned nightmare. You could move billions through this network without anyone catching on.

And even if they did, it'd take years to sort this shit out. It's legitimate in one sense: This criminal enterprise has Lex Luthor–caliber management."

*Why can't anything be easy?* I thought, then said, "You think I can trust this Simon guy?"

"Based on what I've heard, and what you've told me, it's clear he's a heavy hitter. You can trust him as much as you can trust any leader of a shadowy crime syndicate. But it doesn't sound like you've got much choice."

I sighed loudly. Damon had gone out on a limb for me, but I'd still have to fly blind. My plane was boarding and I'd missed priority access. "One last question: How'd you get the info?"

"I asked this girl I've been tryna fuck in the international law division. She told me the name of the company—Silverlake—and pointed me in the right direction. Everything else I found on my own," Damon said.

"She tryna fuck you, too?"

"Remains to be seen. We're getting drinks tomorrow night."

"Well, good luck. And Dame? Thank you."

"Just keep your head on a swivel, Al. You could be getting yourself into some real diabolical shit. I mean, more than usual."

# LET ME RIDE

*Saturday, December 12*

I woke around two in the afternoon. With the blinds closed in my shoebox-size room—I was slumming it at a Marriott near Columbus Circle—it was pitch-black. The red-eye was as bad as advertised and I was exhausted. On par with his usual caginess, Simon—or Herr Hellstrom, as I'd reimagined him following Damon's intel drop—told me he'd "make contact" once I arrived in the city. Figuring he rotated his base of operations frequently, I assumed we wouldn't meet in the same place and chose a centralized location. I checked my iPhone. Nothing. Not even my mom had texted me. If I disappeared, would anybody care? Would anybody notice? Paul and Brad would. Assholes.

I ordered room service—the continental breakfast, judiciously priced at forty-four dollars and ninety-five cents—and watched ESPN. For some reason, North Texas was playing Boston College in the first-ever Tractor Supply Feed Bowl. Who asked for this game? After consuming every single morsel of the spread—when I bagged groceries at Publix, forty-five bucks was a full goddamned day's wage—I commenced my cleansing ritual. I purged all possible execrable fluids, then went for a run on the hotel gym's lone treadmill, then finished up with a steaming-hot shower and shave. By the time I was finished, I looked fresh enough to be the evil boyfriend in a Bollywood flick. The one the beautiful Brown goddess dumps for the taller, handsomer hero, and who's ignominiously drop-kicked out of a helicopter into a volcano.

The waiting game continued. I sat on the double bed in my new shiny black Tom Ford, an early Christmas present to myself, and flipped perfunctorily between bad college football and worse college basketball. I visualized my meeting with Simon, like I'd been taught to visualize football plays in high school and stock market swings in college. What type of intel did he plan to sell me? How much, if any, could I trust? What would I say if I liked what I heard? What would I say if I *didn't*?

Simon had proved he could deliver the goods with the Powerhouse tip. He could still be a con artist and a one-trick pony, of course, but the Illuminati soiree in Connecticut had me sold. Faking that would've been *extraordinarily* difficult. What kept nagging at me was how the money flowed. I desperately wanted to learn the mechanics, and I was fascinated by all the potential details and intricacies.

Safely moving material nonpublic information was as simple as sending a text—presuming you had the good sense to use an encrypted channel. But moving that much cash would surely be orders of magnitude more difficult. In theory, money was just another form of electronic data, but people paid attention to the electrons when they represented billions of US dollars. Damon said the operation looked foolproof, but I had a hard time believing you could nonchalantly launder the GDP of Tajikistan frictionlessly through the financial ether.

Then there was Simon's ridiculous fee structure. There was zero chance I could siphon money out of Prism without Paul noticing. If my plan was to send cash into an anonymous shell company in Macedonia (or wherever the fuck), I needed Simon's holding company, Silverlake, to stake me. That meant they'd take half the earnings, which meant I'd have to double the return I *already* needed to double. *Six hundred million.* In two months. Was that even possible? I began to develop a newfound respect for the world's aristocratic überelite. Running a global financial corruption racket was hard work.

At just past eight that evening, a ghastly pinging sound jolted me awake. The ringtone for a Signal call. Drool had run down my cheek and pooled on the collar of my new Brioni. *Christ.* I shook off my slumber and answered the restricted call without saying anything. A garbled voice gave me a location, Central Park West and 105th Street, and a time, ten, and hung up. Fifty blocks away. I could've walked, but it was fifteen degrees outside. With New York City's endless network of wind tunnels, death via hypothermia—one of the few methods too awful to contemplate—seemed a near certainty.

I re-prettied myself, put on a peacoat and winter hat, wrapped my face in a black scarf, walked a dozen blocks up Amsterdam, and hailed a cab. I paid cash. For the sheer sake of good tradecraft, I once again stayed somewhat off the grid. But this time I was definitely more complacent. Everyone in my orbit committed financial high crimes and misdemeanors in plain sight and got away with it. Why should I bear undue burdens?

I waited at the intersection and watched the glorified gorillas who comprised humanity wade around mundanely and meaninglessly. Fancy tapas. Overpriced cocktails. Superhero movies. Booty calls. A black Navigator with matching tinted windows pulled up to the curb. The front passenger-side door opened. A big dude, the hairless heavy from my last visit, materialized and opened the rear passenger door. I preemptively handed him my phone, and he patted me down and told me to get in. With the wind howling, I stepped into the vehicle and saw Simon's toothy grin.

We exchanged pleasantries, then rode in silence. The Navigator was customized and compartmentalized. The front seats were sealed off by an opaque and retractable privacy mirror, and the usual three rows of seats had been reduced to two. I sat with my back to the glass partition, opposite Simon. A minibar floated between us in a sea of charcoal leather and amber mood lighting.

"Where are we going?" I asked stupidly, because I was nervous.

Simon grabbed a small glass from the minibar, opened a lid on the dash, collected a few pieces of ice, and poured himself some gin. "Would you like one, Mister Al?"

These games had become exhausting. "Thanks for the offer, Herr Hellstrom," I said sternly and deliberately, "but I'm good."

Simon sipped his drink and smirked. "I see you've been doing your homework. Impressive. I always had a good feeling about you."

"Do Trevor and Samus share your enthusiasm?" So much for my calm, calculated visualization of events.

Simon gulped down the rest of his gin, which seemed uncharacteristic. He then slicked back his hair, removed a small capsule from his chest pocket, and poured a few grams of coke onto the top of the minibar. He took a two-dollar bill from the same pocket, cut the powder into three small lines, crouched down in front of me, and disappeared two in quick succession. His eyes grew wide as saucers, and he rubbed the residue from his nose.

"If you're still having doubts about us, Mister Al, please, speak freely," he said, then offered me the stimulant-laced paper.

I squirmed in my seat. I'd only seen cocaine *once* IRL, when I was in sixth grade and Larry, *by far* my mom's sleaziest boyfriend, dangled a bagful in my face and asked if I wanted to make some "extra coin" so I could "impress the girlies." Its mere presence—*a DEA Schedule II substance!*—filled me with anxiety. "Um, no, uh, no thanks," I said. "But I'll have that glass of gin."

"Tell me, Mister Al, what's on your mind?" Simon said. He poured a prodigious serving.

"Well, uh, no offense, but I don't feel like I can trust any of this. Like, I'm flying back and forth to New York on a whim. Sending and receiving cryptic texts. I don't know anything about you or the company you work for, or own, or whatever, and I'm at the point where I need to send you an ungodly amount of money and hope for the best. Can't say I feel great about that.

"Don't get me wrong. That thing you told me about was legit. It was a big deal, and I appreciate it. But I'm in a really bad spot. If this blows up, I'm dead. I'm *literally* dead," I said.

Simon looked at me with sympathetic eyes. An abrupt turn onto 152nd spilled my precious gin. A moment later, the Navigator came to a stop in the middle of the street. I whipped my head around and saw a row of parked cop cars. It was a local police precinct. My heart stopped. I felt light-headed, like I was about to faint. Simon was a Fed! I was fucked! *Fucked!*

"What is this?!" I asked. "Why are we pulling in here?!"

"There's no cause for concern," Simon said coolly.

*No cause for concern!* My brow drenched with sweat. *Fuck, fuck, fuck.* The SUV turned into the parking lot and snaked slowly between rows of black-and-white sedans, SWAT vans, armored trucks, and tanks. *Should I make a break for it?* Simon was fit, but older. He wouldn't be able to stop me. I didn't see any cops waiting for us and the lot was unfenced. The Navigator pulled toward an open garage door. *Now or never.* I twisted around and looked forward, frozen in place, as the vehicle came to a complete stop. The garage sat empty. The bald heavy exited on the passenger side and pushed a button on the wall, sealing the door behind us. The driver killed the ignition. I looked at Simon and attempted to suppress my crippling despair.

"Simon, please tell me what we're doing here."

"Such a jumpy one you are, Mister Al." He chuckled, then inhaled the last line of coke. "What better place is there to conduct business than under the watchful eye of law enforcement?"

*Who watches the watchmen?* "They know we're here?"

"Our organization is far-reaching. We have assets in many unexpected places. These are minor trifles with which you needn't concern yourself. For you, Mister Al, the stakes are much higher. The rewards, much richer."

I looked through the front windshield. The bald henchman was smoking a cigarette with two uniformed beat cops. Each meeting with this guy was less believable than the last. He might still fuck me, but there was no doubt Simon, or Silverlake, or whoever really pulled the strings, was a big-time power player. Snorting lines and scheming *inside* a police precinct?! Talk about a monster flex. I faced Simon and wiped the sweat from my forehead.

"Mister Al, good fortune brought you to me. And afforded you the chance to play the *Great Game* of our time. Few are invited to play this game, because the essential component is trust. We trusted each other once. I provided you with valuable business intelligence, free of charge, and I trusted you to use it wisely, and discreetly. Now we meet again, and we need to trust each other once again. I'm an extremely busy man, Mister Al. The opportunity cost of my time is considerable. By sitting here with you, I'm conveying my trust in you. You must decide if you trust me."

Paul had given me a similarly insane spiel. This must've been what it felt like to be a high school All-American. An endless stream of shady old dudes asking you to trust them while knowing full well they'd fuck you over the first chance they got. How this craziness was happening to me and not some throwaway character on a shitty Netflix dramedy defied my capacity to comprehend. But I'd come this far. No reason to back out now.

"I want to do business with you, Simon. But I can't get comfortable if I'm in the dark. I need to know how everything works."

"You've been to one of our events. We leverage our business intelligence network to create actionable investment insights. We deliver those insights using secure channels."

"What about the money? How does payment work? Where do you send it?"

"We calculate our fee based on the value of the information we provide. You wire said fee—usually in tranches—to account numbers we provide. That's all you need to know."

"What if I can't pay the fee without anyone noticing? Or what if I need you to stake me?" I asked, revealing my limited background in clandestine criminal dealings.

"In such a scenario, we will provide access to accounts with funds already in place. You conduct your transactions as you see fit, then wire the cash—plus our agreed-upon fees—back to a series of separate accounts, which we will also provide."

"I need *a lot* of capital."

"We have ample resources, Mister Al," Simon said. "Let me show you." He removed his phone, clicked on an app I'd never seen before, logged into a web portal of some kind with his thumbprint, scrolled through a series of accounts, clicked on one, and held up the phone. The account contained over two hundred million dollars' worth of liquid assets. "Satisfied?" he asked.

"What bank is that? Where's the account located?"

"This particular account is in Malta. We have several like it all over the world. Luxembourg. Switzerland. Saudi Arabia. Singapore. Access to capital will not be a constraint."

"What happens if I can't pay the fee? Or what if I take a loan and can't pay it back?"

Simon shot me a wide-eyed look. "Needless to say, breaching a contract carries *significant* consequences," he said ominously. "But let us move on from such unsavory matters, which I doubt will be of concern. The relevant issue is this: Are you ready to conduct business, Mister Al?"

The moment of truth.

Every decision I'd ever made, or had made for me, had led here. Every time I made the "right" choice, or took the "hard" path, or opted for the "difficult" route, rendered meaningless. I'd made it. I'd survived a tough neighborhood and a broken family. Breezed through high school and college. Secured an exclusive position at *the* premier hedge fund. And here I sat, glad-handing with the type of man who'd created our modern dystopia. Who gleefully profited from the despair and disenfranchisement of others. Doing the right thing isn't always popular, I'd been told. Yeah, well, doing the right thing had placed me at the mercy of a depraved sociopath. Positioned me to take the fall for a trust fund dipshit who would use his get-out-of-jail-free card to fuck people over with impunity for the rest of his miserable life. Doing the right thing was for suckers. There was a reason Skeletor was doper than He-Man, the Decepticons were more fearsome than the Autobots, and the Sith were more powerful than the Jedi.

And what would happen if I did the "right thing" and told Simon I wasn't interested? Would I get a gold star for good karma? Would my battered conscience stay clean? No, and no. Simon would simply sell his dirty trade secrets to some other hedge fund shitbag, who'd happily make a killing in my stead. The markets were corrupted. The *system* was corrupted. Me taking a noble (and futile) stand wouldn't fix a goddamned thing. It would only accelerate my inevitable defeat. So, was I ready to conduct business?

"Let's do it."

"*Wunderbar!*" Simon reached below his seat and removed a compact briefcase. "Let us waste no more time, *ja*? In this case is a dossier. It contains extraordinarily damaging evidence and describes widespread sexual abuse and rampant corruption that has taken place at a major multinational corporation. This is the *only* copy. No additional information will be provided. The person who compiled this dossier will remain anonymous. The price to obtain this dossier is two million US dollars. Would you like to proceed, Mister Al?"

*Wait, what?!* This was a far cry from the chummy cocktail party dealings I'd observed during my "free trial" in Connecticut. "Uh, is that all you're going to tell me?" I asked. Simon nodded. "Can I take a quick look? You know, 'try before you buy,'" I said, sounding ridiculous to myself.

"Unfortunately, Mister Al, we cannot execute transactions in this manner. If I show you the contents of the dossier, what's to stop you from exploiting this information without us receiving fair compensation?"

"Can you tell me anything else? Without giving too much away?"

Simon smirked. "I must admit, this is among the most comprehensive pieces of business intelligence our R-*und*-R network has ever produced. Because I like you, Mister Al, let's just say the gods and goddesses on Mount Olympus have been very, *very* naughty."

My eyes lit up like I was eight years old on Splash Mountain. "Exactly *how* damaging are the allegations? If you had to quantify."

"Not allegations, Mister Al. Evidence. Extraordinarily damaging evidence."

*Oh my.* "Actionable evidence? Meaning, I can quickly trade on it?"

"That's what I would do," Simon said.

"I'll take it," I said emphatically.

"*Sehr gut.*" Simon opened the briefcase and handed me a spiral-bound document as thick as a college course pack. Then he handed me a single piece of paper with a series of account numbers, followed by a pristine black iPhone. "You will wire the money in ten tranches to the account numbers provided on this sheet. Destroy it when you're finished. Since this is your first transaction, you have one week to send the funds. Please, Mister Al, don't be late."

"Understood."

"From now on, we will conduct transactions remotely. Install Signal on this phone. I will contact you with additional investment opportunities."

"That's it?"

Simon looked over my shoulder at the three meatheads, who were laughing and smoking away. "Please tap the window behind you three times, Mister Al." I did, which prompted the driver to slam the horn. The bald goon darted back to the truck while one of the cops opened the garage door. In an instant we pulled back onto 152nd.

I folded the lone sheet of paper into quarters and slipped it and the new phone into my breast pocket. "You can drop me off at Amsterdam," I told Simon.

He cracked the partition and informed the driver. A few blocks later, the hairless one opened the door and handed me my personal phone. I stepped into the frigid December air and wrapped my scarf tightly around my face.

"It's been a pleasure doing business with you, Mister Al," Simon said. "We'll be in touch." He slammed the door and the Navigator sped off.

I walked ten minutes in the bitter cold, then took refuge in a shoddy all-night diner. I sat at a corner booth in the back, away from the plebes and randos, and ordered a coffee. The dossier had a blank cover page. I flipped it open to the middle. Email correspondence of some kind. I skimmed. As expected, a lot of @olympus.com addresses, but nothing jumped out. If I'd just spent two million dollars on a false bill of goods, at least I'd have a legitimate reason to perform seppuku.

I skipped back to the beginning. Black-and-white pictures. I looked closer. *Dear God.* I turned the pages one by one. Each was more depraved than the last. In my hands, a gold mine.

# INVESTIGATIVE REPORTS

## Monday, December 14

P rism's offices were a ghost town at two thirty in the morning. The cleaning crew worked in the evenings. Fixed income didn't arrive until three. The few times I'd come in this early were when I *knew* shit would go down. Like when a big catalyst or megamerger had been so thoroughly leaked to the media everyone knew the "surprise" announcement in advance. This was different. I'd emailed Paul the evening before and told him we needed to speak urgently, and in person. I said I'd be at the office at three. He never responded, but he undoubtedly saw the message, and I suspected he'd accommodate my request.

Simon's dossier depicted a masterpiece of corporate degeneracy. I read it cover to cover three times. Each analysis produced appalling new insights, which I'd formulated into quite the compelling short thesis. At this point, I simply required Paul's blessing. But in a strange way, I wanted his approval, too. Of course, what I needed most was his intuition. He may have been a deranged psychopath, but the motherfucker knew how to make money. Since he'd put me in this predicament, it only seemed fitting I leverage his disturbed mind to get out of it.

Bathing in the unnatural glow and rhythmic hum of the overhead lights, having only slept a few hours the prior weekend, I stared at my blank computer monitor, lost in thought. Was I asleep? Could I die from exhaustion? If so, how close was I to everlasting relief?

Paul arrived unexpectedly and tapped me on the shoulder. Stunned, I swiveled around, spilled my watered-down Keurig onto the floor, and blurted, "Shit." Paul looked at me, annoyed, and asked if I'd forgotten to take my meds again. *Hilarious.*

"Come to my office, once you get your shit together," he said.

I mopped up the coffee with napkins from Karen's stash, then took the dossier to the bathroom. I micturated, dabbed warm water on my face, and tried to convince myself the person in the mirror knew what the fuck he was doing.

Paul waved me through the glass doors. I'd left my phones at my cube to avoid the security rigamarole and sat down opposite his mammoth desk in the rarely used productivity quadrant. The metropolis outside, hundreds of feet below, idled black and motionless. If New York was the city that never slept, then San Francisco was its crunchy cousin, perpetually hopped up on quaaludes, who went to bed early and did Bikram yoga the next morning.

"What's on your mind, Al," Paul said. He wore a formfitting gray polo and blue slacks, and looked fresh as a daisy, liked he'd already crushed an Ironman, won a van Gogh at Sotheby's, and commissioned a report from the RAND Corporation recommending governments slash worldwide corporate tax rates. That he was so much healthier than me was offensive, though not surprising. The money bought his personal chef, and his personal trainer, and his personal sleep consultant, and the key players in Congress and the DOJ. The money, and the vampire blood.

"You said I needed to run all my trades by you personally." He arched an eyebrow. "Before getting final approval from Compliance." He nodded. "Well, I've got a real doozy for you."

"I'll be the judge of that," he said.

*And the jury, and the executioner, too,* I thought with disdain. "Are you familiar with Olympus Enterprises Incorporated? Ticker: G-O-D-S."

"That rinky-dink theme park in Vegas?"

"Olympian Heights," I confirmed. "But Olympus *Enterprises* doesn't just run a mom-and-pop amusement park these days. A few years ago, the board coaxed Bob Beasley, the longtime CEO of Time Warner, out of retirement and convinced him to become their CEO and executive chairman. As his first order of business, Beasley poached a number of key executives from the competition: Disney, Paramount, Mattel, Netflix, and Warner Bros., to name a few. Next, he revamped the board, restructured the entire business, and raised a boatload of cash via junk bonds, which Olympus has used to aggressively expand its portfolio."

"Good old Bob," Paul said. "Glad to hear he's still got his fastball."

"Under Beasley, Olympus has transformed into a full-blown entertainment conglomerate. They sell action figures and apparel and operate restaurants and cruise ships. The company also produces the top-rated kids' show on Hulu, and they've just broken ground on a brand-new, state-of-the-art amusement park in the Atlanta suburbs."

"Topline?"

"They've quintupled sales over the last two years."

"Cash generation?"

"They've juiced operating margins and free cash flow, though they're leveraged to the gills."

"How's the stock performed?"

"Since Beasley took over? It's increased *twentyfold*. Olympus's market cap recently passed one hundred and fifty billion, and its share price has held steady despite the crash. The Street loves them."

"How come we weren't in on this?" Paul said, agitated.

Good question. "Well, frankly, VICE was built around death and despair, and by all accounts Olympus was on its way to becoming the next Disney. But don't worry. Whatever we missed on the way up, we're about to more than recover on the way down. Take a look at this."

I leaned forward and handed him the copy of the dossier I'd made the night before. Paul removed the paper clip, reclined in his chair, propped his feet up on his desk, and perused. He flipped the pages rapidly until he got to the good parts, which demanded attention. I studied his face while he read. His initial skepticism gave way to surprise, then intrigue, then a sort of lascivious arousal. He put his feet down and sat erect. He stopped on a page about a third of the way through the dossier and stared at it intently. It was *the* page, which contained two breathtaking images. The first was a POV shot of a young girl dressed as Helen of Troy. She was fellating the man holding the camera while another man, in a Minotaur costume, penetrated her from behind. The second, a still from the security footage taken by the ceiling camera, portrayed the same scene from a more incriminating angle.

"Where'd you get this?"

"Do you really want to know?"

Paul looked at me askance. His first instinct was rage, but after a brief moment, he realized that no, in fact, he didn't want to know where I'd gotten it. "How old are these?"

"From what I've pieced together, they were taken sometime last summer. Once you get past the debauched cosplaying, there's a flurry of emails between executives, lawyers, and HR types discussing these sexcapades. Apparently, the college intern who played Aphrodite didn't enjoy being double-penetrated by Zeus and Dionysus and filed a report with the Las Vegas police department. Everything was quickly covered up, and it looks like they bribed all the victims with monetary settlements."

"Victims," Paul scoffed. "What do we do with this, then? The photos are damaging, sure. But if Olympus settled the complaints out of court—which would've included NDAs and confidentiality agreements—there's not much to work with. Nobody cares about a few pervs in middle management boning college girls."

"These people *aren't* middle management. The gentleman there with Helen—holding the camera—that's Bart Guthrie. He's head of global theme parks and merchandising, and rumor has it Beasley's personally tapped him as his successor. Guthrie's also on the board. If you go to the company's investor page, you'll find a slightly more professional picture."

Paul brought up Mr. Guthrie's regal, august headshot on his desktop and muttered, "I'll be damned."

"This isn't an isolated incident, either," I continued. "Elsewhere in the dossier you'll find the exploits of fellow board member Susan Pinochet. She's head of the compensation subcommittee and also sits on the boards of J and J and Honeywell. She was previously a marketing exec in Procter and Gamble's skincare division and, apparently, is a huge fan of *The Iliad*. If you flip to page fifty-four you'll see her in action with Achilles, Patroclus, and Briseis."

"Kinky," Paul said with a smile. "Any other executives implicated?"

"Not according to the dossier."

"Who's in the Minotaur costume?"

"Some poor college kid."

"I certainly wouldn't call him poor, Al. The young man's got a great cock on him. I could fly him out to LA and introduce him to Billy. Lot of potential there."

"That's not my area of expertise," I said hastily. "More to the point, in this dossier we've got two board members, including the heir apparent to the CEO, implicated in a sexual abuse scandal. At the highest levels of the organization, these scumbags have created a culture of fear and exploitation. This is, in NCAA parlance, a *loss of institutional control*.

"But it gets even better—well, worse. Last quarter, these fucking hypocrites unveiled a 'female empowerment' marketing campaign called 'Goddesses Rule the World.' Guthrie's front and center in the TV commercials talking about how Olympus is developing today's young women into tomorrow's business leaders."

"Goddamned liberals have no shame."

"Paul, this has *monster* short written all over it."

He cupped his mouth and leaned back in his chair and thought hard. I knew never to disrupt Paul's reveries. More often than not, his best ideas soon followed. Several long moments passed. "Who else knows about this?"

"My source said there was only one copy of this dossier, but I can't verify that. Who knows how many people put it together and who they might've told."

"You trust this 'source' of yours?"

"Definitely."

Paul exhaled for an absurdly long time. He sat motionless for what seemed like another eternity, then cheerfully said, "Let's make a phone call."

*"Now?"*

Paul pulled out his cell phone and scrolled through his contacts, found who he was looking for, and pressed the call icon. After four rings, the line went to a generic voicemail. Paul mumbled something about "having his cell phone silenced" and dialed a second number. This time, on ring three, a groggy hello.

"Bob! Paul Kingsley, Prism Capital. Sorry for the early morning wake-up call."

"Paul? Paul, it's three o'clock in the morning."

"Carpe diem, Bob! Hey, you're on speaker. I'm sitting here with my top analyst, Big Al Jafar, and we've got a few questions for you."

"They couldn't wait till later?"

"Here's the deal, Bob. My guy Al's been doing some work on you guys, and during his diligence process he's made some pretty startling discoveries. Some potentially ground-shaking revelations, in fact," Paul said, toying with his prey. "It seems Bart Guthrie—your hand-picked golden boy—and fellow board member Susan Pinochet have been dabbling in the Las Vegas talent pool. I'm looking at a couple of photos here. Bart seems to have a bestiality-slash-furry thing going on, while Susan appears to be both bi- and incest-curious. Have you seen these photos, Bob? Magnificent stuff."

A brief pause. "I don't know what you're talking about," Bob said.

"I doubt that's true, Bob. You know, if memory serves, this isn't too dissimilar from that thing you got slapped on the wrist for way back when. It never went public, but you remember what I'm talking about, right?"

"I don't recall."

"That's too bad, Bob. Because it's going to be a real shame when these photos get out. I can't imagine what they'll do to your company's wholesome, family-friendly image. Not to mention your stock price. But you know what'll be *even worse*, Bob? What people will say once they find out you *knew* about these abuses, but turned a blind eye, because you were also implicated. How do you think your shareholders will respond when they realize little Bart here learned how to manage more than theme parks from his beloved mentor?"

The line sat silent for several long beats. Paul winked at me.

"You listen to me very carefully, Paul Kingsley. I will not be bullied by some corrupt two-bit hedge funder. I make one phone call, and DOJ will put its foot so far up your ass, Japanese businessmen will get off on it."

"Wow, Bob, 'two-bit'? That hurts!" Paul said. "Listen, Bob, here's the thing. We don't really care what you did in the past. And we don't want this situation to get any messier than it already is. You don't have to admit to anything, Bob. You just need to tell us you're not going to deny anything."

The air hung thick as molasses while we awaited the legendary CEO's reply. "There will be no denials," he confirmed.

"Thanks a billion, Bob." Paul hung up the phone with the biggest shit-eating grin I'd ever seen splattered across his psychotic face. "It's not often a phone call costs you hundreds of millions of dollars," he said. "I think Bob took it pretty well."

I forced a laugh, then, out of nowhere, Paul jogged around the desk and engulfed me in a warm bear hug. An abusive dad, but a dad nonetheless. I hugged him back.

# C.R.E.A.M.

With the offices filling up and another volatile trading session on the horizon, I thought about Star Wars. Was I Luke? Whose father was a mass murderer and tyrant, but whom he still loved because there was goodness buried deep within him? Or was I Anakin? Whose father was a microbial STD and whose latent rage and antipathy fueled him to devastating ends? Maybe I was neither. Maybe I was a bit player. One of the random Jedi ignominiously slaughtered during the Order 66 purge, whose name was known only to comic nerds and incels. Or maybe I was Jar Jar. A character everyone wished had never been born, but who played an integral part in the destruction of the galaxy.

Another Keurig beckoned—my fourth—when Robbie Cartwright tapped me on the shoulder. Tall and gangly, with inflamed reddish skin and bulging horse teeth, he was Prism's top trader. He had connections to every broker-dealer on the Street and, more usefully, was owed lots of favors by lots of people for lots of different reasons. Robbie traded Paul's personal account, ensuring "the boss"—as Robbie lovingly called him—received the most profitable transaction terms and generated the highest returns.

"The boss wants to see you in his office," Robbie said to me. "Bring the dossier."

We made the long walk in silence. Paul and Brad were lounging on the sofa drinking coffee when we arrived.

"Just the man I was looking for," Paul said. He stood and patted my shoulder. Robbie arched a brow. From the sofa, Brad eyed me like Gollum. "Let's get to work," Paul said, strutting toward his desk. The three of us followed. Robbie and I sat in the two chairs. Brad lingered behind. The city outside remained dark and motionless.

"Bradley, we don't need you right now. Go make sure everyone's fired up and ready to go. We're about to make a fuckload of money."

Brad frowned. "You sure I shouldn't stay? Make sure Habib doesn't get out of line again?"

"His name is Al, Bradley," Paul said. "Now go and check on the others. I'll call if I need you."

"But—"

"Am I fucking stuttering?" Paul exploded. "Robbie, am I stuttering?"

"No, boss, totally clear."

"Al, were my directions unclear?"

I shook my head. Paul flicked his wrist at Brad and shooed him away. The dejected son did as he was told. Maybe I was Darth Maul. The vaguely foreign (read: menacing) and ultimately expendable apprentice to the Emperor.

Paul leaned back in his chair and crossed his legs. He studied us with his piercing blue eyes for a few uncomfortable moments, then nonchalantly said, "Robbie, I want to short one billion dollars of Olympus Enterprises." Robbie eyes bulged more than his teeth. He glanced at me, then back at Paul, then back at me. Paul added, "And I want to do it over the next two days."

"That's fucking insane!" Robbie confirmed. "It's doable. Maybe. But definitely insane."

Paul smiled mischievously. "Show him the dossier, Al." I extended the document as Paul interjected, "Show him the *good* part."

*Right*. Leaning over, I flipped to the dog-eared pages containing the scandalous photos of sexual assault. "This guy here—getting the blow job—he's expected to become Olympus's next CEO. He's currently head of theme parks and on the board. This cougar here's also on the board. She's head of the compensation committee."

Robbie inspected the images, mouthed a waterfall of expletives, looked at Paul, smiled, and asked, "Sure you don't want to short two billion?"

"Could we?"

"If these are real, we can short as much as you want," Robbie enthused.

"Oh, they're real. Al came across them while on a special assignment for me," Paul said, which was sort of true. Robbie eyed me and nodded his head in respect. "Listen, Robbie—all kidding aside—we need to move fast. Realistically, how much could we short without drawing too much attention?"

The expert trader opened the FactSet app on his cell phone, searched for the ticker GODS, and reviewed several of the stock's key trading metrics. "Back of the envelope, given the average daily volume, current price, current short interest, float, et cetera—I could probably tag about five percent per day. That'll whack the stock a little, but our exposure would still be about four hundred million. And that doesn't include options and derivatives."

"Short as much as you can get," Paul said.

"Understood. Is there an announcement coming?" Robbie asked. "Because if we could wait it out a little longer, I could really dig in. Build a *massive* position."

"I'd love nothing more, Robbie. But we don't know who else knows about this. Time is of the essence. Make sure Compliance signs off on everything, then get started. I'll check in later," Paul instructed.

Robbie stood, *saluted*, then set to work on the crucial job of crushing the stock, further spooking global markets, and swindling retirees the world over out of their savings.

I shifted in my chair, butt sweating, and waited for Paul to unveil the next step in his master plan.

"All right, Al, what's our next play?"

*Goddamn it.* "Uh, well, Robbie's setting up the short, and so now we just need to, uh—"

"Need to what?"

"Well, uh, we need to make the stock go down?"

"How do you propose we do that?"

"Uh, leak it to the media, maybe?"

"You're a natural, Al," Paul said. He dug up a number on his cell phone, then placed a speaker call on his landline and held a finger to his lips while awaiting an answer.

After two rings, a woman said, "Paul Kingsley. What do you want this time?"

"I want to help you get that well-deserved Pulitzer, of course."

"I'm listening."

"I've got something big for you, Deb. Enormous. And it's extremely time-sensitive, so you'll need to put your best reporter on it."

"Paul, I don't know if you've noticed, but everything's enormous and time-sensitive these days. We're in the middle of a once-in-a-generation financial crisis. The economy's entering a brutal recession. We've got protests in the streets. CEOs and politicians getting death threats. *And* there's an election on the horizon."

"This tops all that."

"*Really?*"

"Really."

A short pause in the repartee, then Deb grumbled, "This better not be bullshit."

"It's not."

"What do you have? *Exactly.*"

"A dossier. Replete with incontrovertible evidence documenting disgusting, remorseless criminality."

"Who doesn't these days?" she said. "What kind of criminality?"

"The kind that wins a Pulitzer."

"What's your angle?"

"I'm a concerned citizen. Doing his part to make our society more just."

"*Right.* Let me rephrase: What do you expect from me? *Exactly.*"

"Tony Chang. And your commitment to run an exposé as quickly as possible."

"Tony's slammed. You can't have him. But I've got a young whippersnapper for you. Kid's a superstar in the making."

"As long as he's committed to exposing this heinous corruption. I trust you'll move expeditiously?"

"I'll see what I can do."

"Excellent. I'm sending my best associate to New York this evening. Standard operating procedure?"

"Paul, this better not be bullshit."

"Deb, have I ever led you astray?"

The line went dead. Paul smirked. I wasn't sure how to process what I'd just observed. People all over the Street toed the lines of legality to get an edge. That was a given, and everyone knew Prism was the best in the business. But this? Had the scale of the corruption and tomfuckery always been this remorseless? This blatant? Ignorance truly was bliss.

"Listen carefully, Al. You'll make a second copy of this dossier, and you'll give it to a reporter who works for the *Journal*. He'll meet you at nine o'clock tonight at Newark Penn Station—that's in New Jersey, by the way. He'll be wearing a red Bayern Munich scarf around his neck and reading the *Financial Times*.

"You'll approach him and ask how the market for frozen concentrated orange juice futures is doing, and he'll say, 'Never been better.' If he says anything other than 'Never been better,' do *not* give him the dossier. Once that's taken care of, you'll head to Princeton and check into a hotel.

"The next morning, you'll meet with the CEO of some artificial intelligence firm called . . . ah fuck, it doesn't matter. This banker at Cowen's been begging me to meet with them, and I'm sick of blowing him off. Listen to the CEO's pitch and tell him it's all very interesting and you'll report back to me. When you're done, you'll fly back to San Francisco. Lina will book your travel. Any questions?"

*So many questions.* "Nope. Got it."

"Good man."

We stood, then I remembered the most important question of all. "Oh, Paul, I forgot." He looked at me, irritated. "Can I trade on Olympus in my portfolio? You know, for my thing."

"How much?"

"If you're doing a billion, shouldn't I bet everything?"

"I don't know. Should you?"

Always the mind games. "Can I do a hundred?"

"I don't know. Can you?"

"I'd like to do a hundred. Do you approve?"

"Fine. Just make sure to run it by Compliance."

As Paul stepped away from his desk, I interjected again: "One other thing. It's just—you heard Robbie. It'll be a tough trade to pull off. I'll have to compete against him—meaning against you—for shares. If I'm doing this thing in New Jersey, too, then . . ."

"Tell Robbie to short the first hundred million from your account," Paul said. "Now fuck off."

I jogged toward the door, stoked AF.

$$$

Paul's executive assistant, Lina, booked the arrangements. My flight left in four short hours. At Robbie's desk, I placed my order, per Paul's instructions. He looked at me skeptically, but said he'd take care of it. Then I said, "Oh, Robbie, by the way. What's a really stable stock? One that never moves more than five percent one way or another?"

"Why?"

"I want to short something that won't move too much. Free up some extra cash."

"Don't you have plenty of liquidity?"

"I do. I just want to add some low-risk leverage. Juice my returns a little."

"Why don't you buy on margin?" he asked, impatient.

"Uh, yeah, sure, I could do that," I stammered. Fucking traders. I was a *fundamental* analyst. I built complex, elaborate, multifaceted investment theses with simple choices: buy, short, avoid. Anything beyond that was the preserve of traders (gamblers) and quants (gamblers), who couldn't comprehend that "investing" and "trading" (gambling) weren't the same thing. I'd blissfully avoided the nonsense of their day-to-day sprints on the hamster wheel for years, and now I desperately needed their skills and know-how.

"I have this idea I want to test out. It might be dumb, so I don't want to do anything too crazy. I'm just looking to free up a few mil with a super-safe, super-easy-to-cover short."

"Whatever," Robbie said, losing interest. "Try a big pharma like Pfizer or Merck."

"Cool, thanks!"

I hurried back to my desk and scanned the thirty components of the Dow Jones Industrials index. These so-called "blue-chip stocks" rarely fluctuated as is, and Pfizer was the fairest of them all. Ironically, due to the Icarus-inspired crash, Pfizer's stock price had slightly *increased* over the past few weeks. Pharmaceutical shares were considered "defensive"—people needed their 'betes meds during a recession, after all—and were ideal holdings when riding out periods of extreme volatility. These attributes made Pfizer the perfect short for my illicit purposes.

I logged into my portfolio and noticed Robbie had put our brokers fast to work on Olympus. I clicked a few buttons, double-checked a few numbers, then voilà—within a few minutes, I'd also be short sixty-five thousand shares of Pfizer at thirty-one bucks a pop, freeing up over two million dollars.

Once the money magically appeared in my account, I'd send it to Simon's sketchy offshore LLCs. I considered wiring the money into my personal checking account before routing it to its final shady destination—to sever the direct connection to Prism—but then remembered the "headshot" that nearly felled state senator Clay Davis in *The Wire*. Sending the money to myself was a *terrible* idea. Luckily, I'd also learned a few things about British shell companies and money laundering from Damon and Simon, and was feeling much more entrepreneurial.

First, I checked out a loaner laptop from IT. Next, I "borrowed" Dennis's log-in information. He was grabbing a Starbucks with Brad and, more helpfully, always affixed a sticky note with his username, password, and Social Security number to his monitor (tsk, tsk). In an empty conference room, I logged onto the UK's Companies House web page and created my first-ever corporation. Mom and Dad would be so proud! Type: private limited company. Name: Sith Lord Holdings. Director: Nicholas Fury. Shareholder: Anthony Stark. Person with significant control (PSC): Benjamin Kenobi. More of the same for the memorandum and articles of incorporation. *Of course, I'll keep and maintain appropriate records.* I filled in a few more boxes with Star Wars– and comics-themed nonsense and . . . done. Finally, "Dennis" opened a small business account at Wells Fargo to serve as his central "clearinghouse," which was linked to the fake Gmail address I created in his name and verified using the burner phone given to me by Brad. Despite wanting to die most days, sometimes I impressed myself.

To recap: execute the Pfizer short, transfer the money to Dennis's account at Wells Fargo, wire the cash to Sith Lord Holdings LLC, and route it to Simon's offshore accounts. I could repeat this process as desired and clandestinely launder money at my leisure.

The biggest challenge would be hiding the fact that two million dollars had mysteriously vanished from my portfolio. I designed the circuitous Pfizer short to obfuscate things for a few weeks, but eventually Paul would notice. If things worked out, my plan was to replace the money before anyone realized it was gone, and hope nobody paid much attention to the accounting. If things didn't work out, the paper trail showed Dennis getting up to all this monkey business. And if things *really* went south, I was fucked from birth anyway, and could slit my wrists with an X-Acto knife anytime, so did any of this really matter?

# WHO GOT DA PROPS

*Tuesday, December 15*

I touched down at SFO around 7 p.m. The preceding twenty-four hours were a blur, but I'd followed Paul's instructions to the letter. By the time I deplaned and grabbed an Uber to the office, it was past eight. Everyone had long since departed. Everyone except Paul. I made my way to his domain, carry-on in hand, and tapped the glass door. He was playing *Call of Duty* and blaring Led Zeppelin.

"Thought you'd be back sooner," he shouted over the music, without looking, as I entered.

"The morning meeting lasted longer than expected. Then my flight was delayed. Plus, the time change. You know how it goes," I said. Paul turned off the music with a remote control, paused his game, and frowned at me. Then I remembered he didn't, in fact, know how it goes, because he hadn't flown commercial since I was in elementary school.

"How'd the meeting with the AI kid go? What's the company's name, again?"

"Tiger Analytics. It was bullshit. Another Ivy League dropout with an algorithm."

"That's what Zuckerberg is."

"Trust me, Paul, this guy's no Zuckerberg."

He stood to face me, body relaxed, visage tense. "And the other business?"

"Everything went according to plan," I said. "Have you heard anything?"

"You hungry?" he asked, cheerily and abrupt.

I was hungry. Starving, even. But that didn't seem pertinent to the conversation at hand. Paul grabbed a gray Patagonia vest from his desk chair and walked past me into the hallway. I collected my things and followed. We entered the elevator and descended in silence, then made our way to the parking garage in the basement. Paul moved briskly toward his wall of cars. Marvin, sporting a crew cut, razor-thin mustache, and pitch-black suit, was waiting dutifully between an Audi and a Mercedes.

"I'm taking the Lotus," Paul said to him. "Be ready to pick us up when I call," he added curtly.

"Yes sir, Mister Kingsley," Marvin dispassionately replied.

The laconic chauffeur unlocked the ludicrously speedy and absurdly expensive vehicle, then tossed the remote control to Paul. He took a seat behind the wheel and I settled in opposite him.

I'd never been in a Lotus before. It lived up to the hype. Paul throttled the gas as we exited onto California, then sped through red lights and weaved around pedestrians, seemingly intent on getting somebody, or both of us, killed. Would've been a pretty cool way to check out, to be honest. Two minutes later, somehow unscathed, we pulled into the valet line at Medici's, a two-Michelin-star-rated steakhouse. Another minute, and a hostess took my suitcase and my personal effects, including my phones. A minute after that, we were sitting at a secluded table in the back of the dining room. A flurry of staff members delivered two carafes of sparkling water, uncorked a bottle of merlot, set out a selection of small plates, and spoke nary a word.

A waiter appeared, filled our wine and water glasses, and offered us three options: lobster, sea bass, or filet mignon. He described each dish with superfluous adjectives. All were prepared with foreign ingredients and accompanied by extravagant side dishes. We settled on two filets, medium-rare. The restaurant was dark, the atmosphere subdued. Whispered conversations and clanking silverware permeated the air.

"What do you make of it all, Al?" Paul said, then tasted his merlot.

"How do you mean?"

"Your life. San Francisco. The type of work we do." Surely Paul didn't give a good goddamn what I thought about anything—unless it made him a return. "Are you satisfied?"

Had I ever been satisfied? I contemplated eating a bullet every single day, and that was before Paul had dangled fake insider trading charges over my head. "Why are you being so nice to me? A few weeks ago, you threatened to send me to prison."

"Still might. How much you owe now?"

*Owe.* I knew the number to the cent, but said, "About two seventy."

"Big chunk of change. You've got a few months. Think you can pull it off?"

"Depends on how this Olympus play works out. Have you heard anything?" I asked again, deliberately.

Just then, our waiter brought the steaks. They sizzled hot in chives and melted butter. Paul never answered my question, instead delving into his meal, sipping wine and chewing lustily. *Inscrutable.* We ate in near silence. It was *by far* the worst date I'd ever been on: awkward stares, stilted conversation, suspicious intentions. Paul left a third of the exorbitantly priced flesh uneaten, then lit a cigar. I cleaned my plate, and the small plates, like a dishwasher but declined a cigar of my own. Unprompted, the waiter brought dessert wine and two chocolate tarts with vanilla ice cream.

The food was incredible, but I was losing steam. Jet lag and sleep deprivation were working wonders on my battered brain. And being around Paul this long—alone—was exhausting. I thanked him for dinner and tried to break free, but he cut me off. He removed his cell phone from his front pocket and opened his text messages. His fingers strummed the touch screen, its faint glow illuminating his severe face. After a moment of scrolling and tapping, Paul flipped the phone around and showed me the breaking news section of the *WSJ* app.

"Looks like your research is about to pay off," he said.

The headline of the top story read: "EXCLUSIVE: Multiple Olympus Execs Sexually Abused College Interns." *Holy shit.* Everything had felt like a dream until that instant, then suddenly, it was all too real. Paul withdrew the phone and put it back in his front pocket. He stood and slid on his vest. I rose as well, not knowing what came next.

He took two steps toward me and put his hand on my shoulder. "You did good, Al. You did real good."

"Thanks," I mumbled, racked with and rattled by conflicting emotions.

"Robbie and I will take it from here. Go home and relax. You've earned it." He walked past me, then added, "Tell Hector to bill my account. Juanita will grab your stuff and Marvin will give you a ride home."

$$$

When I sat down at my cube at five the next morning, there was palpable excitement in the office. Olympus stock had plummeted a breathtaking 60 percent in pre-market trading, further crushing the Dow and S&P. The entirety of the global media apparatus had seized on the salaciousness of the story. Front-page headlines ran in the *New York Times*, *Los Angeles Times*, *Guardian*, and *Washington Post*, while BuzzFeed, the Daily Beast, and the *New York Post*, among others, plumbed the depths of good taste. Then came the social media backlash. iPhones really needed a crucifixion emoji.

At 5:30 a.m. PT, Olympus put out a press release announcing the "immediate suspension" of Guthrie and Pinochet from all corporate responsibilities, "pending further investigation." True to his word, Beasley hadn't denied anything.

Paul busied himself playing field marshal. He stomped around the office, badgered the traders, and cold-called clients to remind them he was the Street's top fucking dog. I logged onto my portfolio. Robbie had been fast at work unwinding our positions, though he hedged a little since Paul expected a steeper decline once official trading hours commenced. At six on the nose, a "Heard on the Street" column titled "Olympus's Achilles' Heel" appeared. Shortly after, the *Financial Times*'s Lex piled on with "Olympus Shareholders Go Greek." North Korea launched a ballistic missile over Tokyo.

The world outside Prism's offices was crumbling and awash with fear, which was *very* good for business. Inside our pristine hallowed halls, Paul took control of Prism's various portfolios. He was cynical and pessimistic by nature, and the markets rewarded his bearishness. The chaos—Paul's incessant screaming, the blaring televisions, the ringing telephones, the chiming texts—all meant one thing: Money was rolling in.

With Robbie managing my Olympus trades and no major positions in my portfolio, I had little to actually *do*. I slouched forward in my chair and, under my desk, checked my Simon phone for updates. None. I still needed to wire the two million but had a few more days till deadline. I was lost in thought when Keith asked, "Was Olympus your idea, Al?"

I looked up at him, slipping my Simon phone into my front pocket. I stayed mum, loath to take credit for fear of drawing unnecessary attention to my recent activities.

Brad emerged from around our cubes and said, "Great question, Keith. I'd like to know as well. Was Olympus your idea, Habib? Last month you flushed our entire portfolio down the toilet, and now you're on a monster hot streak? Seems a little curious to me. What do you think, Dennis?"

"Very curious," his water polo–playing henchman agreed.

Both twats deserved to be choke-slammed, but I played it cool. "Even dumbasses like me get lucky once in a while."

"You've been a lucky dumbass *three times* in a row," Brad said. "I'd hate to think you've been cutting corners, Habib. Using black edge. Putting my firm in jeopardy." I chose not to dignify his nonsense with a response. "What do you think, Keith? You think Habib's playing it straight?"

"I trust Al," Keith said. "More important, your dad trusts Al. That's good enough for me." A rare airtight argument from my dude.

"Karen?" Brad inquired.

"No comment," she said, eyes glued to her monitor. Nothing but shade from ol' girl. At least she stayed on-brand.

Brad leaned in close, our faces a finger's length apart, and whispered, "I'm on to you, Habib. I know what you've been up to, and I'm going to fuck you right in the ass."

I recoiled reflexively and stood upright to reestablish my personal space. "What the fuck is wrong with you?" I asked, rhetorically.

Just then, Paul descended upon us. Standing in the dead floor space, below the ceiling-mounted televisions and equidistant from the quadrant of cubes, he clapped his hands above his head and settled the room. All eyes fixated upon him. Paul lifted his arm to inspect his watch. Everyone held their breath as the seconds ticked away, wondering which version of the man we'd receive.

"Wait for it . . . ," Paul teased. Seven more seconds. 6:30:00 a.m. PT. Full trading opened in New York City. Billions of transactions executed in seconds. Dark pools, owned by elusive hedge funds in Jersey City, squeezed themselves between buyers and sellers and siphoned enormous amounts of wealth from society while creating no marginal value. Economists called such behavior "rent seeking." Lambasting corporations for such skullduggery was a favorite pastime of the San Francisco liberal elite, though few knew what the nebulous term meant, and most participated in similarly destructive economic activity.

"Ladies and gentlemen, Prism Capital just made seven hundred and fifty million fucking dollars!" Paul intoned. The room erupted. Cheers. Hugs. High fives. For the few privileged women in attendance, unsolicited groping. "And it's all thanks to this man!" Paul said, pointing at me. "Get the fuck over here, Al!"

I stumbled over and met him at the center of the room. He rubbed my head like a puppy's and slapped my back like a newborn's. I smiled coyly.

"Not bad for a guy on the hot seat," he said to the crowd.

The camaraderie, missing since the Icarus nightmare had plunged the digital market and the analog economy into a calamitous death spiral, returned. Everyone in this office was an asshole, but we were assholes together. On the same asshole team. With the same asshole objectives. Seeking out the same asshole rewards. It felt good to be appreciated. Assholes (colleagues) came upon me like a procession, dapping and hyping me up. I received them in funereal fashion while my mind wandered. If Paul's math was right—it always was—about 10 percent of Prism's haul would go toward my debt, which meant I'd generated just over one hundred million dollars in one month's time. Right on track. *I can do this.*

After a few minutes, the celebratory vibe dissipated. A full day of work awaited, and we could never be sure when Paul would switch from the magnanimous Dr. Jekyll to the bloodthirsty Mr. Hyde. Jennie squeezed my shoulder and smiled—her shiny hair smelled like jasmine—and then everyone receded to their cubes, eyeing new and exotic ways to extract more pounds of flesh from the mortally wounded economy. I suddenly craved a Peet's. Before I could grab Keith for a spell of crisp morning air, Brad's T. rex arms barreled into my chest. The force knocked me backward, stunned. I stumbled toward my desk before regaining balance. WTF was his problem now?

"This is bullshit, Dad!" he shouted in Paul's direction. "I can't believe you're going to let Habib get away with this."

Paul gazed at him, his eyes lifeless as a shark's, his face ripe with disappointment. "What are you prattling on about, Bradley?"

"Ever since Habib blew up VICE, he's been trading on insider information. You can't seriously believe he's on a hot streak! He's putting us all at risk!" The office fell silent. A natural circle had formed, everyone raring to watch the schoolyard fight.

"You can prove this?" Paul asked.

"Well . . . no. But—"

"Then Al's just doing the kind of rigorous, thorough, independent research that generates alpha," Paul said. "You might want to try it sometime." Body shot. *Oohs* and *ahhs* from the crowd.

"Dad, listen—"

"This is the type of work we *reward* at Prism Capital. *My* firm. Everyone, show of hands: Who thinks we're some run-of-the-mill hedge fund?" No hands. "Who thinks being ordinary is good enough?" No takers. "Who thinks going the extra mile for our clients is against the rules?" No bidders. Left cross. Grimaces among the spectators.

"That's what I thought," Paul said. "You're starting to sound like those bloodsuckers in Washington, Bradley. If you want to leech off the government's teat instead of doing the hard work required to make something of yourself—like I did—like Al's doing—the door's right there." Right uppercut. Body limp on the canvas. Ten count. The office was quiet as a mausoleum.

"Show's over. Get back to work," Paul ordered.

Bodies scurried like cockroaches. Karen, Keith, and I took our seats, eyes fixed forward on our monitors, pretending to be fast at work. Anything so Paul would leave. The desiccated husk of Brad Kingsley hovered by our cube, flanked by Dennis.

Paul closed the distance between them. In a deliberate voice, loud enough for everyone to hear, he said, "Dennis, take Bradley and fuck off to Ibiza. If he's not willing to do what it takes to succeed at this firm, he shouldn't bother coming back. Al!" My spine straightened and bowels tightened. "Grab your things. We're taking a day trip."

$$$

I sat up in an unfamiliar bed fitted with blindingly white sheets. Sweat formed on my brow. Was I still at the Allure mansion? What time was it? *What day was it?* I owed Simon two million dollars and hoped to Christ I hadn't missed my deadline. My head throbbed and my heart raced. I rubbed the sleep from my eyes and scanned the sterile room. Everything was nondescript, save the gaudy, sex-themed artwork adorning the walls. The clock above the armoire read 8:47 a.m. Where were my phones? Where were my *clothes*? I grabbed a bottle of Evian from the adjacent nightstand and chugged it in one continuous gulp. My body loosened but my mouth remained tacky and dry. I desperately needed a shower, and a mulligan on existence.

After washing my face in one of the bathroom sinks, I discovered most of the attire I'd worn to work the day before in the bathtub. My wallet and phones were nowhere to be found. Paul burst into the room as I was slipping on my damp underwear and slacks. I poked my head around the bathroom door and found him standing beside the bed. He was wearing a sun hat, a long-sleeved T-shirt, cargo shorts, and hiking boots. Worst of all, he looked exceedingly pleased with himself.

"You're quite the party animal," he said. "First time dropping E?"

That explained the pink pills I'd popped, which preceded me getting blackout drunk and doing God knows what with God knows how many porn stars. This was the corrupting influence of guys like Paul. Through sheer force of will—and unlimited wealth—they debased everyone and everything in their orbit, and someone else always paid the price.

The saddest part of this debauched episode was, I'd probably contracted HIV and it wasn't even a death sentence. Thanks to modern medicine, my new viral pal wouldn't kill me *or* keep me unmolested in prison. Another one-sided relationship in a life full of them.

"You up for some fresh air?" Paul asked.

The only acceptable answer was "Sir, yes sir!" so I quietly slid on my socks, shoes, and dress shirt and followed him through the sprawling house to the front door. We exited into the warm SoCal sunshine, and a Jeep Wrangler awaited us in the circular drive. A stunning blonde with an impossible figure sat in the passenger seat. Paul grabbed the wheel, I dutifully climbed in back, and my most surreal surrogate family yet sped off in search of new insanity.

We drove for a dialogue-free hour serenaded by Top 40 pop songs. Paul took the 101 to the 405 to the famed Mulholland Drive and ventured deep into San Vicente Mountain Park. He pulled over at an unmarked section of an unmarked trailhead and hopped out. Sensing my cue, I did the same. The blonde switched seats and Paul told her to meet him at the "missile tower." She departed, and suddenly, we were alone. It was a perfect place for a murder, if only the gods would show mercy.

Paul set off through the unpaved terrain with vigor and I struggled to keep pace in my ill-equipped kit. After a mile that seemed like a marathon, I was parched, famished, and nearly incapacitated, and my state of mind could only reasonably be described as hammered shit. Paul stopped for a moment, swigged greedily from an insulated water bottle, and offered me zero reprieve from the heat. We then slogged on for another interminable mile until a metallic structure came into view. Presumably this was the Cold War relic in question and Paul's latest exercise in sadism was nearing its end.

Atop the tower, we took in a lovely view of the smog-smothered City of Angels. The Jeep idled on the road below, the blonde once again in the passenger seat. Paul downed the rest of his water and let out an exaggerated "Aaaaahhh." I was dying for a drink, though death by dehydration felt disappointingly distant.

Paul turned to me, smiled, and said, "You know what this job's all about, Al?"

I panted and shook my head.

"*Freedom.*" That didn't exactly jibe with my whole hostage situation, but I was too tired to complain. "Doing whatever you want, whenever you want, without constraint. That's freedom, Al." On the cusp of sweating pure salt crystals, I put my hands on my knees and lowered my head from the sun's searing gaze. "One day, you'll be unstoppable."

Paul walked toward the stairs and I started to limp behind. He spun one-eighty and said, "I've got a hot date with Pornhub's most-streamed starlet, Al. This is where I leave you."

*He can't be serious.* "I don't have my phone. Or my wallet," I said, panicked.

"What doesn't kill you makes you stronger."

He patted me on the shoulder, then jogged down the steps, jumped in the Jeep, and sped off. I stood alone, angry, and afraid. If I hiked a few more miles, I'd reach civilization. If I spent the rest of the day in the sun, I'd find salvation.

Either way, I was cooked.

# PART TWO
## 2016

# STATIK

*Monday, January 18*

US markets were closed on MLK Day, but Prism didn't take the day off. The office was stocked but subdued. Everyone pretended to be deep in their research process while they scanned LinkedIn for real jobs. What kind of real job would I want? Presuming I didn't go down for insider trading—or gobble a pack of rat poison. Facebook? Twitter? Apple? Salesforce? Those weren't real jobs. They had *real* offices. Paid *real* wages, which generated *real* fortunes, and transformed San Francisco from a *real* city into a *real* techno-dystopian shithole. Those companies were arguably worse than Prism. We had no scruples and no moral compass, sure, but we didn't kill democracy. At least, that was what I told myself.

I didn't have time to look for a real job, anyway. There were twenty trading sessions until my artificial and arbitrary deadline expired, and I was behind schedule. Simons's R-and-R arrangement had worked as advertised—he texted me intel, "Dennis" wired him money—and nobody at Prism seemed to notice the fuzzy accounting. Problem was, the magnitude of the action had fallen off considerably. The bright and cheerful holiday season, with its ill will toward men and insatiable consumerism, hadn't helped my cause. Normal people—even shadowy, nefarious market manipulators—had better things to do on Christmas Day than eat Dunkin' Donuts, masturbate, and play *Halo* alone.

Nonetheless, the wins trickled in. After the Olympus implosion—which netted almost eighty million for my Special Projects fund—I spent a few hundred thousand dollars of my own money playing "small ball" with Simon. Surprise casino construction in depressed Rust Belt town? I scooped up the municipal bonds just before the announcement. High-flying data-mining company about to miss revenue forecasts? I shorted a few thousand shares the week prior. Niche logistics provider getting acquired by Amazon? I snagged a small but sizable stake in the nick of time.

Paul didn't ask where I got the info, and I didn't bother cooking up elaborate cover stories. Compliance rubber-stamped everything. Saying I talked to a sell-side analyst or saw speculation in the media was justification enough. That the three moves bore the obvious signs of trading on material nonpublic information was an irrelevant aside. The scale—a piddly twelve million dollars in aggregate—was the issue. For the Feds to get interested, I'd come to learn, they needed something meatier, and they needed to catch the perpetrator with the smoking gun in hand.

Even then, they could've had Paul on a wiretap, orchestrating the trades himself, dead to rights, and still come away with fuck all. Paul was politically connected, which meant Prism's white-shoe lawyers would negotiate a puny settlement without an admission of wrongdoing. If you're the Feds in that situation, why bother? The more I understood what really went down, the more I realized Paul was untouchable. The more I realized Paul was untouchable, the more I wondered what in the actual fuck Dennis had done to get on the government's radar.

Emboldened by my inexorable turn to the dark side, I figured out how to make even *more* money on Olympus. With the stock firmly in the gutter, down 50 percent from its pre–institutional rape highs, I convinced Paul and Robbie (and Compliance) to buy a large stake at the depressed price. Then I had Robbie contact his buddy at Morgan Stanley, a trader in the tech sector, who ran a fake Elon Musk Twitter account with seventeen million followers, and suggest Tesla was considering buying Olympus on the cheap and expanding into the media and entertainment business.

Did that rumor make *any* strategic or financial sense? Of course not. But Olympus's stock jumped 10 percent, and Tesla's slid eight, which grabbed the attention of the *real* Elon Musk, who dutifully tweeted, "Good idea??? maybe lololol," which caused Olympus to spike *another* 20 percent before collapsing again a few days later. All told, it was off-brand Iron Man who manipulated the stock market. I'd just gone along for the ride, and generated a cool twenty million for my troubles.

$$$

Around nine, I needed a third coffee. Karen had called off sick, which left Keith to work up a new portfolio strategy for pawnshops and payday lenders. Icarus was in the rearview mirror, and the turning of the calendar had reset the buy-side's annual cost bases. With the alternative finance sector in the proverbial doghouse, getting back in now could reap massive downstream returns for new VICE. In the markets, time healed all wounds. Unless you were one of the Icarus employees who died in the fire. Or an unarmed Icarus protestor who got mowed down by the militarized police. Or an ordinary

American with limited job prospects, buried under endlessly exotic forms of debt, and addicted to painkillers of questionable legality.

Keith and I settled at a black iron table outside Philz on a picture-perfect day. Blue skies, shining sun, and only a vague hint hectares of surrounding forest were ablaze. San Francisco was like a southern hemisphere city: warm during the winter, cold during the summer. Cue requisite Mark Twain quote.

"Which has better fundamentals: PawnBet or SuperPawn?" Keith asked.

Both were run by incompetent, degenerate failsons. Both minted money. Both were fine choices for new VICE. "How much insider trading do you think happens at Prism?" I replied.

Keith's nostrils flared, like he'd caught wind of a decaying animal. "That's a . . . that's a . . . uh, a pretty loaded question, Al."

"Have you ever traded on material nonpublic information?"

"Dude, are you all right?"

"Have you ever knowingly violated securities laws?"

"Are you, like, wearing a wire?"

"For fuck's sake, Keith, I'm not wearing a wire. You want to rub my balls?" He shook his head. "I'm serious. You've *never* gotten a tip from a source inside a company—say, a CFO—and then immediately traded on it?"

"I gather information, glean insights, and synthesize data into an investment thesis," Keith said, his tone suddenly formal and his words suddenly cautious. "That's how we run—ran—VICE. But if you mean, have I ever, like, had a CFO tell me, like, 'We're going to crush guidance so you guys should get in early,' then no, of course not." His eyes darted left, then down at his coffee, then back at me, in a regular, repeating pattern. Keith had joined Prism a few years before me, and I was certain his suspiciously specific example was exactly the kind of thing he'd done before he was assigned to VICE.

"It makes you wonder," I said. "What is material nonpublic information? Isn't anything *not* in the public domain inside information? Or how about this: What is the public domain? If anything not in the public domain *is* inside information, how would we—as investors, traders, whatever you want to call us—differentiate ourselves? If that's the case, isn't the only way to beat the market, by definition, to cheat?"

My monologue worried Keith, and his nose started to bleed. He dabbed his face with a napkin. "I'm not a lawyer, Al. I just try to do my job—which is to make smart, *legal* investment decisions—the best I can. Are you sure you're all right?"

I nodded, and doubted Keith would survive an official FBI interrogation. Speaking of lawyers, I needed to hit up Damon.

$$$

When we were back at our cubes, Paul commenced his rounds. With Prism coming off one of its most lucrative years ever—and among the best in Wall Street history—he was much cheerier these days. Multiple billions of pure profit had a way of improving one's mood. Paul had felt so charitable, in fact, he reversed course and granted everyone performance bonuses. Much of that stemmed from the monster return we'd—*I'd*—generated on Olympus, which made me Mr. Popular around the office. People even called me "Al" without the -Qaeda.

"What are you guys cooking up next?" Paul asked, looming over me and Keith from behind.

We swiveled in unison. Brad and Dennis's absence was conspicuous. They'd returned to the office after the holidays, and ostensibly still worked at Prism, but Brad scarcely made himself present. When he was around, he confined himself to Dan's former office in the old Industrials wing. Dennis flitted to and fro, as before, doing whatever it was he normally did. Fucking up and letting others take the fall, presumably.

"I'm optimizing the alt-finance portfolio," Keith said. "Sector fundamentals still look solid, so there's a lot of potential once it bounces."

"Very nice. Just keep an eye on what's happening in Washington. The commie-crats are pushing hard for new regulations, and the GOP—sensing a populist backlash, and ever the opportunists— might cave."

"Will do."

"Al, what about you?"

"Still brainstorming," I lied. "I've had a lot of success with event-driven moves in biotech, and people are expecting a lot of deals this quarter."

"Always trust your gut, Al," Paul said, power walking away. "I'm expecting another *big* year from you."

"So what *are* you working on?" Keith asked.

"An exit strategy," I said.

$$$

Sitting on the toilet in my favorite stall of my favorite bathroom, fully clothed, I buried my face in my palms and glimpsed the serene water below. What would it feel like to drown? It seemed a truly dreadful way to go. Panic, anxiety, terror, and plenty of time to think about every bad choice you'd ever made. Every horrible thing you'd ever done. Every single person you'd ever wronged. Plenty of time to contemplate whether anyone would miss you. What people would say when they found out you were gone. *Forever.*

Holding my breath for a few seconds in a pool induced an odd, unsettling pain. Surely the full three-minute experience would be nightmarish. But I'd also read that once you accepted there was no hope, and death was inevitable, drowning could be quite peaceful. Not sure how anyone could measure such a thing, but it made a grim sort of sense. No lacerations. No broken body. No charred flesh. No blood. Just weightlessness, then eternity.

I did know one thing for certain: Nobody would care after I died. Of course, my premature passing would be devastating news, and losing a young man in the prime of his life would be such a *tragedy*, but narcissism trumped all. People would only pay attention for a few weeks, at most, then get on with their own lives and go through their own motions until they met their own miserable demises. Even my poor, dear mother—the only family I had—would be hard-pressed to find the time to grieve her dead, pathetic son. Tinder hookups didn't book themselves.

I lifted my head and felt a tear running down my cheek. *Jesus Christ, I am such a pussy. If you want to end it, Al, man the fuck up and do it. Shit or get off the pot.* I got off the pot, went to the sink, and looked in the mirror. My eyes were glassy and bloodshot. I splashed water on my face, blew clear snot from my nose, washed my hands, and wet my hair. A second glance. Better, but still shit. I grabbed my Simon phone and discovered a surprise Signal message.

*Must talk. Urgent.*

*When?* I inquired.

*Freeman's. 94607. 9PM.*

Not the reply I expected. Freeman's could've been anywhere in the world, but that was a California ZIP code. Oakland, to be exact. What was he doing out here? Why did he want to meet in person? He'd specifically said we would become long-distance coconspirators. I started to text back the first of many questions, but stopped. Always better to ask in person.

*Tonight?* I confirmed.

*Yes, tonight.*

$$$

Freeman's was a soul food joint near Oakland's Chinatown. Their fried chicken and collard greens were as good as any this side of the Mississippi, which made it popular with Oakland locals on weeknights and Silicon Valley try-hards on weekends. I'd been twice before, on a Thursday with Damon and a Saturday with Keith. For a European kleptocrat, it seemed a strange place to meet. But the more I thought about it, the more obvious its tactical brilliance became. Oakland had far less surveillance infrastructure—streetlight cameras, facial recognition technology—than San Francisco proper, making it easier to stay incognito. To the extent the Avengers were searching for a globe-trotting champion of financial chicanery, Freeman's in Oakland would be among the last places they'd look.

I walked through the door and was greeted by the thick aroma of buttermilk biscuits and deep-fried batter. A wizened man with a salty beard, the owner, if I recalled correctly, manned the register. I nodded, studied the menu out of habit, and surveyed the room. A couple of two-person booths to my right. A four-person table dead center. Empty. I remembered the hidden nook around the corner to my left. I peeked over and found Simon, seated, perusing a paper copy of the *Journal*. A suited henchman, one I'd never seen before, stood catty-corner to the table.

"Fancy meeting you here, Mister Al."

"What were the odds?"

"Come, sit."

"Aren't you going to order anything?"

Simon seemed thrown off-balance, then shrugged. "Any recommendations?"

I bought biscuits and gravy, fried chicken and waffles, and unsweetened iced teas. I wasn't hungry, but that never stopped me from eating before. Plus, you couldn't use somebody's legitimate place of business to do cross-border financial crime and not buy anything. The fuck was wrong with these people?

I set down the iced teas, waited a few awkward moments at the counter for the order, then returned with the plates and occupied the uncomfortable red plastic chair opposite Simon. I removed my phones, powered them off, and deposited them with the henchman. Simon used a fork to cut a biscuit, topped it with a smidge of gravy, and delicately placed it in his mouth. Europeans—so proper.

I gnawed a makeshift chicken-and-waffle sandwich and, mouth full, asked, "So what's up?"

"I've received information about accounting *irregularities* at a major public corporation. This could be a *significant* business opportunity for you, Mister Al."

Good start, though something felt off. "I thought we were doing everything remote. What brings you to the Bay?"

"I had prior business with another client. Since I was in the area, I thought you might enjoy a little tête-à-tête."

"In Oakland? At a soul food restaurant? That you weren't even going to eat at? What happened to the billionaires' bashes? Like the one in Stamford?"

Simon frowned, annoyed at my skepticism. "Mister Al, certain matters require a greater degree of . . . discretion." He paused, as if that were justification enough. "Anyway, as I was saying, a major investment opportunity has become available. Are you interested?"

"Define major," I said brusquely. "Look, Simon, I'm happy with R and R. You've delivered. But I'd hoped for bigger opportunities. *Much* bigger. Other than Olympus, everything's been small potatoes."

"Funny you should say that, Mister Al," he said. "How about something that makes the Olympian brouhaha seem like 'small potatoes'?"

# MATHEMATICS

*Thursday, January 21*

I sat in the back of a dumpy Thai restaurant in a sad little town called Foster City. I'd scarcely heard of the canal-laden landfill, despite driving past it countless times. It was situated at the midpoint of the peninsula, off the 101, equidistant from San Francisco and Silicon Valley proper. My taxi ride through the town center proved less than exhilarating. There was a Target. And a Costco. And that was it. Visa and Gilead, two Fortune 100 companies, had established headquarters there, too, having surely been lured by some municipal tax scam. The air hung thick and musty, even indoors, and the entire depressing town smelled like Hialeah after a tropical storm.

I was waiting to meet a guy named Ned Song, the CFO of Sweet, a ubiquitous dating app I'd tried a few times with no success (apparently it wasn't the app, it was me). Sweet was created by a Stanford dropout named Lars Heideker, backed by elite Silicon Valley VCs, and headquartered in Palo Alto. The company had gone public last year and—despite the recent market crash—its stock price had tripled, which gave the former unicorn a market capitalization of fifty-seven billion and made it one of Wall Street's hottest darlings.

Ned had been Sweet's CFO for the past two years, managed investors during the IPO, and knew the financials inside and out— and according to Simon, he could produce "concrete evidence the business was built upon a house of cards." I liked the mixed metaphor. Unlike my prior R-and-R dealings, however, this transaction wouldn't be cut and dried. Instead of a "smoking gun"—such as the Olympus dossier—Simon offered me "exclusive access" to Ned. I could call him whenever I wanted, for whatever I wanted, for the fixed sum of five million dollars.

At first, I balked. Why would I want to pussyfoot around with such an arrangement? Either there was a market play to be made, or there wasn't. But Simon insisted this was an opportunity I simply couldn't pass up. I relented, but told him to stake me and knock ten points off my fee. He agreed. Fudging the accounting at Prism was more painful than a few million in extra expenses. Besides, my clock was running out. It was time to go big or go home, where home meant prison or—since my despair and depression had become increasingly debilitating—the morgue.

The tacky silver bells on the door chimed and Ned stepped inside. I recognized him from his photo on Sweet's corporate website. He was a touch shorter than me, with spiky jet-black hair, compacted eyes, and a puckered mouth. Despite his casual attire—cargo pants and a Patagonia fleece pullover—he moved like he was wound too tight. I nodded my head and arched a brow to get his attention, which was sufficient among the small group of diners.

"Did you order anything? I'm starving," Ned said, sitting.

He was thirty-two years old and had already served as CFO of two public companies. If only I'd gotten into Columbia. The waitress brought us jasmine teas. I ordered spicy green curry and brown rice. Ned asked for pad see ew. Solid choice. We sipped our drinks in tenuous silence. I felt an odd sort of deference, him being slightly older and much more successful, even though he was theoretically my indentured servant.

"A mutual friend tells me things aren't all they're cracked up to be at your company," I said, clunky and vague.

He scowled. "The entire business is bullshit."

"Care to be more specific?"

"About which part? The fake user growth? The inflated revenue numbers? Or the missing five hundred million?"

"*Missing?*"

"Well, it's not *technically* missing. It's sitting in an offshore bank account. Maybe in Iran. Or Venezuela. But it's definitely not on our balance sheet, despite what our last ten Q might have you believe."

*Oh dear.* This conversation was already worth every nickel of Simon's fee.

$$\$\$\$$$

We wrapped up our third round of Tsingtaos an hour later. Ned's face was flushed (#theglow) and his eyes hung heavy. I was tipsy, and hardly believed his story. Two out of every three Sweet users were bots. The company publicly reported thirty million "Premium" members, but in reality had two hundred thousand. Management overstated its burgeoning ad business by a spectacular 80 percent. And most hilarious of all, its "Sweet on You" program, which let users buy and send digital tokens to potential matches they were hella interested in, was a full-blown scam. It *was* the site, and not me, after all.

"This sounds like a total clusterfuck," I said, feeling jolly and sated. "Do you guys make any actual money?"

."We've come close to break-even a few quarters, which we, of course, reported as record-setting earnings. Truth is, we're hemorrhaging cash. Lars told our investors we were chasing user growth at the expense of short-term profits. He said when we *just* hit that critical inflection point, and the network effects *finally* kicked in, we'd print money. They believed him, but it never happened. Once Lars realized he couldn't deliver, we started inventing the numbers."

"How many people know?"

"We've had a few internal complaints from people who eventually left. There's a general sense inside we're not doing as well as it seems. But there's a lot of Kool-Aid drinking, too. Most skeptics choose to bail rather than make noise."

"So no government whistleblowers, or anything like that?"

"Not that we know of. We monitor all internal comms, as well as external cell phone use, location data, social media activity, et cetera. We haven't flagged anything."

His utter nonchalance while describing a totalitarian surveillance state would've made Orwell wince. "How'd you hook up with Simon?"

"It's funny. I considered blowing the whistle myself, but then read the horror stories. You blow the whistle, you never work in the Valley again. Plus, there's no guarantee the government will do anything. A friend of a friend of a friend put me in touch with Simon. I figured, if Sweet's going down, why shouldn't I cash in? Not too different from you, right?"

*Gut punch.* Also, accurate. But did it matter? I was selling a soul I never asked for. "What happens next?"

"Remember that five hundred million I said was missing? Lars took it. I don't know where, but it's not coming back, and neither is he. The official story is, he's in Asia looking to expand our offering into new markets. The only thing I can guarantee is this: Wherever Lars is, there's no extradition clause.

"We're auditing the books now. Once that's done, I'll tell the board Lars committed massive accounting fraud and fled the country. Also, that we're insolvent. It'll go as well as you expect. Given the proximity to our fourth-quarter earnings call, I'm going to recommend we rip the Band-Aid off and announce everything at once. I'm pretty sure our corporate counsel will agree."

"When's your earnings call?"

"February sixteenth."

*The exact same day as my "deadline."* The gods were cruel and cynical bastards, indeed. I finished the last sip of my beer. "You can prove all this, right? With emails and bank statements?"

"Beyond a shadow of a doubt."

*Fan-fucking-tastic.* "I'm sending you a Signal message with a list of documents I'll need," I said, typing on my Simon phone while I spoke. "Per my contract, I'll touch base with you at least once per day."

"Not a problem."

I paid the bill with cash. Ned ordered an Uber and I called a Yellow Cab. We exited the restaurant, shook hands out front, and idled uneasily while awaiting our cars. I wandered to the adjacent laundromat. A large, tattooed man was sitting in the window reading *The Economist*. A Hispanic-looking woman with two kids was folding beach towels. The far side of the strip mall included a sushi joint, a laser tag facility, and a high-end jewelry store. Most of the storefronts sat empty. What a bizarro town.

Ned's car collected him. I smiled, waved goodbye, and took his place at the curb. This was it. *The big one.* The one that'd put me over the hump. The one that'd clear my debt and get me off Paul's shitlist. Planning the trade would be a breeze. I needed to make about a hundred and sixty million. Sweet's stock would legit go to zero, which meant I needed to short about a hundred and sixty million, and I had two weeks to do it. A walk in the park compared to what I'd already survived. Things were finally looking up.

# DOG EAT DOG

## *Monday, February 8*

Ned came through with flying colors. I easily convinced Paul the dating app Sweet was an abject fraud, and Prism duly took a short position in the stock equivalent to *one billion* dollars, nearly half of which came from my Special Projects fund. I was out of time and out of fucks. It was all or nothing. Freedom or prison. Glory or suicide.

It'd been an eerily calm period for stock markets. Blue-chip earnings reports trickled in and were generally positive. Political rhetoric had cooled. The world wasn't on the cusp of World War III. Stock prices had remained muted, which was fine. In a few short days, Sweet would blow itself up, I'd cash out, my debt to Paul would be more than settled, and the market would have another aneurysm. The masses would suffer while the privileged few cleaned up. Rinse. Repeat. God Bless America.

I was at my desk, analyzing college basketball box scores, reading about pro wrestling, and listening to *Ready to Die*, when I received a ball-busting FactSet alert: "Sweet (KISS) trading +6.7% on unusual volume." We'd been selling short, which had depressed the stock price, and suddenly the market was going long, which was elevating the stock price. That could become a big fucking problem, real fucking quick.

I nervously scanned the usual channels. No press releases. No takeout rumors. No big-time investor unveiling a large stake. Nothing in the *WSJ* or *FT*. An uneasy feeling welled in my stomach. Sometimes weird shit happened in the stock market, but the universe didn't feel right. I asked Keith if he'd seen or heard anything. Nothing. Karen, same. It was only a matter of time before Paul came rampaging by.

I tracked down Robbie. "What's going on with Sweet?"

"Fuck if I know. It's doing monster volume—double its weekly average." This was bad.

I skimmed Twitter next and noticed Sweet trending in the US. I clicked and scrolled maniacally. Tons of people were stating the fucking obvious—*stock's on fire, bro*—but nobody was offering a reason why. I checked the market price again. Up 8 percent and climbing fast. Why, why, why, what the fuck?

I stood on my chair and looked around at everyone's cubes. Like a SoMa schizophrenic, I shouted, "Does anyone know what's going on with Sweet? Ticker: K-I-S-S. It's up nine percent on no news. Anyone? I could really use some help here." Judgmental murmurs but no answers.

"What the fuck's going on, Al?" Paul barked on cue.

"Working on it," I said. My head and neck dampened.

"Did you check with Robbie?"

I nodded. Paul's reaming was just about to commence when Jennie pointed to the TVs overhead. CNBC flashed a bloodred BREAK-ING NEWS chyron across the bottom of its feed. Keith jogged over and cranked the volume.

" . . . Los Angeles-based hedge fund Seaside Capital just announced it's making a two-hundred-million-dollar PIPE investment in dating app Sweet. It's also requesting a board seat. Jason Beard, Seaside's founder and chief investment officer, described the move as *friendly*, and said the fund would increase its ownership position in the high-flying tech company to approximately four-point-nine percent."

Paul laughed. "Jason's about to nuke his own fund. Serves that cocksucker right."

My fever broke. Before I could agree, the report continued:

"In a related plot twist, a Reddit user calling themselves the Invisible Handjob Sixty-Nine has claimed San Francisco–based hedge fund Prism Capital, run by superstar manager Paul Kingsley, has placed a so-called *monster* short bet against Sweet. The now-viral post encouraged small-time traders to, and I'm paraphrasing here, quote, 'Put that greedy mother-effer out of business,' unquote. It appears an army of mom-and-pop investors are heeding this very call. Sweet's stock is trading at *five times* its typical volume and is up sixteen percent. With more than half the session to go, it promises to be another wild day on Wall Street."

"Turn that shit off," Paul said. "Al, find Robbie and get your asses to my office. *Now!*"

$$$

Robbie and I made nonstop phone calls from Paul's sofa. Nobody knew, or was willing to tell us, how word of Prism's short position had spilled into the open. Unlike "long" positions, which were often willingly disclosed in regulatory filings, and compulsory at certain thresholds (e.g., over 5 percent), there were no legal or regulatory requirements for disclosing bets *against* a company's stock. In theory, a trader could short every single share of a target company without anyone knowing. Hedge funds put forth many explanations for why this was healthy and useful for capital markets, though the simplest and most logical was pure, unadulterated regulatory capture. We certainly hadn't disclosed our "monster" short position in Sweet. Either a loose-lipped broker or somebody *inside* Prism had blabbed.

Paul exhaled in frustration. "Robbie, get back to your desk. I want to know who sold us out."

Prism's top trader departed. Paul motioned for me to empty my pockets and shut down my phone. I complied, making sure he saw. I'd fortuitously left my Simon phone tucked away in my desk, but that also meant I wasn't able to contact Ned and ask him what in the actual fuck was happening.

"How reliable is your source on this?" Paul asked.

How much truth to tell? That was always the dilemma with Paul and, for that matter, everyone. "The intel comes direct from a verified company executive. A *high-level* executive."

"And you're sure it's legit?"

"As sure as I can be in this business."

"This is your ass on the line, Al. You're either sure, or you aren't. Which is it?"

"I'm sure."

Paul huffed. "You got moxie, Al, I'll give you that." He rubbed his eyes with his palms and massaged his face. He looked uncertain for the first time. Vulnerable, even. "Where's the stock now?" he asked. I reminded him my phone was turned off. He removed his own device. "Up twenty-two percent," he confirmed. "I need to think on this one. See what you can dig up. We'll meet back here at nine." He meant p.m. *Fuck my life.* My head sagged and I stood to leave. "Tell Robbie to short another two hundred million. If the stock keeps rising, make it three hundred."

$$$

By quarter to nine, I'd been at my desk for sixteen straight hours. Sweet closed 40 percent higher and Robbie had shorted the entire three hundred million. Our position was catastrophically underwater—imagine owing someone the endowment of a small liberal arts college in New Hampshire—and could still get much, much worse.

Such was the peculiarity of short selling. Because the theoretical price of an individual stock was positive infinity, the theoretical loss on a short position was negative infinity. Those limits problems in high school had finally come in handy. But, like owning a stock that had skyrocketed in value, the gain—or, in our specific case, the loss—was only *real* once it was *realized.* Sweet's stock *would* eventually crash—the sooner the better, of course—and everything leading up to that point would simply be noise.

I texted Ned another litany of questions: *Did you know Seaside was planning to make an investment? Who did you tell about our short? Any word yet on your missing CEO?*

"New phone, Al?"

I jumped like a shotgun had gone off in my ear. "I, uh, cracked the screen on my other one."

"Leave it and come to my office."

Situated in the relaxation station, sipping a brandy, Paul looked chastened and haggard, like a movie star who'd fallen off the wagon. "Where are we, Al?"

*Deep breath.* "Okay, Deepak Patel, who's on Sweet's board, used to be the CEO of a professional networking app called Konnekted—think poor man's LinkedIn. Seaside invested in their IPO, had a board seat, and orchestrated a friendly acquisition by Salesforce after seven months on the Nasdaq. So Deepak has a straight line connection to Jason at Seaside."

"Fine. What else?"

"This Deepak guy surely knows the books are cooked, right? So I figure he does a quick back-alley deal with Seaside to preemptively stabilize the company."

"Why would Jason bite?" Paul asked.

"He trusts Deepak, and he made money on their prior deal."

"And?"

"Deepak lied about how bad the numbers are?" I said, unsure.

"Pretty thin, Al. What about this Reddit horseshit?"

*No fucking clue.* "Still working that angle. My guess is someone at Seaside is front-running the PIPE announcement. Making noise on Reddit from a burner account. You know, classic pump and dump," I said, fumbling for coherence.

Paul rolled his eyes and scoffed. "That doesn't fucking explain how people figured out we were short, Al. That's the crux of the issue here. In case you forgot." I hadn't. But I didn't have any answers, either.

Paul gazed through me like the Eye of Sauron. "You want to know what I think, Al?" I did, actually. "I think we've got a rat." Solid hypothesis. "Some cowardly little snowflake turned on me." Imagine that. "And you know what's really ironic, Al?" About which part? "You're the only person I can trust."

# NATURE OF THE THREAT

## *Thursday, February II*

Sweet's stock shot into the stratosphere over the ensuing days and more than doubled its "undisturbed," pre-Reddit-clusterfuck price. The higher it went, the more Paul shorted. Like a poker player on tilt, he just couldn't let go of this hand. He should've been consolidating his potential losses. Instead, he kept tossing chips into the pot. By last count, we'd put well over two billion dollars—the endowment of a world-class research university—at risk.

Losing a wager of this magnitude could cripple, if not kill, the firm. With less than a week until my deadline, I wondered: *Should I be rooting for the Reddit finance bros?* Paul couldn't pin insider trading charges on me if Prism went belly-up. Maybe I wouldn't have to figuratively and literally self-immolate after all. Like a mobster in witness protection, maybe I'd get a fresh start, in a fresh town. Of course, people far more powerful than the jackasses on Reddit bet against Paul all the time. And lost.

Jennie entered the conference room and took a seat across from me. Sun shined through the all-glass facade and refracted through the blood diamond on her finger. To flush out his elusive "rat," Paul had declared me Chief Inquisitor and ordered me to interview every single Prism employee. I was supposed to figure out who had leaked word of our short.

After "conversing" with half the office, the only things I'd definitively learned were that I was a "sellout" and a "rat fuck" who should "eat shit and die" and "go back to where I came from." That Paul recorded the interviews only amplified my coworkers' brazenness. Better to appear strong and confident while lying than weak and suspicious while telling the truth.

"I'm really sorry we have to do this," I began.

"What the hell's going on, Al? This place is a madhouse," Jennie said.

*No argument there.* "Just a gentle reminder this conversation *is* being recorded."

"So you're the Gestapo now?"

*Ouch.* "Dennis said I was more like Quds Force, which was among the more clever insults he's come up with. I assume he learned about them from *Splinter Cell.*"

This time, my nerdy joke didn't make her laugh. "You've changed, Al. Ever since the Icarus meltdown, you've seemed off. Withdrawn. Distant. Darker—than usual. Plus, I have no idea what Paul's got you doing these days? *Special Projects?* Really?"

"Things are . . . complicated."

"I'm leaving Prism, Al. And I suggest you do the same. This place is effing toxic. There's more to life than money." Said the girl marrying into America's fourth-richest family. It must've been nice gliding through life without a financial care in the world. Never having to worry about losing your house as a child. Not having to work part-time in college. Not having to support your own mother as an adult. Shame on me for not coming from generational wealth. If only I'd pulled a little harder on my bootstraps.

"Have you told Paul?" I asked.

"You said you're recording this, right?" She looked directly at the glass sphere affixed to the ceiling in the corner of the room. "I quit, Paul. Thanks for the opportunity, but this isn't the career for me after all." She looked back at me. "Save yourself, Al. Before it's too late."

Jennie darted out of the conference room and I trailed her back to her cube. She casually powered down her laptop and cell phone and placed framed photos of Preston and her younger sister and a panda bobblehead in her Tumi bag.

"This is a little dramatic, don't you think?" I said.

She looked at me with cautious eyes and extended a business card in my direction. I hesitated, and she nudged it firmly into my chest. She'd written something on the back: *Ferry Building, 15 minutes.* I slid the card in my pants pocket and returned to my cube.

"Find the smoking gun?" Karen asked. I chucked a notebook into my backpack and grabbed my sunglasses.

"Where are you off to?" Keith inquired.

"Heading out for a coffee," I said.

"I'll come with you," Keith said.

"I'm meeting someone. A banker friend."

Keith sulked while I finished gathering my things.

"Dennis was looking for you earlier," Karen said. "Told me it was very important."

I glanced at her. "Did he say what it was about?"

"That it was very important."

$$$

The Ferry Building was cramped, crowded, and claustrophobic. The porchetta sandwich line snaked around the front and obstructed walkways and sightlines. I battled past the high-end cookware kiosk and the overpriced bakery, then the looked-better-than-they-tasted macaron stand and the obligatory Starbucks. No sign of Jennie.

Just when I thought our clandestine rendezvous might've been imagined, she clasped my elbow from behind. We walked in lockstep to the fancy fish market and snagged a secluded table in the corner. She radiated in the dim light. For a few glorious moments, I wondered how it would've felt if we'd been together. If she'd chosen *me*. All hidden notes and secret trysts.

"It's not safe to talk in the office," she said. "Paul's completely lost it. Apparently he has 'spies' everywhere."

"Did you really just quit?"

"I'm emailing my resignation letter at market close. Here's what I've learned about Prism, Al: The longer you stay, the more likely you are to get tangled up in someone else's ratfuckery. Sure, I sucked at picking stocks and my portfolio was a dog and I'll never work on the Street again. Fine, whatever. My hands, and my conscience, are clean."

Too bad I didn't have a multibillion-dollar backup plan. *Has she always been this tone-deaf?* "It's a big decision. I'm happy for you."

"You have to get out, too, Al. Whatever game Paul has you playing, it's going to end badly for you," she said astutely.

"It already has."

"What do you mean?"

How much truth to tell? That recurring, unavoidable question. "The less you know, the better. I don't want you getting tangled up in my—what did you call it? Ratfuckery?"

"Just quit, Al! Surely you have enough saved. Preston's family has connections everywhere. You—"

"Jennie, I'm behind the eight ball and staring down the barrel of a gun. Or whatever. I can't quit. I wish I could. But if I don't discover Paul's 'rat,' and find a way to salvage this insane short against Sweet, then . . . "

The waiter materialized at that most auspicious moment. Jennie ordered two glasses of house red and told him to bring us his three favorite appetizers. She looked at me again with frustrated concern and realized I wouldn't say any more.

"There's something I need to tell you," she said. "Have you seen Brad lately?"

"Just skulking around the office here and there."

Jennie rummaged in her bag and grabbed her phone. She swiped open the screen and flipped it around to show me a picture. "Do you know who they're talking to?" The "they" in question were Brad, Prism's disappointing scion, and Robbie, Prism's world-class trader. Sitting across from them was someone who looked uncannily familiar. It took me a second to place the face, then the realization pummeled me like a Five Star Frog Splash. *No way.* It couldn't be. It didn't make sense.

"When did you take this?"

"Last night." She swiped to the previous photo. "I took this one the night before that. And this one a few days ago."

"But that means . . . *holy shit*! I have to tell Paul. Can you send these to me?"

"*Fuck Paul!* Prism's about to implode, Al. You need to clear the blast radius."

"If Paul goes down, I go with him. Jennie, please. You have to trust me. I *need* to show Paul those photos. And I need to know where you took them."

She furrowed her brow and wore a look of stupefied annoyance. She'd thrown me a life jacket, but like an obstinate toddler, I was too dumb to put it on. The waiter set down our wineglasses.

"There's a beer garden in Dogpatch I pass during my nightly run. A while back I saw Brad there with some guy, but didn't think anything of it. But then I saw Brad and Robbie there with the same guy. And then Brad was there with a different guy. And then the first guy was there with Robbie. At that point I got suspicious and started snapping photos. When this Sweet-Seaside-Reddit circus began, everything clicked."

I was stunned into silence. Whatever the hell was going on was much, *much* worse than I'd imagined. I wished for a heart attack, but my constitution was too sturdy.

"You want to know who Paul's rat is?" Jennie asked. "He's right there in the photo: Brad Kingsley."

# SURVIVAL OF THE FITTEST

I raced from the elevator straight toward Paul's gargantuan office. Sweat seeped from the pores of my unshaven face and dripped off my nose, the result of a breathless sprint down Market and Pine from the Ferry Building. I eyed the electronic device drop box, ignored protocol, and thrust open the door. Paul stood near the humidor, back turned, gazing through the window at the cloudless azure skies. Sitting at his desk, feet propped up, Brad flashed me a devilish grin.

"Habib! Glad you could join us."

"Paul—it's Brad! He's the rat! He's the one who sold us out to Seaside!" I said, panting.

Paul didn't flinch. Brad smirked, then clicked a button on his laptop, which produced a tinny, crackling sound. A voice filled the room. My voice.

"You have supporting documentation, correct?" the recording of me said.

"Spreadsheets, account numbers, the whole shebang. I can show you exactly which numbers are fudged and how we fudged them," the recording of Ned said.

"I'll need all of that," the recording of me said. Brad paused the audio file, hummed mischievously to himself for a moment, then clicked it on again.

"I paid Simon for unlimited access," the recording of me said.

"Whatever you need, I'm your man," the recording of Ned said. "I look forward to working together."

Brad closed the laptop. "I don't know about you, Dad, but it sounds pretty open and shut to me." Paul didn't respond. "Do you have anything to say for yourself, Habib? Any elaborate excuses this time?" Passing kidney stones would've been more pleasant than standing next to these sociopaths.

"What exactly do you want, Bradley?" Paul said.

Brad popped up, grabbed his laptop and a stack of documents, and strutted to the leadership center, where he settled into Paul's favorite spot.

"Come, sit," he said, patting the cushion beside him. "Let us ne-gotiate the terms of your surrender."

Paul sighed and took the seat across from his son. The place where many a Prism employee had been excoriated and executed. I sat next to him. Brad's permanent grin accompanied a purple turtleneck and mustard khakis. Paul manspread across the sofa and forced me to the edge. An air of bored disinterest clung to him.

"Those snippets are but a sampling of the *hours* of recordings I have of Habib and Ned Song, CFO of Sweet Technology Incor-porated, committing textbook insider trading," Brad said. "Habib, before you claim that wasn't you talking to Ned, why don't you take a look at these?"

Brad opened a manila folder and plopped some tastefully shot black-and-whites of Ned and me eating Thai in Foster City onto the coffee table. *Shit.* These must've been taken by the tattooed guy in the laundromat. Of all the places to be caught dead.

"I also have photos of this traitor meeting with some Russian oligarch—presumably the mysterious Simon—in Oakland. And collecting files from Ned in a Costco parking lot," Brad said. "You can keep those, by the way. I've got multiple hard copies and plenty of digital backups."

"I've got a hedge fund to run, Bradley," Paul said. "Why don't you get to the point?"

Brad laughed a dismissive laugh. "The point is, you're *finished,* Dad. Habib trafficked in material nonpublic information, under your direct supervision, and you explicitly ordered Robbie to trade on it. The evidence is *overwhelming.* I give this stuff to the Feds, and *poof*—you're done. Bye-bye, Prism. Hello, prison."

"You practice that line?" I said.

"Fuck off, Habib. You still don't get it, do you? You're expendable. Nobody gives a shit about you."

True fact since day one. I glanced at Paul, who sat still, silent, and serene as a monk. "You go to the Feds, you fry, too," I said. I imagined myself as a tough-talking detective. The kind Hollywood propagandized to perpetuate harmful stereotypes.

"Au contraire, Habib. As the DOJ's key witness, and the man responsible for reforming this corrupt shithole after Dad's gone, my lawyers *guaranteed* me full immunity."

He had a point. DOJ was probing Prism, which was why he and Daddy had set me up to be their fall guy in the first place. The Feds would welcome Brad with open arms. Who better to take down the most wanted man on Wall Street than his own son? It was positively Shakespearean. Paul remained disconcertingly calm. *Amused.*

"Or," Brad said, "we can make this simple. Avoid any *unnecessary* drama."

Paul still wouldn't bite. I had nothing to offer except toothless quips. This conflict was theirs alone. And theirs to resolve. Two powerful, scheming, ultra-rich dickheads, thrashing and smashing any- and everything to get what they wanted, and leaving a junkyard of collateral damage—me, the capital markets, the United States of America—in their wake. Paul crossed his legs and yawned.

"You think I'm fucking around, Dad?!" Paul rolled his eyes, sighed, switched legs. "I'm going to get my lawyers in here, and they're going to draw up new articles of incorporation, with me as Prism's sole proprietor. You're going to bequeath all your beneficial shares to me and surrender your voting rights. You're going to resign from Prism and sign every fucking NDA my lawyers can dream up. And then you're going to fuck off to Florida with the rest of the dinosaurs so I can bring this firm into the twenty-first century."

It sounded like a pretty good plan, to be honest, though Brad hadn't accounted for the immediate and inevitable investor exodus that would occur when the world's greatest stock-picker ceded control of his fund to an entitled, idiotic, unproven shitbag. Surely his trusty lawyers would remember to tweak Prism's lockup periods.

"What about your boyfriend, Dennis?" Paul said. Brad's beady eyes widened. "In your new world order, where you're in charge of Prism—investing in corporate social responsibility or the Green New Deal or whatever you leftist pussies are into—where's Dennis? Will he be a PM? CIO? Chief of staff? Or your personal play toy?"

Brad laughed a nervous laugh. "This isn't about Dennis. This is about the future of Prism, Dad. How you're running it into the ground with thugs like Habib. How I'm saving you from yourself!"

"You think I haven't known about your little crush on Dennis all these years? 'Dennis this' and 'Dennis that.' 'Oh, Dennis is just so great.' All those girls I set you up with. Models. Actresses. All of them would've killed for a piece of your inheritance. But no, you didn't 'click' with any of them. All those trips to the mansion. You having slumber parties with the talent. You think I didn't know what you were up to? They're fucking porn stars, Bradley! You're supposed to *fuck* them, not make pillow talk. I took Al to the mansion one fucking time, and he took care of fucking business. Like a real fucking man!"

Brad glowered at me with an ashen face and a hatred I'd never known. I never realized he was gay. I never realized anyone in San Francisco felt the need to stay in the closet. Then again, I never realized being the unfortunate son of Paul Kingsley wasn't all it was cracked up to be. Everything made so much more sense. I felt sorry for Brad. I pitied myself.

"Do you think I would *ever* let you put your dainty little hands on my firm?" The rhetorical question hung in the air like chlorine gas. Brad bowed his head, eyes sullen. Paul had coiled like a snake, and chose the perfect moment to strike. He wouldn't even spare his lone offspring.

"Now, you listen carefully to my terms, Bradley. You're going to hand over that laptop and those photos. You're going to delete the rest of your copies, digital or otherwise. And you're going to sign every fucking NDA *my* lawyers can dream up, including an affidavit affirming you're psychologically and mentally unstable and you're suffering from severe alcoholism and chronic opioid addiction. You're going to do exactly what I tell you, Bradley. Otherwise, little Dennis will take a nice, long vacation to Sing Sing."

Brad laughed a desperate laugh. The kind that signaled defeat. "Fuck you, *Dad*!"

"Actually, you miserable little pansy, fuck *Dennis*. He might not have put out for you, but those boys inside will have a field day with his lily-white ass. I'll make sure the DA assigns him to gen pop," Paul said.

Dads like this made me think getting abandoned might've been a blessing in disguise. Paul's enormous office suddenly felt choked and claustrophobic, the air filled with spiteful, poisonous pheromones, which triggered generations of epigenetic trauma. Paul had played his hand masterfully. Dennis was on the Feds' radar. Dennis had committed the crimes Paul was lording over me. Dennis was the unrequited apple of Brad's eye, and the weak link in his overzealous power play.

"What assurances will you give me?" Brad said meekly.

"*Assurances?*" Paul cackled like a hyena. "I can *assure* you if you don't hand over that laptop, it'll be the biggest mistake of your life."

"I didn't know," I said to Brad. "I get it: You hate my fucking guts. But, please, listen to your dad. You can't win this one."

Brad's eyes watered and his lips quivered with rage. He handed his device and documentation to Paul.

"Glad you've finally come to your senses," Paul said. "You should thank Al. He just saved your life."

Paul hopped to his desk, scooped up the landline receiver, and barked at Lina to call security. Within seconds, two beefy goons in suits slammed through the doors. "Strip search these two and confiscate any electronic devices," Paul instructed. My Simon phone—*fuck!* While the henchmen began, Paul made a call on his cell phone. "Tell Gerry to get his ass over here as fast as possible. We need a cleanup," he said into the device. "Nobody else leaves this room," Paul told the muscle, then he sprinted into the hallway. It was hard to imagine things getting worse, and I had zero doubt they would.

When I woke up this morning, Brad was the son of my enemy, and clearly my enemy. Now he was the enemy of my enemy and *still* my enemy. Could I summon *any* allies in my futile fight against

Paul? Damon didn't work on the Street—plus, he'd understandably ghosted me the last few times I'd texted him. All I brought him was bad news. The mere thought of Keith going toe-to-toe with Paul Kingsley made me laugh. Karen appeared to be actively rooting for my downfall, though the feelings were mutual. Jennie liked me the way rich yuppies like rescue dogs: They scratch you behind the ears and whisper encouraging words just before you're put to sleep, then have a latte and forget you ever existed. My own mother was like the slutty big sister you had nothing in common with and were too embarrassed to call family. She could barely take care of herself, let alone inconvenience the most malicious man on Wall Street. Maybe assaulting the guards would encourage them to choke me to death. Better that than the alternative. Our Sweet play was billions underwater and my "deadline" was less than a week away.

Brad and I removed our clothes and shoes and tossed them in separate piles. I stood upright, tense, cupping my reproductive organs. Compared to me, Brad's chubby frame sagged like a flaccid, resigned penis. One of the guards donned blue nitrile gloves and probed every bodily orifice and cavity we possessed. The other retrieved some kind of scanning device from the filing cabinet near Paul's desk. He wafted it back and forth over our duds multiple times. After completing their respective tasks, the heavies tossed us our clothes and positioned themselves near the door like pit pulls. Brad and I re-robed. Everyone avoided eye contact at all costs.

The insufferable silence gradually turned deafening. Bereft, and wearing a thousand-yard stare, Brad retreated to the loveseat where his dad livestreamed porn and murdered NPCs. I hid in the humidor on the off chance I'd get lucky and asphyxiate.

A long while later, Paul barreled through the door.

"Where the fuck's Al?" he said.

I emerged from the chamber with a stupid look on my face.

Gerry, an owlish man with streaky white hair wearing a drab gray suit, lingered next to him. He was Prism's "fixer," the merciless lawyer who unfucked fucked-up situations, always in Paul's favor. Two more security guards lumbered into the office with Robbie and Dennis in custody. Dennis was flinging his arms about and shouting macho bullshit like "Get the fuck off me, bro!" and "I'll fucking kill you, bro!" It was very on-brand.

"Everyone's clean," the guard who'd molested us said. He handed Paul a box containing our stolen iPhones and Fitbits. At least Brad hadn't been wearing a wire—silver linings. "This one had two phones on him," the guard said, singling me out. Paul looked at me askance—shit-stained linings. Everyone converged at the desk.

"Gerry has some documents for you gentlemen to sign," Paul said. "No need to read them. Just sign where he tells you."

"What is this bullshit?" Dennis asked.

"This one's a nondisclosure agreement and this one's a sworn affidavit," Gerry said. "You're agreeing not to publicly discuss anything related to Bradley's ill-fated coup attempt, ever again, under threat of legal recrimination."

"I'm not signing a fucking thing!" Dennis said. Gerry looked at Paul. Paul nodded like a Mafia don.

"Well, Dennis, it goes like this. Either you sign right here"—he flipped the page—"right here"—he flipped the page—"and right there, or I send a log of all your trades to District Attorney Holloway, who's a close personal friend to Paul, and to my contacts at the DOJ, who are close personal friends to me. Oh, and I'll also send them a transcript of that call you had with your uncle, Representative Judd Sawyer of Delaware, head of the House Ways and Means Committee, about—what was it again?—oh, right. About that insider tip he gave you. The one where he knew Lockheed would win that NASA contract before it was publicly announced. You remember that one, right?"

Dennis turned white as a ghost and looked primed to puke. Gerry tapped his finger near the first signature line like a stone-cold assassin. Always the quiet ones. Dennis signed. Robbie signed without complaint. Brad glanced at me. I nodded. He signed, too. My turn.

"Can I at least—"

"Sign the fucking papers, Al," Paul ordered. I signed. "Gerry, all good?" The lawyer confirmed. "Bradley, you and Dennis are fired. Run along and fuck each other in the asses somewhere else."

"*WHAT?!*" Brad said. "You won! We did what you wanted!"

"Security, escort Bradley and Dennis from the building," Paul said. "Take their IDs and keycards and make sure IT locks all their accounts. Destroy their phones, too."

"You can't do this to me. I'm your son! *Your only fucking son!*" Paul looked away while the brutes dragged Brad and Dennis down the hallway, kicking and screaming.

"Robbie, I don't have to say it, do I?" Paul asked cryptically. The lanky trader nodded. "You remember Tampa, Robbie?" He did. "The statute of limitations isn't up yet, is it?" It wasn't. "Would you like the Tampa PD to know what really happened to that girl, Robbie?" No. "Listen Robbie, we've got a lot of money on the line. You're the best trader on Wall Street. I need you focused. Are you focused, Robbie?" He was. "Then go back to your station and get to work." He thanked the boss.

Paul was on the warpath. Each execution would be more grotesque and inhumane than the last. I could only imagine what horrors awaited.

# WHO'S GONNA TAKE THE WEIGHT?

*Friday, February 12*

Playing the assailant instead of the victim—for once—felt great. Felt empowering. Felt liberating. Felt dirty. The mystical pink clouds signaling dusk on the peninsula filled the sky. The Japanese Garden nestled inside San Mateo Central Park was serene and peaceful and, most important, empty. Ned sat next to me on a bench near the koi pond, looking anything but Zen. He flipped through the black-and-white photos over and over and over again. When he tired of the visual evidence, he skimmed through the transcript over and over and over again. It was as if he expected the images and words to change if he looked a little closer. A little *harder*. I knew the feeling.

"How can you do this to me?" Ned asked. We both knew the answer. He shuffled the documents a few more times for good measure. "This wasn't part of our agreement," he said.

"Our agreement stands—provided you adhere to the following modifications," I said.

"What does Simon think about this?"

"Simon's a middleman. He doesn't get involved," I said. "I paid to play, but the game's changed. These are the new rules."

"This evidence incriminates you, too. You release these files, you go down with me." Ned's hangdog face drooped like a melting candle.

"Listen, Ned, you're nothing but a pawn in a game you can't control. You're expendable. You think anyone gives a shit about you? You chose the wrong path when you went to Simon. Now much more powerful forces are pulling the strings. You either do what they say, or you burn." *If only I could choke to death on hypocrisy.*

Ned massaged his forehead and exhaled deeply. With his shirt partially untucked and his hair draped over his eyes, he'd abandoned his facade of perfect control. "What exactly do I need to do?"

$$$

"It's done," I said, and took a seat in front of Paul's desk. Through the window, high-rise apartment lights and automobile headlamps assaulted the moonless night.

"Any complications?" he said.

"Nope."

"Drink?"

"Sure."

Paul collected two glasses and poured gin and tonics. "You know, I honestly doubted you could pull this off. But come Tuesday morning, you'll have done the impossible. Recovered three hundred million dollars in three months. Absolutely incredible work. Of course, I'll have generated four *billion* over the same period."

"With my intel," I said, foolishly poking the bear.

"Speaking of which, I've been reviewing the texts in this mystery phone of yours—thanks for unlocking it, by the way." As if I'd had a choice. "Very cryptic. It almost seems like you're doing something illegal. Are you doing something illegal, Al?"

"I'm doing my job."

"Good man," Paul said with a smile. He took a sip. "Then there's just one more piece to this puzzle. Shall it be Keith? Or Karen?"

"Keith or Karen, what?"

This time Paul took a lusty swig of his libation, then powered down my Simon phone and tossed it to me. "The DA needs a body, Al. We can't give them that fuckwit Dennis because he signed the NDA and affidavit. Bradley may be an incompetent moron, but he's still my son. And besides, he also signed the documents. Robbie? Robbie's solid." Paul guzzled the last of his drink, then sucked his teeth. "Of course, that leaves you. But you're my ace, Al. My top guy! Throwing you to the wolves would be self-defeating."

Paul got up and poured himself another drink. My head throbbed, my eyes itched, and my mouth tasted like metal. These long setups always ended with the most depraved punch lines. He settled back into his chair.

"You know, this ridiculous ultimatum was Bradley's idea. Said he got it from some movie he liked. I'll admit, at first, I thought it was stupid. But who can argue with the results? Look at what you achieved once you were properly motivated." Sip. Suck. Smile. "So, do we give the DA Keith? Or do we give the DA Karen?"

"I'll do it," I said impulsively. "I'll admit to the insider trading charges. I made my choices. I'll face the consequences."

"Always so noble, Al. I like that about you people. The focus on the greater good. The *selflessness*. It's why you're such effective suicide bombers," Paul said. "But here's the thing. You make money. Keith and Karen, not so much."

"Then I'll turn myself in to the Feds. I'll say I masterminded the entire thing. And that I worked alone."

"How about Jennie? Maybe we turn her over to the DA. She did resign abruptly. And she refused to cooperate with our recent internal investigation, which you so expertly conducted on my behalf. Seems pretty suspicious to me, Al. Don't you think?"

*Leverage.* This motherfucker always had it, and there was never any escape. My guts twisted in knots. Begging and pleading never helped. Threatening always made things worse. Abstaining wasn't an option.

"Keith," I said flatly. Karen may have been a venomous thundercunt, but society had conditioned me to protect White women at all costs, and my misguided sense of chivalry always triumphed. Like me, Keith had made his insider trading bed long ago. He and Dennis also facilitated the stripper debacle at my birthday party. *Sorry, bruh.*

"Good choice, Al. Very logical. Dennis received privileged information from his uncle and unwittingly passed it to Keith, a close work associate. Dennis is guilty of being a loudmouthed moron, sure, but according to his own sworn statement, he's also a drug-addled manic-depressive. Keith committed the real crimes. Keith knowingly traded using black edge. A rotten apple in our ranks. Who'd have imagined?" Sip. Suck. Smile.

"Glad we finally got to the bottom of this, Al. By the way, I'm taking the Cessna to the mansion tonight. Want to come along?"

*$$$*

## Sunday, February 14

Today was the big day.

In a few hours, techie douchebags would sip mimosas in Pac Heights and Sweet CFO Ned Song would deliver a master class in market manipulation to the foolish Redditors who thought they could take down Paul Kingsley and the mighty Prism Capital. It would all be over soon. And not just this accounting-fraud, father-son, triple-double cross, meme-stock madness. I would officially complete my personalized Bataan Death March, which I'd been arbitrarily sentenced to because . . . because I blew a bunch of money on unlucky bets? Because Paul needed to make an example of me? Because I was Brown? Or stupid? Talentless? Or, perhaps even more insane, because I was *smart*. Because I was capable. Talented. Whatever Paul's reasoning, I was about to complete—I was about to *crush*—his ridiculous gauntlet. I should've been happy.

Instead, I tossed and turned in bed, wide awake, assessing the feasibility of suicide via hanging. It wasn't practical. People did it in the movies and made it look easy, but it took *a lot* of planning and precision. Screw up the strangulation, and not only would I *not* die, I'd end up with neurological damage from the lack of oxygen to the brain. Life was hard enough with (allegedly) functional cognition.

Drop hanging, where the goal was to quickly snap the neck, seemed reasonable. But getting the setup right proved quite labor-intensive. And finding a secluded location with retail-store-high ceilings and sturdy support joists wasn't easy. Even if I nailed all the steps, with my luck, I'd end up paralyzed and institutionalized. Most likely, I'd make my attempt using a subpar setup, fall on my ass, and have to explain away the resulting scars on my neck for the rest of my pitiful life. I crossed hanging off my list. Too difficult.

I grabbed my phone from my laundry hamper/nightstand, typed "how to access the dark web" into an incognito search tab, and immediately felt ridiculous. To conduct any transactions, such as purchasing an unregistered Glock G17 9mm pistol with the serial number removed, I needed specialized equipment. Like a VPN. And Bitcoin or some shit. Even then I wondered: *Where would I have it shipped? How could I trust the seller? Jesus H. Christ, why was everything so goddamned complicated?* Figuring out how to commit suicide only amplified my anxiety and depression. If I was going to buck up and finally get it over with, I'd have to procure my weapon of self-destruction the old-fashioned way. From a "drug dealer." In the "inner city." As American as apple pie.

$$$

Half a day later, the sun seared through Paul's office windows. He, Robbie, and I were sitting three abreast on the sofa in the relaxation station, preparing to watch whistleblowing CFO Ned Song deliver an impromptu press conference detailing "troubling financial irregularities at Sweet Technology Incorporated."

Paul was the picture of joviality: red polo, khaki shorts, and white dock shoes, a gin in one hand and a cigar in the other. The only thing missing was the porn star on his arm. Robbie seemed more subdued. Restless. But that made sense: He'd be quite the busy man the next few days and, apparently, lived in constant fear that Paul would have him hauled away for being a sexual predator. I felt repulsed sitting next to him, refused to make eye contact, and fidgeted aimlessly.

Prism was set to make *billions* more dollars. In a single day. On my work. Our trade would be lionized as an all-time great in Wall Street's annals. Rivaling *The Big Short*. I would complete the impossible task Paul had laid before me, and assuming he kept his word, I'd inherit my very own portfolio. In a few years, I'd run my own fund and manage my own money. I'd be rich beyond belief, with bountiful, busty women at my beck and call. A heteronormative Caucasian success story for the ages. It was all in front of me, and I felt nothing but contempt. For Paul. For Brad. For Dennis. For Robbie. For Ned. And, most of all, for myself. *How did I end up like this?*

"I'm standing here today because I want to do the right thing," Ned said on the television screen. "Doing the right thing isn't always easy. Sometimes doing the right thing carries costs. Immense costs. Both personal and professional. For yourself and for your family. But what I've learned over the years is this: No matter the cost, doing the right thing is always *just*. And that's why I want to share some shocking revelations about my company, Sweet Technology Incorporated."

A bravura, and comically on the nose, performance from Ned ensued. Worthy of crocodile tears and golf claps. He calmly, and diligently, explained how rogue CEO Lars Heideker had embezzled funds through undisclosed illicit channels. How Lars had lied to shareholders, suppliers, and subordinates alike. How Lars had cooked the books while the board cheered him on, asleep at the switch. And, most important, how only one man—Ned Song—had possessed the courage to step up and put an end to this despicable corporate malfeasance. Everyone was the hero of their own story— everyone except me.

Ned neared the end of his sermon. Paul's phone tirelessly blew up with texts and tweets and breaking news alerts. He muted the TV and read aloud from a *Wall Street Journal* story masterfully titled "Big Tech's St. Valentine's Day Massacre." The piece was exquisitely written by the young, up-and-coming whippersnapper who'd collected the Olympus dossier from me in New Jersey. I'd always wondered how journalists wrote these breaking news stories so fast. It'd never occurred to me they were fed the desired narrative in advance, to appease whichever power broker was most in favor at the given moment. The fourth estate's tail wagging the First Amendment's dog.

Paul finished reading, then adjusted his crotch. "I need a cigarette after that," he said.

Robbie laughed.

I stared blankly at the humidor. Could I kill Paul with my bare hands? He was taller, but I was heavier, and had youth on my side. Would Robbie help me? Or would he help Paul? Did it matter? If I stuffed them both in the wooden box, how long would it take for someone to find their bodies? Would I have time to flee the country? Would I want to?

# BURNING SEASON

*Tuesday, February 16*

My drop-dead day had *finally* arrived. Prism's offices crackled with an electric air, like when the home team had an insurmountable lead in game seven and was dribbling out the clock with each perfunctory possession, sending the crowd into an ever-heightened frenzy, ready to taste championship glory. Everyone in the office had gathered around the cubes, under the televisions, and was standing at attention. Paul, our Warrior King, would soon inspire us with his words, before leading us into battle. Noticeably absent: Jennie, Keith, and Dennis. Brad most of all. I tuned out Paul's lamentations, proclamations, and excoriations. Unlike the rest of the crowd, I knew exactly how we'd arrived on this celebratory stage. *Graft*, not genius, had positioned Prism for another massive payday. My graft.

Monday was Presidents' Day, a US market holiday, which

meant the whole world had waited two days with bated breath to witness the scale of Sweet's meltdown. When pre-market trading opened, the faux company's stock price had plunged 90 percent. Volumes soared. Paul could've had Robbie unload our shares—after checking with Compliance, of course—at will, and Prism would've booked over a billion dollars in profit. But he didn't. Robbie stood with the rest of us, casually dressed in a flannel and jeans, awaiting further orders. Paul's sixth sense must've been at work again. He must've known shit would *really* hit the fan when formal trading commenced. And why settle for anything less than maximum carnage? It would be a betrayal of his fiduciary—no, his *moral*—duty to do otherwise.

I rubbed my hands through my hair. It was shaggy and unkempt and uncut. If I put a bullet hole in my forehead, would it matter how my locks flowed? Paul finished his soliloquy by shouting me out to the crowd. "The Comeback Kid," he called me, which elicited cheers and an ovation. I waved adoringly at my phony fans and superficial supporters. It was all performance. Paul orchestrated these stunts to nullify his persistent sadism. He forced us to pretend Prism was one big, happy, dysfunctional family. But festering underneath the smiles and the handshakes and the backslapping there was only one genuine emotion: *jealousy*. This crowd of Ivy League strivers and sycophants would've killed to be where I was. After the jealousy came resentment. How had *this fucking guy*, of all people, become Paul's favorite son?

The markets opened with—depending on your perspective—a bang. If the Icarus crash had cut the fat, and the Olympus crash had cut into muscle, then the Sweet crash would ground up the bones. The so-called sophisticated institutional investors, the Fidelitys and the Wellingtons and the T. Rowe Prices of the world, immediately panicked and dumped millions of shares on anyone stupid enough to take them. Every buyer needed a seller, and since markets were "efficient," there was always a sucker ready to get fleeced.

The voluminous trading volumes triggered the automated trading algorithms, which further crushed the fraudulent dating company's share price, exacerbated the liquidity death spiral, and caused the heroes of Reddit—the guys and gals who'd planned to stick it to Paul Kingsley and take back capitalism for the working class—to capitulate. Within minutes, Sweet's share price had plummeted a spectacular 97 percent. It would've been physically impossible to burn tens of billions of dollars of paper cash so quickly. The contagion spread like measles in Sonoma and bombed the Nasdaq's value back to the pre-internet Stone Age. All hail the Invisible Hand.

About an hour into the trading session, Sweet's board tried to sneak a laughable 8-K filing, SEC code for communicating news of a "material event," past the market:

*In light of these extraordinary market events, and some minor accounting irregularities discovered during our routine year-end audit, management intends to indefinitely delay the filing of its 10-K report. While management expects any adjustments to prior financial statements to be inconsequential, in accordance with SEC guidelines, investors are cautioned not to rely upon previously issued financial statements.*

*Minor! Inconsequential!* Who could fathom what Sweet's hapless, unqualified board expected to transpire after that absurd missive. Considering their CEO was missing in action and their CFO had just sold them out, they didn't have many options. When Bloomberg and the rest of the data aggregators got wind of the filing, Sweet's stock somehow fell further, achieving a near perfect 99 percent decline.

Party vibes permeated the office. Prism had gone from the brink of collapse at breakfast to record-setting returns by brunch. Everyone would drink, smoke, snort, and fuck themselves into oblivion later that evening. I sat at my cube and scrolled LinkedIn postings. *Director, business development, Google.* Pass. *VP, financial planning and analysis, Oracle.* Pass. Then I remembered: *Icarus needs a CFO!* Burning to death in their fire seemed more appealing. I wasn't qualified to do any of those jobs. More important, I didn't *want* to do any of those jobs.

An overwhelming sense of urgency gripped me. Like that feeling of staying too long at a bad party. Or the last day of high school with senioritis at full bore. I needed to get away from Prism. *Now.*

I texted Simon and let him know I wanted to settle my balance. He responded immediately with a series of account numbers and the final bill. Unfortunately, Dennis's computer and log-in information were no longer available for risk-free embezzling. IT hadn't confiscated Keith's laptop yet, but I didn't know his credentials. I debated asking Karen, VICE's sole survivor, if she knew them, but thought better of it. No need to plant suspicious seeds. Plus, Karen wouldn't make eye contact with me, having rightly assumed I was to blame for railroading the colleagues she didn't even like.

I wired Simon's outstanding balance from my Prism portfolio to the small business account I'd opened in Dennis's name at Wells Fargo. He was a well-established white-collar criminal with chronic substance abuse problems, which would divert attention away from my wrongdoing. When the money became available, I'd head to a public library in some random peninsula town, get a library card in Dennis's name—I could pass for a Dennis—and use the free public Wi-Fi to transfer the money to Simon via his network of shell companies. My business with him and his bullshit R-and-R front company would be concluded.

When Paul came looking for the money, and there was no doubt he would, I'd feign ignorance, blame Dennis, and refer him to my own sworn affidavit, which indicated I abused myriad memory-altering substances. Blackmail went in both directions. Multiple loose ends simultaneously and brilliantly tied.

With less than an hour to go in the trading session and Prism's money-minting long concluded, I strolled down the hall to Paul's office with my head held high. For the first time in a long time, I felt something strange. *Hope.* I had more control than I'd realized. I didn't have to do this anymore. I'd built a large financial buffer for myself. Developed and honed transferable skills. And had a solid résumé. Prism was just a job. As Jennie, and Damon, and even my mom had tried to tell me, there was more to life than money.

Paul was seated by the humidor, studying the centerfold in a classic *Hustler* magazine, when I tapped on the glass door. He waved me inside and we congregated at his desk. He gripped a neat glass of gin. I held a single sheet of paper.

"Helluva day, huh, Al," he said. "How's it feel?"

Prototypical of Paul to ask a vague question, meriting a number of possible responses. "The trade, obviously, was awesome," I said. "And personally, it's a *massive* relief. Achieving my goal. Clearing up my 'debt.' I'm really looking forward to a fresh start."

"What's that you're holding?"

"Well, um, I want to talk to you about my future," I said. "The last couple months have been *insane.* Hectic. Stressful. For a while, I worried I wouldn't be able to recover the VICE funds. But—*with your guidance*—we pulled through. Survived. Thrived, even. And now I'm thinking about what's next. Like, what do I want to be when I grow up?"

"Hand me the paper, Al." Cautiously, I complied. Paul skimmed the lone paragraph and chuckled. Then he ripped it in half, then quarters, then eighths. "No can do, Al. You're too valuable to the firm."

*Not good.* "Okay, well, um—please don't take this the wrong way, Paul—but that's my choice. We're square. Settled up. Copacetic. I've been thinking a lot, and this isn't the path I want to pursue."

"Fucking millennials. You want a raise, Al? To manage a team? A bigger portfolio? Done. You've earned it. But you can't quit."

*Fucking boomers!* "Paul, working at Prism has been an absolute privilege. You're the best in the business, bar none. I've learned a lifetime in a few short years," I said, ready to vomit in my mouth for my crass obsequiousness. "But it's my decision to make, and it's final. This is what's best for me."

Paul forced an exaggerated sigh. "Still not getting it, are you, Al? What do you think this whole charade—you being *held hostage*—has been about?" My throat tightened, like it was wrapped in a noose. I knew I needed to walk on eggshells during this conversation, but something else was at play. And no matter how many times I parried, Paul would gaslight me onto some new plane of insanity.

"This entire gauntlet," Paul continued, "the ultimatum, the threats, the pressure, the deadlines, all of it was a test. It was my direct challenge to you. To prove to me, and to yourself, you have what it takes to be the best. *You were never going down for insider trading.* That was a head fake. A motivational tool. An incentive for you to take your game to the next level. And you more than surpassed expectations. *Nobody* at Prism can do what you do, Al. Well, except me, of course."

A wave of nausea slammed into me. Bile crept from my gut into my brain. I felt dizzy. Rattled. Confused. "What about the insider trading investigation? The one Brad told me about after the Icarus crash?"

"I cleared that up with Holloway months ago," Paul said. He dropped this information as if it were a minor detail. Not relevant to the plot at all. My existence had officially turned into the shittiest M. Night Shyamalan movie of all time.

"I don't understand," I said, because I didn't.

"You want to know the real trick to this business, Al? Get lots of people to owe you lots of favors," he said. "Speaking of which . . . "

Paul opened his desk drawer and removed the same manila folder Brad had tried to blackmail us with. My heart stopped beating. My eyes stung with rage and tears. *No, no, no, no, no, no, no, no, no.*

"You remember what's in here, right?"

"Paul, this isn't fair. I did what you asked. I made back the money. I signed the documents," I said, babbling and begging. "I just want a fresh start. I don't want to work on the Street. You'll never hear from me again. I promise. *Please.*"

"That's nice, Al. But listen. The biggest difference between me and Bradley is this: When I say I'm going to fuck you six ways from Sunday, I do." He looked euphoric, like one of those Scandinavian horror movie psychopaths. "You're tired, Al. Emotional. You've been through hell. But *this* is what's best for you. A few years ago, you were a smart kid with a chip on his shoulder, hungry to prove himself. Now look at you. You're the rainmaker of Prism Capital. You're a man to be feared. Admired. *Respected.* Journalists. Politicians. Movie stars. They'll all know your name. You can't just throw that away, Al. I won't let you."

Paul took a long swig of his gin, then wiped his mouth with his sleeve like a drunk. "Prism is your home, Al. Prism is where you belong."

# ILL VIBE

*Saturday, February 20*

I was in a pensive mood.

During the past three months, I'd lost a fuckton of money, made a fuckton more, built a potential rap sheet long enough to make Tony Soprano blush, and proved to my crazy ass boss, and supposedly myself, I was misanthropic enough to become a Master of the Universe. And yet, what about my life had changed? I was still a depressed half-breed with a tragic backstory, who was consumed by suicidal ideation and questioned every moment he chose to remain alive.

And what about Paul's life had changed? I'd run through his manufactured hell, and in the process made him dizzying amounts of money, even though he was already one of the world's richest men. *Why?* What had Paul achieved? Why was he like this? What made him tick? All those micro curiosities got me thinking about a macro question.

*What was White culture?*

In the crumbling society outside Prism Capital's hallowed halls, disenfranchised and persecuted minorities held hands with self-effacing "allies" and asked this very question. Their point, as I understood it, was to examine why the US had socially regressed. To explain the rise of ethno-Christian nationalism, akin to the foundation of the Nazi Party in Weimar Germany. To ask why so-called "White people" refused to acknowledge their past transgressions. Empathize. *Apologize.*

I'd pondered those same culture war questions for years. I was half White. Birthed by a White child. I went to high school and college with primarily White people. Worked alongside predominantly White people, and had a direct window into "Whiteness" since the day I was born. My name was Ali Jafar, but I was ostensibly a "White guy." But was I *really* White? *Could* I really be White? If the answer was yes, then what was my culture? Because humans viewed the world through a White lens, non-White cultures were reduced to racist stereotypes. "Black culture" was fried chicken, gun violence, and basketball. "Hispanic culture" was tacos, drug trafficking, and fútbol. "Asian culture" was fried rice, subservience, and Ping-Pong. "My people's" culture was curry, call centers, and cricket. But what were the White stereotypes? Apple pie, perfect SATs, and baseball? What *defined* White culture?

*Property rights.*

White culture was property rights. White people loved to *own* shit. Stocks. Bonds. Commodities. Real estate. Land. People. White culture's animating philosophy was right in the open, clear for all to see. When *The Economist* bloviated about adhering to the "rule of law," what they really meant were governments, corporations, courts, and other White-dominated institutions needed to protect White financial interests. When the US military went abroad in search of foreign monsters to slay, it was to protect "our"—meaning the White—way of life. When politicians denounced protesters after police murdered another Black person in cold blood, they pointed to the property damage and the disruptions to "small business own-ers." In the aftermath of the Icarus nightmare, the *real* tragedy was the market crash, not the loss of (sub)human lives.

Property. That was how Paul saw me. I was an asset to be owned. And my sole purpose was to be leveraged, at his behest, to produce more assets for him to own. And no matter how many assets I pro-duced, and no matter how much wealth he accumulated, he'd never have enough.

$$$

I removed my headphones and killed the screen on my phone. I could only watch so many YouTube tutorials explaining how to accurately fire a handgun before zoning out. I debated masturbating. Would've been the third time that day, which seemed excessive. Maybe later.

After the Sweet bonanza, and my failed parole hearing, I told Paul I needed a few days off. He said to take as much time as I wanted. Right. I was still his prisoner, but at least I wasn't under the gun. Figuratively speaking. The time away was nice, though I could've spent it more wisely. I could've been at home, remembering how to do my job, before the days of Simon, R and R, and wanton financial felonies. I could've been in Sydney, blowing cash at bars and nightclubs, trying to hook up with tall blond surfer chicks, and pretending to have a good time. I could've been at the Allure man-sion. I could've been anywhere more interesting than where I was: New York City. The greatest city in the world, where "greatest" meant most superficial, most materialistic, and most rat-infested.

Another meeting with Simon beckoned. He'd texted a few days earlier and said he had a massive scoop for me. Something so big, so unbelievable, so controversial, we just had to discuss it in person. Sure, fine, great, whatever. What else was I gonna do? Play by the rules? *Lolz*. The world operated on one principle: power. And I possessed none.

I rolled out of the comfy king-size bed I'd wallowed in for most of the day. I'd splurged on the midtown Sofitel, even booked the luxury suite. Why not? If inspiration struck, and I mustered the courage to sexually asphyxiate myself to death, I wanted my carcass to be found in a *classy* joint. The kind of place where investment bankers and IMF chiefs sexually assaulted the staff and (obviously) got away with it.

In the bathroom, I masturbated to a few of the Allure stars I'd met in the flesh. They seemed to enjoy their jobs. They certainly added more value to society than anything I did at Prism. Afterward, I conducted my typical grooming routine, but dressed down for the occasion, opting for jeans and a hoodie. It was still miserably cold, and I planned to walk to the rendezvous point in Chelsea. Despite my myriad misgivings about the Big Apple, a collective energy permeated the bustling streets. Being here always felt *exciting*, and conjured memories of my simpler days as an undergraduate. Also, few things stressed me out more than the NYC subway system.

The closest I'd ever come to a legitimate suicide attempt was in the Union Square station during my junior year of college. I was in the throes of a deeply depressive episode—precipitated by a poisonous slurry of personal and professional rejection—and the concept of suicide suddenly graduated from daily abstraction to permanent solution. The 6 train was barreling down the track, and I'd dangled a curious foot over the ledge. All I needed to do was lean forward a little farther, and I was just about to when a random guy grabbed me by the shoulder, pulled me back, and said, "Hey, buddy, watch your step, huh?" Fucking New Yorkers.

*$$$*

After walking halfway to my destination, I wished I'd taken my final plunge onto the subway tracks. The city's legendary wind tunnels had turned the dry winter air into quadrillions of invisible razor blades, exfoliating the exposed patches of my genetically nonpredisposed skin.

I ordered a cappuccino at Starbucks and sat by the glass facade, watching the violent and chaotic traffic on Seventh Avenue. Operators of cars, delivery trucks, and taxi cabs threatened to kill each other while jockeying for an arm's length of asphalt. All in the hopes of arriving at their destination a fraction of a second sooner. Strolling into the intersection struck me as a potentially potent form of euthanasia. Surely one of these morons could finish the job. It'd look like an accident, too. I was a tourist, after all. My mom would no longer receive the monthly stipend I sent her, but she also wouldn't have to haggle with my life insurance provider over the sizable payout. Not that she deserved either. But a pretty decent plan.

I sipped the bitter beverage and contemplated the downsides of death by traffic. My biggest fear, as always, was nonlethal paralysis and mutilation. The method needed to be foolproof. New York City taxi drivers simply weren't trustworthy enough.

My phone buzzed.

*Do anything fun for valentines day any hot dates?????*

I affixed a thumbs-down to my mom's message. *Obviously you haven't been following the markets.*

She affixed a thumbs-down to my message and called. I declined and texted her I was busy. Another thumbs-down. We hadn't talked in months. This wasn't unusual. Our relationship was a long slog of disdain and disappointment interrupted by fleeting, unexpected spells of genuine affection. We were currently entrenched in the unpleasant part of the cycle, and more prosaically, she'd developed an uncanny ability to bother me right as I was preparing to commit an elaborate financial crime.

I exited the Starbucks around 8 p.m., tossed my empty cup into an overflowing trash can, and made my way south. Google Maps said the address was near the Fashion Institute of Technology. Fortuitous. Maybe a Swedish supermodel would spot me, realize I was the exotic, ethnically ambiguous plaything she'd always wanted, and whisk me away from all this madness. Maybe America would become a just, equitable, and inclusive society while she was at it.

I arrived at Simon's address. A residential building tucked away on a rare, sleepy block. I had to give him credit—the guy didn't cut corners. Simon stayed perpetually on the move, which made him elusive. And incognito. The marks of a true professional. I admired his tradecraft but also wondered why he bothered. I'd surrendered any hope of staying off the grid at this point. Or maybe, deep down, I wanted to get caught. Maybe prison, brutal and inhumane as it surely was, was the only (nonlethal) way to escape Paul Kingsley.

I typed the security code Simon had provided into the keypad. A moment later that awful, ubiquitous buzzing noise—half semitruck horn, half duck quack, half shot-clock expiration—blared into my ears. I ventured into the foyer, past the unmanned security desk, down the dank hallway, and onto the elevator, which obviously smelled like piss. Sixteenth floor. The rooms were demarcated with letters instead of numbers, which made me wonder how the addresses read on postage. This place really brought the shithole energy. Simon must've needed *deep* cover.

I knocked thrice at my destination. A large man opened the door and stood to the side. I recognized his entirely bald head.

One of Simon's recurring henchmen. Straight ahead were two more heavyset goons. I ambled into the squalid room. Simon was seated on a tan metal folding chair and an empty duplicate idled across from him. He looked *wrecked*. Face unshaven. Hair unstyled. And wearing a short-sleeved dress shirt right off the T.J.Maxx rack. Apparently, we'd all decided to dress down for the occasion.

I stepped toward him, expecting his Eurotrash shtick. He just glared at me. Silent. Scornful. The door closed and the deadbolt turned. Three goons formed an impenetrable wall behind me. Suddenly, everything felt off. All the warning signs flashed at once. My fight-or-flight response kicked in. I turned one-eighty, ducked under the goon closest to the door, and sprinted for the exit. The hairless one locked his sweaty arm around my neck and lifted me off the ground like a rag doll. *Hard. To. Breathe.* I should've been happy. The end had finally arrived. But that wasn't how instinct worked. I fought desperately. Kicked and flailed.

"Ali Jafar," Simon said, his thick Boston accent all kinds of wrong. "You're in a world of shit."

I struggled to stay conscious. *Who the fuck are these guys?* Were they actually trying to kill me? I balled my fist and smashed it into the henchman's nose. It distracted him just enough to loosen his grip, which allowed me to bite his forearm with every bit of prehistoric primate inside me. He screeched and let go. I fell to my knees, popped up as fast as I could—gasping—and stumbled toward the door. I twisted the deadbolt and yanked the handle and a loud clang sent everything black.

# GOT

ce water coursed down the back of my neck. *What the fuck!* My head throbbed and my hoodie was soaked. I jammed my shoulder blades together and rubbed the back of my skull, which swelled like a balloon. Blurred vision made it hard to figure out where I was, but apparently, I'd been propped up at a dining-room table in the same musty, moldy apartment where Simon and his thugs had ambushed me. Unfortunately, my intrinsic will to live was strong, and I'd clung to life. Simon materialized across the table. He still looked like shit, but this time he wore a smug, satisfied grin.

"Ali 'Al' Jafar. Aka Mister Al," the man I knew as Simon said. His updated voice suggested he was a noxious Celtics fan from Southie. "How's the head?"

"Who the fuck are you?" I said.

"Head seems fine," he said. "Well, Al—is it all right if I call you Al?—okay, good. Here's the deal. You know me as Herr Simon

Hellstrom, founder of R *und* R," he said, briefly switching to his German accent. "Shadowy information broker and ruler of the financial underworld. Thing is, my real name is FBI Special Agent Joey Sabato. And you've been a *very* bad boy."

"Bullshit." My interlocutor produced his badge. Sure as shit, the name read *Joseph R. Sabato*. The other three men flashed their badges as well. I suppressed my urge to puke. "Those are clearly fake. You," I said, pointing at Simon, or Joey, or whoever the fuck he was, "fed me inside information and helped me destroy multiple companies. I saw you do coke, for fuck's sake."

"Listen, Al," Simon/Joey said. "We've got you dead to rights. Securities violations. Wire fraud. Embezzlement. The whole nine yards. To put it mildly, you're fucked."

"Lawyer," I said. "I want to talk to a lawyer. I know my rights." All those Scorsese flicks had finally paid off.

"You haven't been charged with any crimes—*yet*," Simon/Joey said. "So there's no need for Miranda rights and due process and all that socialist bullshit."

"If I'm not being charged, you can't hold me. I want to—"

"I suggest you shut the fuck up for two fucking seconds, okay, fuckboy?" he replied. "You're not being charged. But you walk out that door, we call the DA, he does some paperwork, and we show up in San Francisco and take you away in cuffs. You can talk to as many lawyers as you want from prison."

"Or, better yet, we charge you right fuckin' now and send your Muslim ass to Guantanamo," the hairless goon said. The dental imprints in his arm were an obvious sore spot.

"We've accumulated enough evidence for the DA to put you away for *decades*," *Joey* continued. His stupid accent and douchebag demeanor screamed "Masshole," and as much as I wanted to, I could no longer delude myself into thinking he was a European

kleptocrat. "We've got text messages. Photographs. Audio recordings. Wire transfers. Convicting you would be the easiest case in the
history of the Southern District. But here's the good news, Al: The
Department of Justice doesn't give a fuck about you. The Department of Justice does, however, give a fuck about your boss, Paul
Kingsley. He's been in our crosshairs for a *long* time. And you're
going to deliver his head to us on a platter."

My mind raced, calculating all the angles. All the permutations.
All the ways I was totally, utterly, completely fucked. Was this the
absolute worst-case scenario? Definitely. The stress soaked my body
in cortisol. Suddenly, it was sensory overload. The sulfurous smell
of the tap water gagged me. The fluorescent hue of the lights pummeled me. The swelling in my brain disoriented me. I sprayed blood-
speckled vomit onto the table and into Joey's lap. He jumped back
and cursed his god. Face flushed and eyes bloodshot, I heaved till I
choked. My mouth tasted like grapefruit mixed with paint thinner.
Somehow, this dump heap of an apartment smelled even worse.

"Jesus fucking Christ, are you finished?" Joey said.

"Water. I need water."

"Richie, get him some water," Joey said.

*Richie?* "Delicato?" I said.

"Flattered you remembered me, tough guy—though that's not
my last name," Richie said from the sink. "Not feeling so slick now,
are you?"

He walked over and handed me the glass. I knew that fat fuck
looked familiar. He was the goombah who drove me to the Illuminati shindig in Connecticut. *Motherfucker.* These assholes
*were* FBI agents, and they'd pulled off a vintage John le Carré
double-double cross. I replayed each episode with Simon in my
head, and the extent of their operation crystallized. They'd been
watching me. Following me. Studying me. Grooming me like a

preteen for a Florida congressman. Everyone I'd interacted with since meeting Simon could've been in on it. The African mining baron. The Clockwork CFO. Ned. Maybe even Brad and Dennis. Or Keith. Jennie?! *Damon.*

I gargled the water at the kitchen sink and spit out residual flecks of sick. "Entrapment," I said. "You guys entrapped me."

"Get a load of this fucking guy," Richie said to his comrades. They had a hearty laugh.

"You're a smart kid, Al. But you ain't wriggling your way out of this one," Joey said.

He dabbed a wet towel on his pants to clean off the vomit and ended up looking like he'd pissed himself. He then walked from the kitchen into the living room, picked up the folding chair from the floor, opened it, set it in its original place, and motioned for me to join him. The conspicuous dent in its back support reminded me I had a throbbing headache. The bald henchman guarded the door, presumably hoping I'd try to escape again. Richie and the other meathead lingered near the table. I took a seat.

"I'll level with you, Al. You've made mistakes. *Big* mistakes. But deep down, you're a good kid," Joey said. "The guy you work for? Paul? He's not a good guy. In fact, he's a real piece of shit. A leech on the financial system. A guy who fucks over everyone for his own benefit."

"Why don't you tell me something I don't know?" *Act tough,* I told myself, channeling every interrogation scene from every action movie I'd ever watched. The electroshock torture in *Lethal Weapon* held an extra-special place in my heart. Perhaps I, too, could fake my own death and stage a daring escape.

"How about this? With your cooperation, we can finally take the sonofabitch down," Joey said. "You know how long we've been after this guy, Al? Damn near a decade. We've tried *everything*. Wire taps. Surveillance. CIs. You name it. But nothing sticks. Fucker's made of Teflon. That's why we need your help."

"*Help?*" I exaggerated a fake, drawn-out laugh. "Paul's got his tentacles in everything. He's on speed dial with the San Francisco DA and the California governor. He owns half of Congress through lobbying. If anyone gets in his way, he *buries* them. I've watched it happen. He's untouchable."

"Why don't *you* tell us something *we* don't know?" Joey said. He forced a haggard smile. "I like you, Al. And I want to help you."

"Is that why you smashed a chair over my head?"

"*Richie* smashed a chair over your head," Joey said. "And since you violently resisted our invitation to chat, his actions were completely justified."

"You took a chunk outta my fuckin' arm, too," the bald one said. Quite an exaggeration. Teeth marks, sure. But a chunk? Drama queen.

"You took a chunk out of Slick's arm, too," Joey said.

I instantly felt bad. I hadn't bitten anyone in malice since preschool. It was a horrible decision, made in haste. "Sorry, Mister Slick," I said. "I just . . . panicked."

Slick nodded and grunted, which I assumed was caveman for "apology accepted."

"And Richie's sorry for whacking you over the head with a chair, aren't you, Richie?" Joey said. Richie was sorry, too. Total overkill. Crime of passion. "See, Al. We're not the bad guys here. We're the good guys. And *you're* a good guy. A good guy who did some bad things. That's why you need to help us. So we can help you."

$$$

Our back-and-forth went on for what felt like hours. Joey lobbed legitimate threats. I countered with false braggadocio. There were

227

no clocks in the room, they'd confiscated my phones, and it'd been dark when I arrived. In the city that never slept, that made it impossible to know the time. I assumed it was near midnight, since my Bay Area circadian rhythm was pleading for rest. Deflection and obfuscation had run their course. Or maybe Joey had worn me down. Either way, I finally caved.

"Let's assume—for the sake of argument—I play ball. What exactly do you want from me?"

Joey straightened his back and sat tall. His eyes were stoic, his demeanor serious. "I'm about to share extremely confidential and sensitive information with you, Al. I'm sharing this information because I *know* you're going to aid our investigation."

"For the record, I haven't agreed to anything," I said. "You've also been holding me against my will for God knows how long, which I'll be sure to share with my lawyer."

Joey chuckled. "The tough-guy act is cute. But you can drop it. I've been doing this a long time. You could hire Johnnie fucking Cochran. One look at the shit sandwich you're about to eat, and he'd beg us for a plea deal."

His casual certainty was disconcerting. He was right, and I knew it. Had known it. Had avoided admitting it. "Shouldn't you offer me immunity, then?" I asked. "Or . . . something?"

"That's for your lawyer to work out with the DA," Joey said with a smile. Was I caught in a *Catch-22* paradox? The concept was widely misunderstood, so I couldn't say for sure. But my predicament was, like the inimitable Captain Yossarian's, *FUBAR*.

"Believe it or not, Al, I don't like making threats." I didn't believe him. "But let me be crystal-fucking-clear: If you divulge any of the information I'm about to share with you to anyone outside this room, or if you in any way compromise the integrity of our investigation, or in any way betray our trust, I personally guarantee you'll spend the rest of your life in prison. Do you understand?" Moments like this were the highlight of Joey's miserable, sad-sack existence. Lording power over the compromised. He probably had a hard-on. I nodded.

"It goes like this, Al. For the past few years, me and my team have been conducting an elaborate sting operation using the FBI code name House of Cucks. I came up with that myself. Pretty clever, huh?" It was pretty clever, but I remained stone-faced and refused to grant him the satisfaction. "Anyway, as a result of this operation, we've bagged and flipped dozens of corrupt executives, dirty bankers, rogue hedgies—anyone fucking around in the markets falls within our purview." So the FBI's plan was to arrest everyone on the Street. Smart strategy.

Joey leaned closer and looked me square in the eyes. "But the target of this operation has always been one man: Paul Kingsley. The founder of Prism Capital. The most dangerous man on Wall Street. Your boss." Check that—the FBI's plan was to arrest the Homelander, the one supervillain who was too cunning, too strong, and too diabolical to ever face justice. Stupid strategy.

Joey paused and cracked his knuckles. "As I mentioned before, traditional methods haven't worked. That's why—"

"For the love of God, please tell me you tapped his office phone?" I said, incredulous.

"We were up on a wire for eighteen months," Joey said. "The vast majority of Paul's calls involved phone sex, and the rest were him bossing around his son or his assistants. Some left-wing judge said we didn't have a case and refused to re-up our FISA."

"What about his cell phone? Did you hear our call with Bob Beasley?"

"Every word."

"*Then why the fuck haven't you arrested him?*"

"Well, thanks to my work as 'Simon,' we've had Beasley under surveillance for months," Joey said. "But Paul didn't say or do anything illegal during your call. Cavorting with a crook isn't a crime."

*Catch-22* suddenly seemed quaint. "*Cavorting!* What about the Olympus dossier? What about the sex photos and the blackmail and the timing of Prism's trades? It's all right there!"

"We can't use the Olympus dossier to pin *criminal* charges on Paul," Joey said. "But we can use the Olympus dossier to pin criminal charges on *you.*"

"*Me?!* I thought the DOJ didn't give a fuck about me," I said, aghast. "Wait, am I supposed to believe you clowns cratered the stock market—*twice*—and the best you can do is arrest *me*? Are you even close to nabbing Paul?"

"Call it the gale of creative destruction," Richie said from the kitchen.

*Killer line.* I scoffed. "And what, I'm just collateral damage?"

"We're making an omelet, Al," Joey said. "And to make an omelet, you gotta break a few eggs."

I felt nauseous. Light-headed. Like just before my Brad-induced hospital stay. Too many blows to the head were catching up with me. Chronic traumatic encephalopathy would inevitably kill me, but it'd take too long. I sank my face into my hands. I wanted to cry, but couldn't stomach the joy it would've brought these contemptible fucks.

"I know what you're thinking, Al," Joey said. "We got the dossier. The timing of the trades. The *magnitude* of the trades. The call to Beasley. On paper, it's all so fucking obvious. And in one sense, you're right. The pansies at the SEC have more than enough evidence to level a hefty and totally fucking irrelevant fine on Prism Capital."

"But we wouldn't get Paul," Richie said, pulling up a chair next to Joey.

"But we wouldn't get Paul," Joey agreed. "See, billionaire scum-bags like him consider fines the cost of doing business. They pay, they move on, they keep cheating. I got sick of that pattern, so I decided to think outside the box. Hence, R *und* R." Joey rubbed his hands through his hair and crossed his legs. "Once we created a service to make these greedy fucks even richer, they came to us."

"That's how we stumbled across the Olympus dossier," Richie said. "Some soulless shitbird in middle management hand-delivered the evidence to us. Said he was looking to cash out."

"We sent him on an eighteen-month sabbatical instead," Joey said.

"Remember your pal Ned Song?" Richie said. The pit in my stomach turned into a black hole. If only I could spontaneously collapse into nothingness. "Agents in San Fran picked him up a few days ago."

"Now he's going to prison for a long, *long* time," Joey said. "See, Al, Ned *knew* Sweet was a house of cards. He could've gone to the legitimate authorities any time. But he chose to go to Simon." Joey smiled like his alter ego, satisfied with himself. "Funny enough, we were about to grab you for Olympus when Ned told us about Sweet. It only made sense to reel him in first, which also strengthened our case against you."

"Our operation works like the food chain, Al," Richie said.

"We catch a small fish, like Ned, then we use him to catch a bigger fish, like you," Joey said.

"Paul Kingsley's the biggest fish of all," Richie said.

"Our white whale," Joey said. Whales were obviously mammals, and Joey obviously hadn't finished *Moby-Dick*. Both data points augured poorly.

"But here's the thing, Al," Joey continued. "We can't catch Paul from the outside. He's too smart, and too insulated. He surrounds himself with goons and thugs and yes-men willing to do his dirty work. People who can take the fall for him."

"Like a Mafia boss," Richie said.

Joey reached into the back pocket of his jeans and removed my switchblade comb. It was snapped in half. He set the useless plastic threads on the table and twiddled the metallic handle like a fidget spinner. "Do you know how to take down a Mafia boss, Al?"

"You breach his inner sanctum," Richie said. "Earn his trust. Get close. And when he's least expecting it . . ."

". . . you stick the knife in." Joey tossed me the last vestige of my broken childhood. "You're going to be our assassin on the inside, Al. And we're going to hand you the knife."

# CODE OF THE STREETS

*Sunday, February 21*

hilly air gusted near the empty bleachers overlooking the Bay. Alcatraz floated serenely in the distance. Desolate. Isolated. Dark. The derelict prison and I had a lot in common. In more civilized times I'd have ended up a permanent resident, rooming with mob bosses, drug barons, and the occasional serial killer. Navigating the various criminal factions until I got shanked to death. But these weren't civilized times. Alcatraz was a gaudy tourist attraction, and the FBI was strong-arming me into their fruitless crusade against white-collar crime. Against Paul. A campaign as likely to succeed as Taiwan invading China.

Joey and his gang had made one thing more than apparent: The freedom I continued to enjoy required my cooperation and rested upon their largesse. I needed a lawyer, stat. But before I retained one, I needed to talk to the one I knew best. Someone I—perhaps erroneously—considered my closest friend.

A gorgeous sun was setting over the Bay. The intensifying breeze cut through my fleece as I surveyed the area. My pulse quickened with each flickering shadow. Each passing jogger or dog walker. *Keep the adrenaline high. Stay frosty.*

Finally, I spotted him. The rare Black man traversing the Marina. His Armani suit sans tie another dead giveaway. I stood and shined my phone's flashlight in his direction. He nodded and quickened pace to close the remaining distance. We met at the top row of the aquatic amphitheater. He stopped a gurney's length away. No smiles. No dap. We eyed each other awkwardly.

"You come alone?" Damon asked.

I nodded and stepped closer. "You?"

Supposedly he had. If it was contempt that killed marriages, it was suspicion that killed friendships. "This is a ridiculous question, Al, and I hate to ask it, but—are you wearing a wire?"

I lunged at Damon and grabbed the collar of his dress shirt with both hands. "You sold me out, Dame! You fucked me!" The bottom of his chin sat level with my eyes. The fine hairs of his stubble in high definition. I pushed forward until Damon's back slammed into the concrete wall surrounding the open-air auditorium. I was apparently attacking my one and only friend, another ill-advised decision in an ill-advised life.

Damon grunted, then rolled his eyes toward me, then slapped the palm of his hand into my face. I flexed my biceps and leaned my full weight into him. Another thud into my cheekbone. Then another. My eyes widened. Elbows loosened. I let go of his shirt and stepped backward. Damon slouched forward, then stood up straight.

"Did you just slap me?" The question sounded more absurd than intended.

"You good?" Damon said, his breaths labored.

I nodded in quick bursts like a bobblehead. He pulled the collar of his jacket forward and dusted off his shoulders. Suddenly this entire rendezvous seemed more ridiculous than life-threatening. I burst into cacophonous laughter. I didn't belong at Alcatraz. I belonged in a goddamned mental asylum. Damon laughed slowly, then loudly. Just two men of color having stress-induced nervous breakdowns by the Ghirardelli factory. Typical day in the Bay.

Our maniacal laughter dissipated. "I need to know, Al. Are you mic'ed up?"

"Seems I should ask you the same question," I said. "Though I can't imagine the FBI needs any more dirt on me." Damon waited, then leaned his head forward and widened his eyes. "No, Dame, I'm not wearing a wire. You want to rub me down?"

*Fuck that*, he said without words. "Hold up, why would you think *I'm* wearing a wire?"

"You sent me to Simon," I said. "Aren't you working with the FBI?"

"*Me?* Bruh, I'm fucking pinched, too."

"What do you mean?"

"I mean your boy Simon—aka FBI Special Agent Joey fucking Sabato—knocked on my door a few weeks ago and told me I had two choices: cooperate with his investigation, or start practicing law in Zimbabwe. Racist fuck."

My knees wobbled and the ground beneath me turned to quicksand. I plopped onto the last row of concrete bleachers. "That doesn't make any sense," I muttered.

"Actually, it makes perfect sense. Simon, R and R—it was the Feds the whole time. They must've *planted* the files I gave you. Then started rumors around Triple C to see who'd get dirty."

"Did Joey tell you that?"

Damon scoffed and sat down next to me. "He told me they *knew* I passed you the info about Simon. Then he started leaning on me. Said I'd tell him everything I knew about you and your work at Prism. And that I'd keep this conversation to myself unless I wanted my boss to know I leaked files to a crooked hedge funder."

"What'd you do?"

"Fuck you mean? I told him everything, which thankfully wasn't much," Damon said. "It's not like I had a choice, Al."

"*Damn*," I said. "I'm sorry for doubting you. And for grabbing you. I'm just . . . I'm fucked up. I don't know who to trust."

"You look like shit," Damon said. "When's the last time you slept?"

*Soundly?* "Dame, I'm fucking *got*, got. I dealt directly with Joey. The FBI has recordings, text messages, phone calls. Enough to send me to prison for a *long fucking time*."

Damon mouthed a *fuck*, his relief matching his pity. His encounter with the law had been rosy by comparison. Then his shoulders tensed and the blood drained from his face. "Do they know I tipped you on Clockwork?"

"It never came up," I said. "But that doesn't mean—"

"No, no. That's *exactly* what it means," Damon said. "There's no way they'd let me walk if they knew."

His certitude struck me as wishful thinking, but I didn't press. He was clearly glad our roles weren't reversed. I couldn't blame him. "So you're off the board, then," I said, part question.

"It makes sense, right? Paul's the target. And they're using you to get to him."

"How do you know that?" I asked, suspicions aroused again.

"This is FBI one-oh-one shit, Al," Damon said. "The exact playbook they used to take down Joey the Greek and Gary Greenberg." The former was a Mafia don in New Hampshire and the latter a Ponzi-schemer in Philadelphia. Both were felled by undercover lieutenants. Both ate bullets soon after. Homicide and suicide, respectively. At least the future looked brighter.

"You lawyered up?" Damon asked.

"Not yet. I haven't been charged with anything."

"You will be. The justice system relies on people not understanding it. They want you to make bad decisions, with limited information, so you fuck up. Then you're in worse shape. Listen—do *not* talk to Joey until you've hired the best lawyer money can buy."

"Any recommendations?"

"Alan Dershowitz, if he'll take you."

"Seriously?"

"No, he won't take you. Your case is a loser," Damon said. "You'll have to plead out, Al. Agree to fully cooperate with the investigation and have your lawyer beg the DA for the best deal you can get."

"That's it? First you said I couldn't fight Paul. Now I can't fight the Feds?"

"How are they any different? You've got the wrong name and the wrong background and you're taking on a powerful institution. But in this case, the Feds got you cold. You go in front of a grand jury, you go to trial. You go to trial, you get convicted. You get convicted, you get ten years," Damon said. "Fight as hard as you want, Al. But this is America. You'll lose."

*Ten years.* A lost decade atop a wasted life. Death before dishonor had never made more sense. "Where's that leave you?" I asked.

"I'm going to keep my head down and hope and pray they want nothing to do with my Black ass," Damon said. My shoulders slumped, and my head sagged, and my vibe needed life support. "I'm sorry, Al. I didn't mean to set you up. On purpose."

"Intent. That's what the law's all about, right?"

Damon told me to grab my cell phone while he removed his own. He read aloud a number and I texted it to myself. "I know I'm not the most trustworthy source for information these days, but call this dude Blake at Janice Brown Miller. He's a friend of mine from law school. Tell him I said you need the best representation they can offer."

We stood and hugged tight, like it was the last time we'd see each other. Damon walked off and disappeared into the shadows of a drab brick building. I was like an angel of death, radioactive to the touch, vanquishing friends, allies, and foes alike. Damon. Jennie. Keith. Brad. Dennis. And then there were three. Paul. Joey. Me. I stared into the choppy black water. Cold and unforgiving. The pier jutted far from the shoreline. If I swam toward the floating hell, I wouldn't make it.

# YA PLAYIN' YASELF

*Monday, February 29*

Joey, Richie, and I rode a private service elevator to the lowest level of the parking garage. Oily sweat beaded on the back of Richie's thick neck. The stench of his microbiome accosted me. Joey's distorted face reflected on the chrome interior like a fun house mirror. The elevator settled and the doors opened. Richie stepped through first and made a beeline toward the warehouse of cars. Joey said to hang back and wait. He asked if I needed to piss. Told me we had a long drive ahead. I asked where we were going. No answer.

We'd just finished meeting with Dave Bradshaw, the district attorney for the Southern District of New York, in his Lower Manhattan office. He and my lawyer, Leslie Miller, a renowned criminal defense attorney and partner at vampiric mercenaries-for-hire Janice Brown Miller, had hashed out the details of a cooperation and plea agreement. Considering their back-and-forth included the planning of a covert sting operation, the proper functioning of the wealthiest capital market in the history of the world, and my literal freedom, the encounter had proved disconcertingly dull. A far cry from the television shows retired boomers and desperate housewives binge-watched. Took less time than a typical ad-packed episode, too. When it ended, I was billed the equivalent of three months' rent.

Before the meeting, Miller had advised me to say nothing unless addressed directly. Bradshaw asked me one question: Did I truly wish to atone for my sins? I answered in the affirmative. Bradshaw seemed satisfied. The meeting adjourned shortly after. In the hallway, my high-priced defense attorney told me, since I'd agreed to cooperate, absolute worst case, I'd get twelve years and do eight. Best case, five and three. *What the fuck happened to full immunity?* That would be possible if, and *only if*, Paul Kingsley went down, Bradshaw got a glowing write-up in the *New York Times*, and the judge signed off on the plea deal.

In a nutshell, the best days of my life—most of which involved contemplating suicide and wondering why my mother hadn't done the rational thing and aborted me—were in the rearview mirror. Miller darted off to fleece another guilty client. Bradshaw to oversee another miscarriage of justice. Executing the government's hatchet work, and administering actual justice, had somehow fallen on my shoulders.

A matte black sedan, unicolor from front to back, including windows, pulled up in front of the elevators. Joey opened the door and invited me inside. I sat behind Richie, savoring the strangely satisfying new-car smell. Probably a carcinogen. Joey sat beside me and closed the door and again asked if I needed to piss.

"Are we *driving* back to San Francisco?" I said, annoyed.

"Worse," he said. "Newark."

The three of us rode in silence. Richie navigated the chaotic Manhattan streets with ease. Even made smooth work of the Holland Tunnel. I suspected he'd been an actual driver before joining the US secret police. Joey started yammering when we entered Jersey City. He told me I was doing the right thing. Like I had a choice. He told me we'd finally get Paul. Sure. He told me he was tight with the DA, and would put in a good word for me when everything was said and done. I nodded along, reminding myself Joey wasn't my friend. He, too, was the enemy of my enemy, and still my enemy. Funny how that kept working out.

"You know why we targeted you, Al?" Joey said. Tastier bait, but I refrained. "You're not like them. You're an outsider."

"They never accepted you," Richie said from the driver's seat.

"And they'll never accept you," Joey added. "No matter how well you perform. No matter how much money you make for them."

Oh great, even run-of-the-mill cops had resorted to pop psychology. "Malcolm Gladwell teaching at Quantico these days?" I said.

"You ever hear the name Harold Shinawatra?" Joey asked.

*Poor Harold.* Everyone at Prism knew his sad, pathetic tale. Something about Joey's suspiciously perfect pronunciation of the Thai surname triggered my spider-sense. "Doesn't ring a bell."

Richie abruptly smashed the brakes to avoid rear-ending a New Jersey Transit bus. He sped around the stationary vehicle while calmly and expertly muttering racial epithets at the driver, who turned out to be a rotund White woman. Definitely a former driver.

Joey huffed and rolled his eyes. "You're a shit liar, Al. And I can tell you're a shit liar because you speak unnaturally slow, and you blink twice as many times as normal when you're doing it. You think Paul won't pick up on that? Do you *want* to end up in jail?" I shook my head. My eyes widened and pulse quickened. "Harold Shinawatra—what do you know about him?"

"He was a tech analyst. Blew up his portfolio and Paul had him blacklisted. Last I heard he had a nervous breakdown and was living in Bangkok with his mom," I said, practicing my lying face while telling the truth.

"*Wrong!*" Richie said.

"He runs a private wealth business out of his mansion in Singapore," Joey said. "Also does a little consulting work for us on the side."

"Smart guy," Richie said. They let the silence linger.

Harold's meltdown happened shortly after I joined Prism. It predated the launch of VICE, Dennis's congressional infractions, and Brad's ultimately hollow threat to take me down for insider trading. Joey said they'd been after Paul for *years*.

"I'm not your first mole, am I?"

"*Bingo!*" Richie said. My guts tightened. This rabbit hole kept getting deeper and danker.

"Harold blew the whistle years ago," Joey said. "Gave us the initial evidence we needed to set up wiretaps, round-the-clock surveillance, you name it. It was enough to generate some decent-size fines and a slap on the wrist from the SEC. But it wasn't enough to get Paul. You know why, Al?" Joey paused again, waiting for me to answer the ostensibly rhetorical question. One second. Two seconds. Three seconds. "Because Paul didn't give a flying fuck about Harold," Joey said.

"But *you*," Richie said. "You're his golden boy."

"Paul sided with you over his own son," Joey said.

"He's been teaching you all the tricks of the trade," Richie said.

"Preparing you to manage your own portfolio. And one day set you up with your own fund," Joey said.

The black sedan had become an interrogation room. A prison on wheels. And their bad cop–bad cop routine had pounded my fragile mind into submission. I needed air, and pushed the power window button to no avail. My body hotted up and sweat rolled down my temples. My chest constricted and my dress shirt dampened. Richie eyed me in the rearview mirror. Joey leaned toward me, glaring, a half smirk carved into his jagged face.

"This time it's different," Joey said.

The most famous last words on Wall Street. Used by everyone from traders to journalists to Federal Reserve chairs to justify how the current market crash fundamentally differed from the previous market crash. To find the upsides and silver linings to whatever the ongoing crisis happened to be. To explain how this time everything would be okay. How we'd learned, improved, and grown. These were the lies everyone told themselves so they could navigate a world devoid of meaning. So they could traverse an industry built on excess. Where greed and venality were the heroes, and fairness and conscientiousness were the villains. This was the lie Joey and Richie were telling me now. Explaining how I would succeed, where Harold—*Harolds?*—had failed.

"Paul likes you, Al," Joey said. "He sees himself in you. You're hungry. Smart. Loyal."

"The son he always wanted," Richie said.

"Paul was an outsider, too," Joey said. "Born to a fireman and a schoolteacher. Went to public school in bumfuck Missouri. Had summer jobs. Paid his way through college. The extravagant billionaire persona is a facade. Deep down, he's an insecure little boy trying to prove himself."

"Just like you," Richie said.

I'd doubted these two. Underrated them. And for my arrogance, they'd broken me down. I wiped away the forming tears.

"What you're feeling," Joey said. "Channel it. *Harness* it. Because you'll need it all to take down Paul Kingsley."

The car stopped at a security checkpoint. A Soviet-era compound stood confidently under the gray morning sky. Wrought-iron fencing with tall, angled bars and barbed wire encircled the facility. Richie rolled down his window and flashed his badge to the station guard. The metallic gate retracted. We drove into the empty parking lot, past the entrance and its three colorful flags, then into another underground garage. Richie parked lengthwise across the row of handicapped spots.

Millions of questions swirled around in my head, but I chose to ask the most pertinent: "What really happened to Harold Shinawatra?"

Joey sighed.

"Paul got suspicious," Richie said. "Sicced Brad on him."

"Sounds familiar," I said.

"Harold couldn't handle the pressure," Joey said. "He started having anxiety attacks and didn't want to cooperate anymore. Since he was a whistleblower, we had to let him walk."

"And that's why it's different this time," I said. "I can't escape."

Richie winked at me via the rearview mirror. He exited the car and opened Joey's door. The two Feds waited while I clambered out the opposite side.

"Harold took his money, changed his name, and started his own fund halfway across the world," Joey said.

"He's doing quite well for himself," Richie said.

"There's hope for you yet," Joey said.

# DRESS TO KILL

*Friday, March 4*

*A*ct normal. Be yourself. Pretend it's not there. That was Joey's soundest, most consistent advice. It made sense. Paul was paranoid at the best of times, and these weren't those. On the other hand, what passed for normal behavior these days? Normal was Joey, as Simon, sending me illicit information, which I pawned off as my own research. Normal was financial engineering, market manipulation, money laundering, and wire fraud. Normal was alienating my only friend and my only family member. Normal was waiting to find the courage to end it all. To reject the terrible existence thrust upon me against my will. To correct the poor choices of others, which had been compounded by the poor choices of my own. The sun hadn't risen and billions of dollars' worth of electrons had traded hands. I needed a coffee.

At my desk, stimulant in hand, I sat perpendicular to my computer monitor, propped my feet on Keith's orphaned chair, and pretended to read emails on my phone. Dennis's vacant desk stood catty-corner, and in the periphery, I glimpsed Karen's thick mop of dirty-blond hair. She faced straight into her monitor, per usual, but bowed her head low, which meant she was selectively responding to her adoring fans. I kept a safe distance and my defenses on high alert in her presence. I had enough enemies as is, and experience implored me to never cross a White woman. Especially one with hundreds of thousands of rapacious IG and Twitter followers at the ready.

Fourth-quarter earnings season had just wrapped, and no banker in their right mind advised fundraising during a historic bear market, so news flow was muted. Ever magnanimous, Paul had carved out *three hundred million* and handed me the keys to my very own fund. I had full autonomy. As long as Compliance approved my trades, of course. The target return was an ambitious, if achievable, 30 percent annualized. But everything was relative. That goal sounded quaint compared to the ordeal I'd just survived, but only the dirtiest players on Wall Street could dream of accomplishing it.

On the plus side, I'd *arrived*. Achieved—no, surpassed—the goals I'd set for myself when I graduated from college. I was disinclined to care. My lawyer was haggling with the DA over how long I should spend in prison. My imminent indictment and tragic suicide would render my alleged success moot.

To minimize distractions, I allocated all three hundred million to two popular Vanguard ETFs—the total stock index fund, and the total bond index fund—in a sixty-forty split, like a savvy, disciplined, passive long-term investor should. With the market enjoying its latest dead cat bounce and the Federal Reserve threatening negative interest rates for the first time in history, I booked a solid

20 percent return in a few weeks. Cheating was by far the most lucrative investment strategy on Wall Street. Barring that, like most things in life, it was better to be lucky than good.

My third coffee necessitated a trip to the men's room. I took the long route to the opposite half of the office, which looked still as a frozen lake. Internet had fucked off to either lunch or Las Vegas. A new Dalí graced the wall, Paul's latest present to himself for being the smartest man in the world. I studied the painting's Surrealist elements. In the bottom corner of the chaotic scene, a man wore a lobster on his head.

I micturated, then ventured into the long hall leading to Paul's lair. At the end, a large Black man stood menacingly in front of the door. I approached cautiously. At arm's length, I reached into my pants pockets, gathered my phones for the TSA receptacle, and told the newest hired muscle I needed an audience with the boss.

"Nobody's allowed in Mister Kingsley's office."

"Right now? Or, like, *ever?*"

He didn't budge. My plan to capture Paul committing crimes via the miniature recording device nestled under my testicles had run into some significant snags. I racked my brain for a convenient lie as to why I needed to see Paul urgently. None emerged. The glass door opened. Paul patted the guard on the shoulder and told him to keep up the good work. He looked at me and smiled his Patrick Bateman smile.

"You like massages, Al?"

$$$

I drove Paul's Lotus down Geary to the Vista del Mar neighborhood on the far side of the peninsula. The sun warmed the back of my neck. We spent the entirety of the ride talking about baseball. I paid little attention to the dying sport, but Paul possessed uncanny knowledge of past America's favorite pastime. He rooted for the Dodgers—risky for a San Francisco resident given the fan bases' penchants for stabbing each other—and coveted a sizable stake in the franchise. The existing ownership syndicate had cockblocked his advances numerous times. After lamenting this unfair persecution, he went on sweeping expositions about the merits of advanced analytics, the problems with tanking as a rebuilding strategy, and the dysfunctional market for streaming and television rights. I hoped Joey could build a case on this.

Our destination, a Turkish bathhouse, was situated between a Safeway and a locksmith. How did Paul find these places? I parked the Lotus in an open space out front. We approached the nondescript facade and two of Paul's new security goons greeted us. They must've tailed us in a separate car. *Great.* They knew. Or would soon. Fear and relief bubbled in equal measure. The end was nigh, one way or another.

The four of us walked down a dank, dark hallway lined with teal tiles. At the concierge's desk, an attractive middle-aged woman with light brown hair and green eyes, presumably Turkish but probably Ukrainian, acknowledged Paul with a slight nod and a subtle smile.

She led us down a stairwell to a private room. Inside, the tacky tiling gave way to shiny marble, mood lighting, incense, and blindingly white towels. A rectangular Jacuzzi swallowed most of the floor, its brilliant cyan water beckoning. The hostess/mistress departed. Paul walked to the other side of the pool, removed his cufflinks, and rolled his sleeves to the forearm. He crouched to inspect the temperature. Pleased, he stood and flicked his pointer finger toward the bath.

A sudden thrust into each of my shoulder blades sent me hurtling into the water. I sank to my chest but kept my head afloat.

My clothes, wallet, phones, hidden recording device—everything was drenched. I shouted rhetorical questions laden with obscenities. Paul laughed.

"Dunk your head," one of the goons said. He was round and thick and multicolored tattoos crept out of his suit and up his neck.

"Fuck you."

"Dunk it. Or I dunk it for you."

I declined his counteroffer and submerged. Evacuating the entirety of my lungs, I stayed underwater as long as I could, which ended up being about ten seconds. I surfaced and sucked air like a shop vac. Drowning was definitely out. I waded to an empty side of the bath and scaled the ledge. Cool water gushed through my saturated sport coat, which weighed heavy on my sagging brain and body.

"Take your clothes off," Paul said.

*Think fast, Al!* Questioning Paul's orders rarely went well. Defiance equaled incrimination. I removed my jacket, then shirts, slacks, and socks. I left my boxer briefs on. They fastened the FBI-issued surveillance device to my derf.

"Underwear, too," the fat goon said. I scoffed.

"Do you know how many cocks I've seen?" Paul said. "You're not special, Al. Take them off."

*Fuck, fuck, fuck, fuck, fuck—got it!* I grabbed my penis in an exaggerated manner with both hands and removed my last article of clothing crotch-first, like a mental patient. I bent down, shivered demonstrably, let the soggy black boxers hang at my knees, and used my dominant foot to push them down to the marble floor. In an adroit movement befitting a decathlete, I clasped the recorder between my two biggest little piggies, made a fist with my toes—*Die Hard*–style—and held on for dear life. My prehensile toes, a useless vestigial trait I shared with my distant cousins, the lemurs of Madagascar, had finally proved useful. I then tugged lustily on my foreskin to awaken my poor, lonely, shriveled member, which had retracted from the cold. The guards looked up like they were pissing at urinals.

"Decent piece of hardware you got there, Al," Paul said. "Firm up that tummy and you'd have half a chance in the skin biz."

"*Thanks?*" I said.

"Check him," Paul ordered.

One of the goons sifted through my clothes while the other shined a small flashlight in my ears, nose, and asshole.

"He's clean," the first goon said after a thorough inspection. He handed Paul my sopping wallet and phones.

"Throw him a towel," Paul said.

The flashlight-wielding goon complied. I wrapped the fluffy white cotton around the lower half of my body. Paul told Inspector Goon to discard my clothes in the dumpster out back and asked if I wanted to talk shop before or after our happy endings.

"I need to use the bathroom," I said.

Paul huffed. "Piss in the pool."

"I need to take a shit. I swallowed too much chlorine, or something."

Paul sighed like I was Brad and blasphemed. "You, go with him," he said to Flashlight Guy.

I limped gingerly toward the exit with the device curled tightly between my toes, selling hard the idea I was about to lose control of my bowels. Flashlight Guy followed at an exaggerated distance.

The men's lavatory was a private room down the end of an adjacent hall. I twisted open the doorknob, leaned my shoulder into the door, dropped my towel, then lunged ass-first onto the toilet and feigned relief. The door closed behind Flashlight Guy. He stood by the sink, eyes to the heavens.

"Dude, I can't go with you standing there." He said nothing. "Haven't you had a close enough look at my asshole?" Silence. "Well, if you're just going to stand there, why don't you make yourself useful and give me a blumpkin?" I said, wiggling my dick at him. He looked down for a split second, then stepped forward and slapped me across the temple with his open paw.

"Hurry up," he said, and exited the bathroom.

I stood and locked the deadbolt behind him, then unclenched my cramping foot. A searing pain ran up my shin and into my knee. I roared loudly, as if cursing Montezuma's Revenge, and tried not to laugh. Someone painfully shitting themselves was never *not* hilarious. I knelt down on the cold black marble and bashed my fist onto the miniature recording device until it shattered into pieces. I deposited the first several into the toilet and flushed. Success. I waited a few moments, dropped in the remaining fragments, pissed on them for good measure, and flushed again.

Step one in the FBI's master plan to take out Paul Kingsley had literally gone down the toilet. The merger between two dying grocery store chains, which "Simon" had told me about, which I was supposed to discuss with Paul, while wearing a hidden wire, which would dead to rights incriminate him and save my skin, would simply become another profitable feather in Prism's financial cap.

*What if I wander into the woods in like . . . Wyoming?* Like in one of those fabricated reality shows? I barely survived when Paul jettisoned me at a state park in Los Angeles. I was a city guy. A *pussy.* I wouldn't last a week in the proper wilderness. Getting mauled by a grizzly bear seemed nobler than getting mauled by the state.

I dabbed my head and neck with warm water until it ran down my chest and back, put on my towel, then opened the bathroom door. Flashlight Guy snarled, still fantasizing about the sexual favors he'd promised me. He shoved me twice on our short walk down the hall. Flirtatious type. Back in the Jacuzzi room, the hostess/mistress stood next to three striking women in silk robes: a redhead, a blonde, and an East Asian.

"Where's Paul?" I asked.

"Which do you like?" she said.

All of them. None of them. The hostess/mistress insisted. The Asian made me think of Jennie. Who had Paul chosen? Was this another demented test? Was I supposed to get a massage?

"Her," I said, pointing to the redhead. She had milky-white skin with freckles and bright blue eyes. I'd never been with a redhead before, and I needed to check things off my bucket list as quickly as possible.

# SOUND OF DA POLICE

*Saturday, March 26*

"Maybe you're confused about what we're doing here," Joey said with his patented condescension. "Is that it?" He, Richie, and I were sitting in a dreary, window-free conference room with off-white walls and morose brown carpeting at the FBI's main field office outside Sacramento. "If the goal was to charge Paul Kingsley with soliciting prostitutes—well, this'd be the best-run operation in the history of the fucking bureau! I'd be nominated for fucking director. Isn't that right, Richie?"

The slovenly one nodded. He'd soaked through his shirt and looked like a block of prosciutto that'd sat in the sun too long. The office smelled accordingly. Joey's exasperation was palpable. He hemmed and hawed and flailed in his seat, looking more haggard and exhausted than usual. Apparently, neither of these morons had figured out they were no match for Paul Kingsley.

"Don't you have anything to say for yourself?" Joey said.

"I've met with Paul three times since I *agreed*"—air quotes—"to cooperate. All three times he made me strip naked before talking business."

"Oh, poor Al! It's so stressful fucking whores on the DOJ's dime," Joey said. "You're not even wearing the backup wire!"

"Are you fu— Do you *want* me to get caught?" I said, flabbergasted. "Or did you forget I saved your bullshit operation at the Turkish bathhouse?"

"He's got a point, Joe," Richie said.

"And, for the record, one of the women was a porn star."

Eggs would've fried on Joey's beet-red face. He leaned back in his chair, rubbed his eyes with the backs of his hands like a kitten, and practiced his Lamaze breaths. Richie dabbed sweat from his temple with a yellow-stained handkerchief.

"Look, ever since the Valentine's Day Massacre, Paul's been ultra-paranoid. He's got a round-the-clock security detail. Nobody's allowed in his office. He never talks business on the phone. He won't even send a goddamned text message. And you see how he's treating me—his alleged golden boy," I said. "I can't get to him. You need to find another way."

"There is no other way," Joey sighed.

A pathetic silence smothered the room. These dunce caps *actually* believed they were on the cusp of taking down Paul Kingsley. The equivalent of Gotham beat cops capturing Batman.

"I'm planning to turn myself in to Chris Holloway, the DA for the Northern District of California," I said. Joey's head shot up. His eyes bulged like he'd been thrust into the vacuum of space.

I had no incentive to play this nonsense game any longer. Charting this irreversible path would force me to use the Glock tucked safely in the unopened gym bag on my kitchen counter. The one I'd purchased in Oakland after meeting with Damon for the last time. The one I'd thought about incessantly but was too scared to touch, let alone fire. The one tailor-made for turning my macabre fascination into a personalized final solution.

"I don't care if I go to prison," I said. "I deserve it." The first statement was a lie, but the second was true.

"Listen to me, very, carefully, Al," Joey said. "You will not say one fucking word to Holloway."

I laughed. What could he possibly lord over a latent corpse?

"He can't help you," Richie said.

"Oh, great. More shit cop, shittier cop? You guys enjoy getting worked by Paul the rest of your lives. I've got more important things to do." I stood to leave, part serious, part bluff, all apathy.

"Holloway's a dead man walking," Joey said.

My muscles froze.

"He bought Intel options with info acquired through Simon's network," Richie said. "We caught that fucker red-handed."

I slouched back into my chair, stupefied. "You're going to charge a federal district attorney?"

Joey exhaled deeply. "We've pinched a shit ton of execs and hedgies, Al. But the corruption goes way beyond that. Prosecutors. Judges. Politicians. You can't imagine the scale." He ran his hands through his hair, then propped his elbows on the table and leaned forward. "We've been building this case for *years*, Al. Patiently and methodically. The last man standing is Paul Kingsley."

"He's like Shredder. Or Magneto. The final boss," Richie said.

"After you nail him, we'll roll up the entire network. *Hundreds* of people will go to prison."

"It'll be the biggest white-collar corruption case in history," Richie said.

"But it all depends on you, Al," Joey said.

"We need you, pal," Richie said.

*Need.* They didn't need me. They *wanted* me. And not because of who I was or what made me uniquely me. They wanted me because of what *I* could do for *them.* That was the common denominator in all my failed relationships. The FBI wanted me to get Paul. Paul wanted me to make money. Brad wanted me to kick around so he could feel better about himself. My mother wanted me to rationalize her bad luck and bad decisions. My entire existence was transactional, and in every transaction I got ripped off.

"Why should I continue to help you?"

"You're a good kid, Al," Joey said.

"A tough-as-nails kid," Richie said.

"We know all about you," Joey said. "Born to a single mom. Aced high school. Paid your way through college. Fought your way onto Wall Street. You were dealt a tough hand and you made something of yourself. And you want to throw it all away?"

"According to my lawyer, I'm going to jail no matter what."

"We all have to make sacrifices, Al," Joey said. "Deep down, you *know* it's better to do the right thing. To make the hard choice."

Conceding the effectiveness of their pop psychology pained me. I did like making hard choices. I'd spent a lifetime convincing myself I was tougher than everyone else. Tenacious. Indefatigable. *Stronger.* Attributes that differentiated me from the pack. And look at me now. My best possible future included a multiyear prison sentence. I reminded myself none of this mattered. The sooner I got back to my apartment, the sooner I could wash my hands of Paul, Prism, the FBI, all of it. Just play along for the cameras a little bit more.

"What do we do now?" I asked, morbidly curious.

Joey sighed and smiled like a man who hadn't impregnated his au pair after all. "Follow me," he said.

The three of us exited the conference room and walked down

a maze of corridors until we arrived at a door labeled "EQUIP-MENT" in stenciled black letters. My heart thumped with childlike enthusiasm. Joey swiped his keycard, depressed the door lever, and walked inside. I followed, half expecting to see walls jam-packed with machine guns, bazookas, and incendiary grenades, like in the movies. Instead, I discovered a rat's nest of AV cables, errant mice and keyboards, and derelict desktops older than myself. A musty odor clung to the cramped room, which was surely draped in asbestos.

Joey rummaged through a mess of open-topped cardboard boxes looking for God knows what. I asked Richie why the FBI didn't just assassinate Paul and pretend it was an accident. He told me, with a straight face, America was a nation committed to the "rule of law." I debated whether to laugh or cry. Joey found his buried treasure with a triumphant "a-ha." He held up a gallon-size Ziploc bag stuffed with black rectangular devices and charging cables for us to admire. He signed the pen-and-paper inventory log and we departed.

"We'll have to do this old-school," Joey said, back in the conference room.

He emptied the contents of the plastic bag onto the wobbly fiberboard table and sorted the items by size. The four smallest pieces were no bigger than flecks of lint, imperceptible to the untrained eye. The largest rectangular block was the size of a slice of rye bread and resembled a mobile charge bank. Last, but certainly not least, Joey showed me a nondescript pen, the kind hotels and pharmaceutical companies passed out like PEZ. The built-in microphone sat at the top, while the battery was smartly embedded inside the shaft. The miniature recording device also doubled as a real pen, Joey explained excitedly.

His demonstration underwhelmed. I always figured, in the unlikely event I found myself learning to use sophisticated government surveillance technology in an epic training montage, the experience would be much, much doper. Where was the microscopic drone that looked like a mosquito and flew around Paul's office recording his every move and every word? Or the *Predator*-style infrared body-heat sensor that monitored movement through walls? Why didn't that pen come with a built-in rocket-propelled grenade? And where were the condoms that doubled as plastic explosives? The FBI was lame AF. No wonder crime paid.

"Distribute these little microphones around Paul's office. Make sure they're hidden, but not obstructed—otherwise, we won't be able to hear anything," Joey said. "Place the pen near Paul's desk. On a bookshelf. Or in a desk drawer. Finally, put this big guy wherever Paul spends most of his time. Make sense?"

This was quite possibly the stupidest plan in the government's long, sordid history of infringing upon civil liberties. The *Mission: Impossible* franchise required less suspension of disbelief. Prism's offices teemed with CCTV security cameras. Paul's bunker was protected with a brand-new keycard system and was guarded 24-7 by Blackwater rejects. Worst of all, even if I breached those defenses, accessed the office, and followed Joey's directions to the letter, all they'd hear was Paul jerking off to live porn streams.

"I think you're overlooking something pretty important here. *Paul's office has better security than Fort fucking Knox.*"

"You're a clever guy," Richie said. "Get creative."

"Is this a joke? This must be a joke, right?" They didn't respond. "Why don't you just raid Paul's office? I thought you FBI goons loved that shit."

"And find what?" Joey said sharply. "What clear and incontrovertible evidence of criminal activity does Paul keep in his office?" The rhetorical question lingered.

"We search and seize, we come up empty-handed. Paul and every other fucker on Wall Street figures out we're on to them, and our criminal case is shot. *At best*, the SEC fines the fuck out of him," Joey said. "You know what happens then, Al? The sonofabitch makes *even more* money. We've seen this script.

"Martz.

"Rodriguez.

"Cohen.

"Brown.

"Whitney.

"Do you know how many of those guys are in prison? *Zero*. You need to quit fucking whining, Al, and step the fuck up."

I fidgeted in my seat, wiped my brow, cleared my throat. *Remember, just play along.* "How would I get past his security systems? I'm not a trained spy."

"We'll work out a plan—*together*," Joey said. "All you need to do is execute it."

"And if it doesn't work?"

Joey sighed. "Al, this is our best, and probably last, chance to bury Paul Kingsley. To earn back your freedom. To do the *right* thing. Isn't that motivation enough? Isn't that worth a shot?"

Soon I'd be a cadaver, which made this utterly absurd conversation as irrelevant as it was insane. *Just don't think about it.*

Don't think about the fact that the same federal government, which was all too happy to spend trillions blowing up civilians in my ancestor's backyard with Predator drones and satellite-controlled missiles, couldn't be bothered to prevent one ultra-rich asshole from destroying the integrity and credibility of the world's largest capital market.

Don't think about why the monumental task of stopping him had fallen to me.

Don't think about the mess.

Don't think about who'd discover my body.

Don't think about my mom. Or how she'd feel when she found out. Or what she'd say. Or if they'd make her fly to San Francisco and identify my remains.

Don't think about what Damon would say. Or Jennie. Or Keith. Or Joey. Or Paul.

The Good Lord and the Invisible Hand worked in mysterious ways.

Just don't think about it.

# SUICIDAL THOUGHTS

*Sunday, April 10*

I twiddled the handle of my broken switchblade comb. Its plastic-and-steel frame drew heat from my fingers. I clasped it tightly and lifted my arm, centering the flat edge against my temple. Higher. Higher. Too high. Still didn't feel right. I placed it under my chin. To be effective from this position, I needed to angle the barrel. Otherwise, I'd end up in prison with half a face. That juxtaposition seemed even more awkward. I relocated the imaginary barrel to the center of my forehead. My arms felt teratogenic. Too short to ensure an accurate, straightaway discharge. I flipped it back to the side of my head. Centered, above the ear. Best bet.

Steady. *Steady.* Visualize the end. No more pain. Be brave. Just for a second. Then it'd all be over. I closed my eyes, mouthed an imaginary *bang*, and considered the bullet ripping through my skull and brain tissue. In an instant I'd cease to exist. Perhaps a favorite childhood memory would race between my failing synapses, like in that famous *New Yorker* story. Perhaps I'd regret this irreversible choice the second it was made. But would that really matter? My entire life had been one long sequence of uninterrupted mistakes. The sunk cost of existence.

The microwave clock read just past midnight. Three in the morning on the East Coast. A definitive no-man's-land for America's stock market gladiators. At this exact moment I was supposed to leave my apartment and execute Joey and Richie's ridiculous "plan." The one where I snuck past the lone security thug. And danced around the prying eyes of the security cameras. And broke into Paul's office using the keycard I'd stolen from Lina's purse. And planted clandestine recording devices at hidden—yet accessible—points around Paul's gargantuan office. And absconded into the shadows without anyone ever knowing, rendering the mission a resounding success. Joey and Richie played too much *Metal Gear*. They were also complete fucking imbeciles.

$$$

I masturbated, evacuated, shaved, and showered. Each perfunctory task carried with it a hopeful, wistful finality, like the last day of high school. This was the *last time* I'd ever strut into first period. The *last time* I'd ever listen to morning announcements. The *last time* I'd ever see that girl I liked but never asked out. Or that douchebag I hated but never fought. I dressed in my favorite baby blue shirt and patterned tie, my sharpest navy blue Armani suit, and my shiniest brown dress shoes and matching belt. Then I peed again, touched up my shave, and pomaded my hair to perfection. Somebody—probably one of the neighbors I'd never met and never would—would discover the mess. The least I could do was put a hole through my head with dignity.

The face in the bathroom mirror smiled back at me. "Live fast, die young, leave a good-looking corpse," I said aloud.

Giddy thoughts of relief swept over me as I headed to the kitchen. The gym bag sat ominously on the counter, undisturbed since the day I'd brought it home. I inhaled and exhaled deeply, then shadow-boxed in place to hype myself up. My old game-day routine. After collecting the bag, I settled down on my shitty IKEA futon, which sat adjacent to my shitty IKEA coffee table and opposite my overpriced flat-screen TV. The carefully selected location obstructed the view from my lone, lonely window.

I removed the box of bullets from the bag and spilled them across the table. I picked up the handgun. It was deceptively heavy and black as a shark's eye. I clicked the safety back and forth a few times and left it in the off position for good. The trigger pulled with ease. I lodged bullets into the pistol's magazine and loaded the weapon. The moment of truth—set in motion the nanosecond I was unjustly thrust into this godforsaken world—had arrived.

I should've felt relief.

I should've been at peace.

Panic enveloped me. Followed by anxiety and nausea.

I'd never fired the gun—only watched countless YouTube videos and action movies. Did it work properly? Was the ammunition live? I realized I should've done a test run. But wasn't suicide a once-in-a-lifetime experience?

I placed the pistol on the table next to the remaining bullets and frantically paced my apartment. Tears swelled in my eyes. Another poorly constructed plan in a poorly constructed life. I couldn't even shuffle off this mortal coil without fucking everything up. I jetted down the hall to my bedroom, then back to the kitchen, then back to the living room. I thought about the wife I'd never marry and the honeymoon I'd never take and the kids I'd never sire and the house I'd never buy, then impulsively picked up the pistol and jammed it into my temple and tried to pull the trigger, but my finger froze in place. I fought back tears and I couldn't breathe and I dry heaved and threw the gun into the kitchen, shattering my coffee carafe and scattering shards of glass everywhere. I darted to the bathroom and puked pure stomach bile.

When only searing pain inched up my esophagus I stood and looked in the mirror. Pale skin, bloodshot eyes, and a mouth dripping with off-yellow secretion gazed back. Not exactly a fashionable corpse. I splashed cold water on my face and rinsed out my mouth and walked back to the kitchen. The gun sat motionless on the cheap linoleum floor, surrounded by broken glass. An odd crime scene. The transgression was helplessness and the victim was unharmed. I flipped off the kitchen light, maundered to the futon, and collapsed onto its uncomfortable cushions. Exhaustion crushed me like the original Terminator. I stared at the ceiling, cursing my cowardice.

$$\$\$\$$$

Vibrating on my hip startled, then annoyed, then insisted I wake up. The awful taste in my mouth and the expensive, uncomfortable suit clinging to my body reminded me I was, unfortunately, alive. Darkness smothered the room as I fumbled in my pocket for my phone. I glanced at the too-bright screen with strained eyes. Insult had tagged in injury, and they were preparing to deliver their double finisher.

The name on screen read *Kate Murphy*. Better known colloquially as "Mom."

Her timing never ceased to amaze. The obvious—*rational*—thing to do was push decline. Maybe I could dig my hole with the FBI a little deeper. The handgun still offered a permanent reprieve—if I could only find the nerve. Maybe my mom's call was divine motivation. Maybe her voice would be the catalyst I needed to figuratively then literally pull the trigger.

"Al, sweetie? Are you there? I've been trying to reach you *forever.*"

"I know."

"You've been avoiding me."

*Now, why would I do that?* "I've been under a lot of stress. At work."

"That awful job's going to put you in an early grave," she said. Irony had died, but I lived on. "I saw something on the news about your boss. They said he single-handedly bankrupted that poor on-line dating company. They had a great app, too. I met my friend Carlos on it."

"Poor company," I scoffed. "It was a fake. A house of cards. *Fraudulent.*"

"Well, Carlos is *very* real."

The obvious solution finally hit me. I just needed to take the pistol and threaten Joey and Richie. They were trained to shoot first and ask questions later—the darker the threat, the quicker the draw. I'd be put out of my misery in a New York minute.

"Al?"

"I'm busy with work and—"

"You're always busy with work. Too busy to come home for Thanksgiving. Too busy to come home for *Christmas.* Too busy to call me on my birthday!"

"When was—"

"Don't interrupt me, Al. I'm your mother and I'm talking."

"You can't—"

"*All you do is work.* All you *talk* about is work. Work this and work that. And for what, Al? Money? Respect? What good is money if you don't have time to spend it? What good is respect if nobody actually cares about you? What about your *family?*"

"Thanks to you, I never had any family!"

"I'm your family, Al!" she said. Her voice cracked. "I know you think I'm stupid and selfish and you wonder why you got stuck with a White trash mom like me."

She sobbed fully into the phone. "I've made a lot of mistakes in my life, Al. But you. You're the *one thing* I know I got right. You're the best thing that ever happened to me. I'm worried about you. And I miss you. I love you."

Her words stung like vinegar in an open wound. I wanted to cry, too. And not an errant tear or two. The kind of ugly, unrestrained, cathartic cry that wiped the slate clean and nullified decades of dysfunction. Rendered moot a childhood of perpetual neglect and intermittent abuse. But I'd been dismissed and deceived too many times to let myself be vulnerable. I'd learned to harden my heart. Protect myself from pain.

"I'm in trouble. A *lot* of trouble."

"At work?" She sounded hopeful.

"Worse."

"*Worse?*" She sounded concerned. "Just tell me what you need, Al. Tell me how I can help."

I paused for a moment, then sarcastically said, "What do they do on your soap operas, again? When the hero's being blackmailed by an evil billionaire and also a fugitive on the run from the FBI?"

"*The FBI?*"

As if on cue a barrage of texts from Joey blanketed my phone screen.

*Howd it go?*
*Did you pull it off?*
*Were not getting a signal*
*Call me ASAP*

I sat upright on the futon. "I don't know what to do."

"You listen to me, Al. People like us have to fight and claw and kick and scratch for everything. *Nothing* comes easy. Ever since you were a little boy you never backed down from a challenge. And I'm *so* proud of you. And of everything you've accomplished.

"No matter what kind of trouble you're in, no matter how big, I know you'll fight to the bitter end. And I know you'll do the right thing," she said, her voice strengthening. "And if that doesn't work, steal a bunch of money, fake your own death, and move to Switzerland. That's what they do in my stories."

Rays of sunlight streaked through my sad little window and another volley of texts badgered my phone.

"I really do have to go, Mom."

"You know I always love you."

I ended the call. I hadn't told my mom I loved her since middle school. I hadn't even called her "Mom" since the ninth grade. Emotionally distancing myself was a survival method. She was my mother, but I didn't have a say in the matter. I didn't *have* to love her. And I sure as shit didn't have to validate her choices. But did she make those choices? She was a child masquerading as an adult. Emotionally frozen in time at six years old, when her dad bailed on her, and sixteen years old, when a stranger robbed her of her innocence and stole her potential.

I thought of Dr. Manhattan and the "thermodynamic miracle." Nobody chose to be born. Nobody chose their uniquely tragic circumstances. *Every* life was a disaster. *Every* life was an unmitigated clusterfuck. But every life was also a statistical impossibility. A mathematical marvel. Every life deserved validation. Every life deserved *love*.

For the first time in years I felt something other than crushing despair. Or hopelessness. Or that I was a bit player watching my life helplessly unfold before me. I stood and stretched my legs, skimmed

Joey's wall of texts, and looked again at the gun on the kitchen floor. I stripped off my coat and tie and dress shirt and walked to the bathroom and stared in the mirror.

On the surface I looked nothing like my mom, and yet in the contours of my face, I saw a striking resemblance. We were fucked-up people, no doubt, but we were *survivors*. My mom had been dealt a much shittier hand than me, but she chose to keep playing. I'd reached my do-and-die moment, but I chose to keep living. We always chose to fight, no matter how devastating the consequences, no matter how overwhelming the odds.

I studied the man in the mirror.

He had plenty of fight left in him.

# THE SETUP

Joey called and texted countless times. He and Richie were operating out of the FBI's Sacramento office, which meant I needed to feed them an excuse explaining why I hadn't completed last night's "secret mission" before they knocked at my door. I hadn't thought this far in advance. I was supposed to be dead. Best-laid plans.

On my notepad, I doodled a less-than-useful murder board and wrote Paul's name in big, bold, capital letters smack-dab in the center. Channeling my inner Lester Freamon hadn't produced the killer insight or spark of inspiration I needed to extricate myself from the mess I'd made of my life. And while my mom had jolted me out of my depressive death spiral, and reminded me I wasn't totally alone on this planet gone mad, neither she nor Damon nor Jennie—who all loitered on my board's outermost rim of relevance—had much to offer when it came to outfoxing the FBI and Paul Kingsley. Ol' Dirty

Bastard's "Brooklyn Zoo" thumped from my Bluetooth speaker. *Think, goddamn it.*

I dropped the notepad on the futon, entered the kitchen, and kicked pieces of glass into a pile by the dishwasher. I removed the pistol from the floor and stuffed it into the gym bag along with the loose bullets. Once I figured out how to steal a bunch of money, fake my own death, and move to Switzerland, I'd figure out how to offload my hardware. The Bay was the obvious—though environmentally unfriendly—choice. The haunting piano of Wu-Tang's "C.R.E.A.M." filled the room. *Think, goddamn it.*

I grabbed the notepad again and gazed at my messy diagram. My stomach panged from hunger and my head throbbed from caffeine withdrawal. Was there anyone left to rally to my cause? Even if the corrupt, complicit, and incompetent cops weren't out to get me, they tended to create more problems than they solved. Paul had neutralized my only allies inside Prism. RIP, Jennie and Keith. Every hedge fund rival on the Street wanted Paul's head on a plate—none more so than Seaside's Jason Beard—but they'd all taken a beating during the Sweet meltdown. The market's zero-sum game meant their losses were Paul's gains. And just like in poker, you only attacked the player with the biggest stack of chips when you held a no-doubt winning hand. Me—Ali Jafar, obscure, token-minority analyst, who was tragically and coincidentally named after characters from *Aladdin*, and was under the thumb of the most powerful man on Wall Street, and was in the crosshairs of the most powerful law enforcement agency in the world, who had no leverage or kompromat or inside information, and lacked any semblance of a silver bullet—was the farthest thing from a no-doubt winning hand imaginable. Method Man's "Biscuits" boomed in the background. *Think, goddamn it.*

A heavy fist pounded on my door. They'd arrived earlier than I expected. No sense delaying the inevitable. I stuffed my notepad in my work bag and threw the door open wide. Joey barged inside and stood with his back to me in the middle of my tiny living room. Richie waddled in behind him and took a seat on my futon. I closed the door and, wanting to play proper host, regretfully informed them my coffeemaker was broken.

"Where, the fuck, have you been?" Joey said.

"I can explain," I lied.

"Did you plant the fucking bugs?!" Joey asked, which should've been his first question, and which I answered in the negative.

I could practically feel the heat emanating from his face as he launched into one of his patented diatribes. He accused me of sabotaging his operation, collaborating with the enemy, being a lazy, entitled millennial, and failing to grasp the seriousness of the consequences I faced, including how he'd personally arrange for me to be violated on a daily basis during my one-way extended-stay trip to Sing Sing.

He paused to catch his breath and prepare for another salvo.

"Paul was in his office," I said. My bluff stunned us both, and Joey went silent for several agonizing seconds. Before he or Richie could challenge my dubious assertion, I doubled down. "He was live streaming an interracial gang bang. Three Black dudes, three White dudes, one blonde, and one brunette. It was pretty intense. I'm sure you can imagine." More uncomfortable silence. I could practically hear the gears in Joey's head cranking, wondering how to respond to such a claim, as I tripled down. "Lina told me Paul was supposed to be on a trip to Jamaica. That's why I planned the operation for this weekend. But when I got to Paul's office I saw him through the glass. Sitting on his couch, buck-ass naked, tugging away. In crisp, clear, four-K definition."

"We get the picture," Joey said.

"Obviously, given the circumstances, I aborted the mission."

"Obviously."

In my fugue state, our roles had suddenly reversed, and I took great pleasure in tormenting Joey. I let the silence deafen. Allowed the tension and uncertainty and confusion to compound, and seized the power in our abusive, one-dimensional relationship. It was more effective and intoxicating than any upper or antidepressant I'd ever taken. *This* I could get used to.

After another protracted lull, Joey assured me I still had to plant the bugs, or else I'd rot in prison when I wasn't being molested. But this time his voice lacked conviction. Without me, he had no chance of bringing down Paul Kingsley. Without me, he'd wasted years of his life cosplaying someone clever, blown millions in taxpayer money, and destroyed billions of *shareholder value*. Without me, he was just another ineffective cog in the FBI's impotent machinery, soon to be relegated to a desk job in the defunded tax crimes division. I was the one on the dangle, but Joey needed me a lot more than I needed him.

The newly leveled playing field reminded me of a famous idiom: When you owe the bank a little bit of money, the bank has the leverage; when you owe the bank *a lot* of money, you have the leverage. I'd always wielded the leverage. It'd just taken me too long to realize it. What I unequivocally understood was this: No matter what happened, I was done getting pushed around. By Joey. By Paul. By this unjust, inequitable, and insane world. They could destroy me, but not before I destroyed them first.

I thanked Joey and Richie for stopping by, and showed them the door.

$$$

I hit the gym for weights and Pilates and had Amazon same-day deliver a proper vacuum and a fancy cappuccino machine. These were likely my final weeks—*days?*—of freedom and I didn't want to squander them in squalor. Why had I chosen such an austere lifestyle? What *was* the money for? Deprivation hadn't made me stronger, just miserable. There'd be plenty of time for self-denial and self-flagellation in prison. And who knows—maybe I *deserved* to have a few nice things before my life imploded.

I plopped down on my shitty IKEA futon and placed an open tray of Oreos on my coffee table like Teddy KGB. I dunked one in steamed half-and-half, devoured it whole, and stared at the wall, which I'd converted into a professional-grade murder board. Using pushpins and color-coded three-by-five notecards, I'd created a triangle denoting my predicament's principal belligerents: Paul, Joey, me. No matter how long and how hard I looked, however, they always annihilated me in a brutal pincer attack.

I once again added Damon, Jennie, and my mom to the periphery. It felt good to have comrades, even if they were outclassed and overmatched. Then I remembered to add Keith and Karen, though ostensibly for comic relief. Keith was as useless as an incel at an orgy, and I wasn't sure who Karen hated more: me or Paul. That enemy of my enemy is my enemy shit was getting old. Finally, I tossed up Marvin, Paul's driver, on a whim and added "Allure porn stars" for my debauched amusement. At least they connected directly to Paul, and there was hypothetical strength in delusional numbers.

To stretch the bounds of my sanity, I dropped in some bit players. Rival hedge fund managers. Corrupt politicians. The dipshit head of the SEC. It amounted to little more than performance art. Nobody was coming to save me. I downed another Oreo and thought of the Glock in the gym bag. Why not ice Paul? The FBI sure as shit wasn't going to save the country from his financial terrorism. With a body to my name, I'd go inside with significantly more rep.

I buried the thought and started feeling sorry for myself again, taking solace from the fact I didn't have to go to work anymore. Paul couldn't blackmail me for crimes the FBI knew I'd committed, now could he? *Fuck Paul.* And fuck the FBI, too. Cowards all of them. I thought about calling back my duplicitous lawyer and telling her I didn't want the DA's bullshit plea deal. And then telling those sad-sack motherfuckers at the DOJ to prosecute me to the fullest extent of the law. Better yet, I considered leaking *everything* to the press. Just going out with one gigantic middle finger to the entire corrupt enterprise. Removing uncertainty was the one silver lining of being completely screwed. I was going down, but I could go down swinging.

In reflective, pathetic moments I often wondered if having a dad would've changed the trajectory of my life. Everyone around me had a dad. You didn't take AP Calculus without a dad. You didn't go to NYU without a dad. You didn't get a job at Prism Capital without a dad. Would my dad have supported me along the way? Would he have helped me avoid my current predicament? Or, if the future really was preordained by venal cosmic forces, would he have offered a meaningful insight, or encouraging pep talk, or reassuring lies about how it'd all be okay, before I spent my prime years in prison? Maybe he would've had enough ill-gotten gains to buy my freedom, like a Russian oligarch's kid? How about a single chance to tell me he loved me?

All those rent-a-dads my mom had cycled through played like a sad highlight reel in my head. All the teachers and coaches and professors and bosses I'd looked up to in the pitiful hope they'd fill the permanent void. That they'd treat me like a son instead of a stranger. Or, worst of all, a charity case. I jammed two more Oreos in my mouth, then studied the murder board and the gym bag. I was back to vacillating between hope and hopelessness. Classic symptoms of bipolar disorder, which I'd never suffered, and major clinical depression, which had swaddled me since birth, no matter how many drugs the pharmaceutical industry threw at me.

I saw my mom's card on the board. She didn't have a dad, either.

Then I looked at the gym bag.

I saw Damon and Jennie and Keith and Karen. They had dads. Perhaps, coincidentally, they weren't heading to prison.

Then I looked at the gym bag.

I saw Joey and Richie. I bet they had dads, too. Proud Goldwater and Nixon voters.

Then I looked at the gym bag.

I saw Paul. I wondered: Did his dad bail? Was that why he was so damaged? Or maybe he did have a dad. A dad like him. Abusive. Manipulative. A full-blown—

I stuffed one final Oreo into my face and grabbed a pen. I wrote "Brad" on a notecard and added it below Paul's name. I connected Brad to Robbie, and linked Robbie to Paul. I stood and faced my haphazard schematic and forgot about the gym bag. The battlefield had suddenly shifted. But a connection was missing. I grabbed another card and excitedly scribbled "Fucking Preston." Chekhov's billionaire dipshit created a straight line from me to Jennie to Preston to Brad to Paul. A Suicide Squad of white-collar misfits coalesced before my very eyes. A disgruntled failson, a ruthlessly efficient trader, an ace lawyer, Wall Street's savviest social media strategist, and an armed semiterrorist with a rage-filled soul and nothing left to lose. All apoplectically aimed at Paul Kingsley.

I began formulating the most implausible *Mission: Impossible*–style caper ever conceived.

A crew like this had the skills and wherewithal to wreak havoc.

A crew like this could bring the ruckus.

# VERBAL INTERCOURSE

*Sunday, April 10*

Late that evening, and well past my Bay Area bedtime, Damon and I were holed up in a shitty room at a shitty Holiday Inn Express in a shitty peninsula town just south of SFO, a shitty airport. I'd come equipped with an all-new phone, brand-new attire, a fistful of cash, and a plan crazy enough to give Danny Ocean pause. I'd hoped, probably in vain, my latest attempts at spycraft had prevented Paul and/or the FBI and/or anyone else who was interested in fucking me over from tracking my movements.

Damon had been knee-deep in paperwork on a megamerger between two insurance companies for the past few months. The deal was sure to close, though any remotely competent FTC chair would've blocked it without blinking. Aside from the fact that I was distracting him from his day job, Damon had made it clear—multiple times—he wasn't exactly enthralled by the prospect of becoming an active participant in my farcical conspiracy against one of the world's wealthiest, most spiteful men. He was my best friend, sure, but he wasn't totally fucking insane.

Eventually, after much gentle coaxing and much guileful guilt-tripping, I convinced him to collude. First, by assuring him his name would never be linked to my preposterous scheming, and second, by agreeing to pony up for a candy-red Lamborghini if I pulled this off. And no, I hadn't forgotten about the Ferrari I'd already promised him for his troubles.

We'd spent hours discussing the legal documents and affidavits I needed him to prepare: changes of control, transfers of beneficial ownership, nondisclosure agreements, and indemnification clauses, among others. These white-collar weapons of mass destruction formed the crucial linchpins in my outrageous scheme. But even with my livelihood on the line, the tedious process of parsing and poring over the legalese caused my exhausted eyes to glaze over—more than once.

"Are you paying attention, Al?" Damon snapped.

"I don't know how you do this every day without becoming suicidal," I said.

"And I don't know why I agree to help your punk ass every time you come to me with some *Wolf of Wall Street* shit."

I laughed, then Damon joined me. We were worn out and getting loopier by the second.

"Dame, honestly, I appreciate you," I said. I'd entered the borrowed-time phase of my existence and was feeling unusually sincere.

"I'm a diamond in a dung pile, Al, and don't you forget it," he said, then tweaked an errant word on the document we'd been reviewing. "You think the others will play ball?"

"It's a coordinated-action problem. None of us is as strong as all of us, and all of us have scores to settle with Paul Kingsley."

"Bruh, is everything you say from an action movie?"

We laughed even harder.

$$$

## Monday, April 11

While Damon worked feverishly behind the scenes, I rounded up a few more essential collaborators. To explain my absence from the office, I texted Paul from my original phone and told him I was first meeting with the CEO of a digital advertising start-up in Redwood City, then with a partner at a PE firm in Menlo Park. To placate the FBI, I texted Joey from my "Simon" phone and told him I was planning to plant the bugs in Paul's office over the coming weekend. To attempt to save my ass, I texted Jennie from my new phone, told her I needed a massive favor, and asked if she could meet for a clandestine coffee in Cow Hollow.

After nuzzling together at an undersize table, which was situated behind a shelf full of used books, I coolly and calmly conveyed to her the CliffsNotes version of my double life as an insider trader turned FBI informant turned rogue agent of chaos hellbent on burning it all down.

"Jesus Christ, Al, that's fucking insane," Jennie said, perhaps understating the events underpinning the past six months of my life. "That explains why you were so cagey the day I quit."

"The last thing I wanted was to mix you up in this nightmare," I said, struggling not to stare at her supple lips. "When I tried to turn myself in, Paul threatened to go after you next."

"Ugh, what a scumbag," she said. "Though, you know I can take care of myself, right, Al?"

*Great.* My old-fashioned attempt at chivalry had come off as chauvinism. "I know," I said flatly. I also knew she was joining one of a dozen-odd families in the entire world capable of sparring with Paul Kingsley, a considerable tactical advantage she continued to take for granted, which continued to rub me the wrong way.

"So, what's your plan? What do you need from me?"

"I actually need a favor from Preston," I said. *Fucking Preston.* "I need him to schedule a meeting. And I need him to do it today."

"That's it?"

"The trick is, he's going to say he's attending the meeting in question, but I'm going to attend in his place. Think you can help me?"

"For you, Al? Anything," she said, missing the irony.

$$$

A few hours later, when I was supposed to be yukking it up with some PE ghoul in Menlo Park, I met Keith at the busiest part of the Fisherman's Wharf tourist district. Keith didn't know—and didn't need to know—I'd thrown him to Paul, and Paul had thrown him to the FBI. That was because the FBI's wolves never devoured him. And *that* was because Joey and Richie were about to take down District Attorney Holloway for insider trading and had much bigger fish to fry. Keith, who was mostly innocent and definitely harmless, was the least important person on their hit list.

All Keith knew was he'd abruptly lost his prestigious perch at Prism. And all I told him was, to get his old job back, he just needed to be in one very specific place, at one very exact time, and complete one very simple task. My former cubemate was understandably skeptical, as evidenced by the single drop of blood that'd crept out of his nose. But with no better career prospects lined up, he was also on board.

$$$

## *Tuesday, April 12*

The following day, I dropped by Karen's desk and said we needed to discuss something urgent. I suggested we grab lunch outside the office, which would, of course, be my treat. Karen explained, with her renowned compassion, that as a bona fide IG influencer and high-profile Twitter personality, her free time was simply too precious to waste with the likes of me. If I really desired her company, I could book a consultation on her website during non-Prism hours.

For the low, low price of five hundred bucks I did just that, reserving a thirty-minute time slot at her WeWork. I passed the rest of the seemingly endless workday reading *Monday Night RAW* recaps, exchanging texts with Damon and Jennie, and pretending to look motivated.

At seven that evening, Karen and I were sitting across from each other at an oval table designed for four. She looked prim and proper, as always, wearing a navy suit, a crème blouse, and a bun wound tight enough to stop a cannonball. On the table in front of her sat an open notebook, an influencer-approved pen, and her most lethal implement of choice: the priciest iPhone on the market. She pushed start on the device's digital timer, then clasped her hands and placed her wrists on the table like a schoolgirl. *This obviously isn't going to go well*, I told myself, *so why not throw caution to the wind?*

"I'm about to say something utterly insane," I began, then swallowed and sat up extra straight. "I'm going to take out Paul, and I need your help."

Her face was expressionless for a moment, then she started giggling, which turned into laughing, which escalated to cackling through the hand she'd brought to her mouth. I'd never seen her so emotive. She was like an evil Gillian Flynn character come to life.

"I'm serious, Karen. Me and a few others are tired of Paul's bullshit and we're ready to fight back." This made her laugh even harder.

"Did you know Paul was planning to pin insider trading charges on you before I stopped him?" I said, presenting a slightly more positive spin on the truth.

"And shall I presume you were the one who committed said insider trading offenses?" Karen asked, gathering herself.

"Not in that particular instance," I said. "But that's not the point. It's only a matter of time before Paul turns on you, too. You have no idea how much shit I've been through since Icarus."

"If I remember correctly, Al, Icarus was your baby. *You* were the one who blew up VICE, and *you* were the one who sparked Paul's ire in the first place, which turned you into . . . whatever it is you've become," she said, waving a hand at me like a condescending composer. "As you can see, I'm doing quite well for myself. So whatever idiotic bullshit you're planning, you can count me out. Also, half your time's up, and the slot after you is booked."

I laughed to myself and pitied the poor bastard who would one day marry this beautiful blond ballbuster. More pressingly, I wondered what I could say to pique her unflappable self-interest. Reciprocity was a dud and self-preservation wasn't cutting it, which left just one option.

"How would you like to become the youngest chief investment officer in Wall Street history?"

She shifted in her seat and looked interested at last. "At Prism?"

"Listen, Karen, we're going after Paul with or without you. But we could really, *really* use your social media superpowers."

"Not sure I like the sound of that."

"You will," I said. "Especially once I explain how you're going to become the Instagram-worthy face of high finance."

She smirked reflexively, and I hoped this naked appeal to her ego had struck a nerve. Karen picked up her phone and typed adroitly for several moments. Then she eyed me in an oddly and unexpectedly seductive manner.

"I canceled the rest of this evening's appointments," she said. "Why don't you tell me about this little adventure of yours?"

$$\$\$\$$$

## Wednesday, April 13

I saved the hardest piece of the puzzle for last.

Jennie and I stood atop the concrete stairs outside the Center for the Arts at Yerba Buena Gardens. Situated at the corner of Mission and 3rd Street, the location provided the perfect vantage point to get the drop on my quarry. We sipped cappuccinos while we waited. She looked stunning in profile.

"He's not going to show," I said.

"Don't be such a downer, Al."

Story of my life. "Preston reached out directly, right?"

Jennie looked at me and smiled that killer smile. *Fucking Preston.* I downed the remainder of my tepid cappuccino and felt jittery. From the caffeine. From the nerves. From the fact that my final chance to wrest back my freedom—my final chance to impose a modicum of justice on this unjust world—rested in the hands of a mercurial dipshit failson. A twisted by-product of nepotism and neglect and greed and generational trauma. An inferior rival who hated my guts. A son begat by the very psychopath trying to destroy me. Brad Kingsley.

Jennie smacked my shoulder excitedly. "There he is!"

Sure enough, little Bradley exited his Uber and sauntered down Mission on his way to the grassy area between the Gardens and the Metreon shopping complex. He thought he was meeting Preston near the entrance to the AMC. Thought they'd grab overpriced cocktails at a gauche bar teeming with faux-oak furnishings and technolibertarian twats. Thought they'd discuss the possibility of Brad becoming the managing director at one of Preston's plentiful family trusts. Poor little Bradley thought wrong. The only question was how dramatically he'd respond to his rude awakening.

"This isn't going to work," I said.

Jennie moved in close and wrapped her arms around me, squeezing tight. I reciprocated for what felt like a blissful eternity. How come I couldn't die like this? She peered deep into my eyes as we unclasped. I waited for her to plant a generous kiss on my lips. For her to vindicate my patience and fulfill my unrequited affection. For my knees to wobble and electricity to course through my body and for all this madness to have been worth it.

She stepped back and smiled and offered me a big-sisterly, "You got this, Al."

$$$

Brad idled by the movie theater entrance and gazed into his phone to appear busy. Important. Sought. He'd shed his typical garish attire for a more restrained light gray suit and UCLA-blue dress shirt. Informal interview dress. I wondered whether his fight-or-flight response would activate. I expected him to tell me to fuck all the way off, of course. But it'd be downright Homeric if, after all my hemming and hawing about whether I should prematurely end my futile, pointless life, I capitulated to the Camus-esque construct of "Existence is meaningless, sure, but fuck it, why not stick around and see what happens?" just in time for hapless, pathetic Bradley Kingsley to cut me down.

I ventured past the former Prism heir to the orthogonal cross-walk and approached from behind. In position to pounce, I hesitated. Brad stood aimless amid the lush foliage and endless blue sky. He looked up at regular intervals to see if Preston had arrived. Each passing moment his posture tensed, and he appeared more desperate. His body language revealed a man who'd been stood up by his date. A man who wasn't worth the effort. The longer I watched, the sorrier I felt for him. He'd had the entire world handed to him on a platinum platter, and yet every single day of his doomed existence he was more sad and desperate and broken and alone than I'd ever been.

"Preston's not going to make it," I said.

The sound of my voice spun Brad around like an enraged matador. "What the fuck are you doing here?"

"I have a business proposition for you."

"That's fucking rich," Brad said. His eyes darted in all directions.

I lifted up my shirt and sweater and rotated around, then pulled up each of my pants legs. "You can check my crotch if you want, but I promise I'm not wearing a wire."

Brad scoffed. "I don't know what game you're playing this time, Habib, but I'm not interested."

He turned to walk in the opposite direction. I lunged forward and gripped his elbow and he screamed, "Don't fucking touch me, you two-faced piece of shit!" and punched at my wrist until I let go. He stared at me with murderous intent while I scrambled for words. Onlookers gawked and increased their distance and hurried by.

I patted Brad's shoulder and straightened his jacket sleeve and stepped back to a safe distance and implored him to calm down while he stomped and yelled obscenities like a deranged toddler. When he'd exhausted himself, I tried a new tack.

"This concerns Paul, and the future of Prism. I need your help."

"I haven't seen Dad in months. I'm not allowed to visit Prism's offices. He doesn't respond to my emails. He blocked my fucking phone number!" Brad said, aghast and pitiful. "And you want *my* help?"

"You're the only one who's suffered?" I shot back. "Did you forget about the little blackmail operation you and Daddy dreamt up for me? Or how about what you did to Harold? You remember Harold, right? Or how about Keith? Or your boyfriend, Dennis?"

"Fuck you."

"No, fuck *you*, Brad," I said. "It was all fun and games when Daddy had your back, wasn't it?"

"I don't have to listen—"

"*Paul* fucked you, Brad. *Your* father. He only cares about himself. He'll destroy anyone who threatens his wealth and power. Including you. *His own son.*"

"Don't say that!" Brad said. His head drooped and his voice cracked. "You don't know him."

Oh, but I did. All too well. Proximity had blinded Brad to Paul's legion of faults the same way it'd blinded me to my mom's myriad redeeming qualities. Paul was a globe-trotting financial rock star who offered his son the world. My mom was a White trash hairstylist who burdened me with existence. We were too close to be objective, and too desperate to justify our circumstances with self-rationalizing and self-destructive narratives. But I was seeing the world a lot more clearly. It was time for Brad to wake up, too.

I placed a firm hand on his shoulder and leaned in close. "I've got a plan to take your dad out once and for all." Brad's puppy dog eyes locked onto mine. "If you want to run whatever's left of Prism when I'm finished, you should listen to what I have to say."

$$$

Two hours and two bottles of malbec later—tucked away in the private dining room, and protected from the faux-oak furnishings and technolibertarian twats—Brad still needed convincing.

"So let me get this straight. I help you, and the FBI sends Dad to prison for the rest of his life. I do nothing, and the FBI sends *you* to prison for the rest of your life. Why should I help, again?"

"What do you get, Brad? My life gets ruined and you get to gloat and say you beat me. Awesome. Great. Congratulations. Then what? Your dad shut you out and took your future hostage with NDAs and noncompetes. He'll never let you run Prism, and nobody on the Street will touch you. Receive any exciting job offers lately?"

Brad frowned, then shook the last drops of red wine into his empty glass. "I could go to law school. Start fresh."

"This isn't about you. Or me," I said. "It's about *Paul*. It's about taking a goddamned stand."

"I can't knowingly send my dad to prison, Ha— Al. He's my dad, for Christ's sake."

"We don't get to choose our parents. You think I *wanted* to be abandoned by a gutless coward? I doubt you *wanted* a grade-A psychopath for a father. We didn't choose them, but we can choose to be better than them."

"Jesus, Al, that's pretty fucking cheesy."

"It is cheesy," I said firmly. "It's also true. If we don't stop Paul—if we don't stop *your dad*—he'll keep cheating and exploiting and fucking everyone over. And he'll always have leverage over us."

Brad leaned back and exhaled a deep sigh. He retreated suddenly into his phone, as if our conversation had magically resolved. We sat in silence for a while, and that ever-present sense of failure crept into my mind. *I knew this wouldn't work.* At least I'd proved myself right on that front. I flagged the waiter and ordered an $800 bottle of rosé, which I imagined would be in short supply in Sing Sing.

I poured a glass for myself and one for Brad. I asked him who he was texting, but he ignored me and continued to type away. His chubby fingers moved with disconcerting alacrity. Maybe he was alerting Paul to my master plan. Didn't matter. No part of this debacle was Brad's fault. He, like me, was a product of his environment. Expecting him to find religion—to go full Oedipus, without a MILF as his reward—made it clear I'd gone insane. I wafted the glass under my nose to admire the sommelier's handiwork. The aroma struck me as suspiciously similar to my go-to merlot from Trader Joe's.

I took a long, libidinous swig and considered what kind of jail-house tats might confer me some clout.

Brad abruptly set his phone down. "Wait, Robbie's already agreed to help you?" he said, stunned.

"He's been hard at work since Monday morning," I said. "I told you, Brad, I'm not fucking around."

He rubbed a hand through his hair and breathed deeply for several moments. Then he leaned in close. "And you're sure we can take him out? Like, *sure* sure."

Buoyed by his response, but incapable of telling a bald-faced lie, I said, "We owe it to ourselves to try."

Brad sat back, sighed, smirked, and sipped the freshly poured wine. A few moments later, he said, "Then what's our first step?"

# BRING THE PAIN

*Friday, April 15*

I stood beneath a shady patch of trees and watched the road like a hawk. The midday sun beat down on the pavement with relentless intensity, heating and distorting the air. All the pieces were in place. Our planning was immaculate. Damon and I had checked and double-checked and triple-checked the documentation. The rest of the crew had their marching orders and were awaiting my signal to proceed. My newest phone had patchy reception but more than enough battery. Like most human affairs, the biggest constraint was time. US banks closed in less than an hour. *Where the fuck are they?*

Sweat dripped from my brow and my anxiety kicked into high gear. I reminded myself I was playing with house money. Literally. I'd already lost, so all I could do was win. It was a nice sentiment. But also bullshit. I looked at the gym bag near my feet. Like the specter of death, the gun inside seemed to follow me everywhere. Waiting for the opportune moment.

At quarter past noon, everything felt wrong. No texts. No calls. *Nothing.* Brad—that slimy fucking snake in the grass—must've betrayed me. It was only fitting. I was digging into my pocket for my phone when a black Mercedes materialized in the distance. The vehicle glided smoothly down Edgewood, crossed Cañada, and turned toward me onto Old Cañada Road. My heartbeat spiked and my mind raced as the car approached. I took deep breaths as moisture beaded on my face and saturated the inside of my clothes. The sedan slowed to a crawl and veered onto the dirt. Marvin lowered the driver's side window, nodded to me, and cut the ignition. *Showtime, kid.*

I walked toward the vehicle but stopped several car lengths away. I dropped the gym bag back at my feet and cocked my cell phone in my right hand. Marvin turned and said something to the passenger in the back seat, then pointed toward me. I hummed the hook to "Bring the Pain" over and over and over until the rear door of the sedan flung open and Paul stepped out. He closed the door behind him and ambled toward me until we stood about eight feet apart, like boxers at opposite ends of a ring. I wore a stoic facade while my guts twisted and the logic center of my brain repeatedly wondered: *What in the actual fuck was I thinking?*

"Somebody finally got to Marvin," Paul said. "He was the one person I trusted. Occupational hazard."

"I want out, Paul," I said, deliberately, desperately trying to steel my nerves.

"Out? Why? Itching to start your prison sentence?"

*Stay cool. Stick to the plan. Don't let him goad me.* I bent down, unzipped the gym bag, and removed a clipboard affixed with a pen and a thick paper document. "I have an agreement for you to sign."

"You don't think I know the Feds pinched you?" *Just stay cool, Al.* "Do you actually think I'm that fucking stupid?"

I cleared my throat. "This agreement invalidates my prior confession and includes a new NDA, which supersedes the previous one. All you need to do is sign your name a few times. Then we can go our separate ways." *Just keep breathing.*

"And all I need to do is make one phone call," Paul said, calm, cool, and collected as Hannibal Lecter. "I can have a hundred cops here in minutes. Think you and Marvin will walk away from that unscathed?"

I took a deep breath. *Fuck it.* "Speaking of phone calls." I pushed the green button on my device, tapped the speaker icon, and held it high so Paul could hear over the I-280 hum. "I guess we'll do this the hard way."

Two excruciating rings.

"Hey, Dad." Paul grimaced reflexively, betraying his hitherto sense of control. "Dad? You there?"

"Bradley."

"Great to hear your voice, Dad. Listen, I know you're very busy, so I'll keep this brief. Al and I have a little deal for you: You sign the paperwork he's holding, and everyone lives happily ever after. Easy-peasy."

"Bradley, I suggest you think very carefully before speaking again."

"Oh, I've been thinking, Dad. A whole lot. And see, Al and I realized we have a common problem: *you.* And we also figured out a way to solve our problem, which is why we really need you to sign that agreement. It's nothing fancy. Just a simple retraction and an ironclad NDA. Sign it, and nobody ever knows what happened. Refuse and, well, things might get messy."

Paul reached into his pocket and removed his phone, and I said, "I wouldn't do that if I were you."

He froze and glared at me and just couldn't resist. "Or what?"

"Brad, have Robbie send the first tranche."

"Robbie?" Paul muttered.

"And . . . done," Brad said.

"Congratulations, Paul. You just donated *one billion dollars* to UNICEF," I said. "You're quite the philanthropist."

"Bullshit. Bradley!" Paul shouted in my direction. "Bradley! Where are you?"

"I'm in your office, Dad. Your chair's quite comfortable. Think I'll keep it."

"Impossible."

Paul's phone immediately began chiming and pinging and buzzing like a defective slot machine. He scrolled frantically, pushed a button, and held the device to his ear. A second later, a faint, staticky version of Brad's voice emanated from my phone's speaker. "Paul Kingsley's office. Hello? Hello? Sorry, you must have the wrong number." *Click*. Paul's shoulders slumped and he lowered his hand in slow-motion disbelief. The cacophony of alerts and notifications on his phone continued unabated.

"All you need to do is sign, and you can save yourself a whole lot of heartache," I said.

He stepped closer and shouted expletive-laden warnings at Brad's disembodied voice. I scooped up the gym bag and caught a fleeting glimpse of the Glock's shiny black finish. I backpedaled to maintain a comfortable distance and told Brad to fire off the second tranche. He confirmed the transfers and I said, "Wow, Paul—*one-point-five billion* to Greenpeace! I never pegged you as a tree hugger."

"You're lying!"

"Karen, how's our engagement?" I asked.

"Prism's Twitter account has officially gone viral," she said via my phone. "Let's see: We've got fifty thousand likes—and counting—and we've been retweeted by the *Journal*, the *Times*, NPR, Dan Rather, and Taylor Swift."

"*Nice*," I said.

"And yours truly, of course," Karen said. "Ooh, Obama just retweeted us."

Paul's beet-red face tickled me pink. "Ready to sign?" I asked.

"Robbie!"

"Robbie doesn't work for you anymore, Dad."

"Bradley, you listen to me. You stop this nonsense right now—"

"He still needs convincing," I said.

"—or I'll—"

"You ever heard of Moms Demand Action, Dad?"

"—*fucking bury you!*"

"Because you just donated two billion dollars to their cause," Brad said.

"Might be enough to get the Second Amendment repealed," I added.

"I'm going to murder all of you."

I laughed. The more threats Paul made, the less threatening he became. When we stripped away his multibillion-dollar security blanket, he was just another angry boomer raging on Facebook.

"Well, Paul, that's half of your holdings in Prism. Poof. Gone," I said. "You're truly making the world a better place."

"I'll fu—"

"You won't do a goddamned thing!" I said. "Brad, who's next on the list? The NAACP? Or is it the ACLU?"

"Stop!" Paul said. "Stop. Just . . . stop."

He slumped over and suddenly looked frail and haggard, like he'd aged decades in minutes. I tossed the pen and clipboard at his feet and told him to sign the highlighted signature boxes, which Damon had conveniently demarcated with bright yellow tape. Paul silenced the alarms blaring on his phone and slid the device into his pocket. He collected then oriented the document right-side up and attempted to skim.

"Sign the fucking papers, Paul. Or we nuke the rest of your fund."

He paused and glowered. Defiant and petulant to the very end. Several *long* seconds passed. No movement. I brought my phone to my face and told Brad to prepare for the next transfer. Paul stared me down and mouthed empty death threats. Ironic, since I was the one packing heat. Before we could threaten another donation, Paul signed the first section. Then the second. Then the third and the fourth. The weight of galaxies lifted from my shoulders. *We got him.*

"Toss it back to me," I said.

Paul complied. Relief and joy and the sweet, delectable taste of revenge swept over my body. I tapped off speaker mode and placed the sunbaked phone to my ear. I grinned diabolically at Paul and gleefully told Brad we got what we needed. "Begin phase two," I said quietly, and disconnected the call.

Phone in pocket, I collected the clipboard and confirmed Paul had signed in the requisite places. I waved to Marvin and told Paul it was a pleasure doing business with him. He glared at me and seethed, but stood frozen in place, declining, after all, his prime opportunity to kill me with his bare hands.

At the end, Paul Kingsley proved he was nothing but a classic bully, whose entire persona was constructed upon the classic bully tactics of fear and intimidation. But unlike a proper strongman, the source of Paul's power was financial, not corporeal. His assets weren't guarded by tanks or fighter jets or nuclear weapons. No soldiers or sailors or league of assassins would lay down their lives to protect his fortune.

His money, and his power, simply resided on digital ledgers at financial institutions around the country. It was accessible, liquid, subject to the whims and vagaries of modern capitalism, and ripe for the taking—if only someone were crazy enough to try. Robbie had full autonomy and authority over Paul's personal accounts, and after I'd approached him bright and early on Monday morning, and explained to him how we could finally extricate ourselves from Paul's sadistic clutches, he began leveraging every available tool and deploying every available trading strategy to disburse as many of Paul's funds as quickly as possible, when the time was right.

In advance of our showdown, Robbie had trimmed positions, liquidated holdings, entered opaque contracts, and purchased esoteric derivatives. When Paul left with Marvin a short while ago, Robbie immediately began divesting shares, transferring accounts, and wiring cash. He'd executed everything right under Paul's oblivious nose, because who the fuck would be stupid enough, and *ballsy* enough, to cross him?

The answer, of course, was me—with more than a little help from my friends.

Exactly how much of Paul's wealth Robbie had just distributed, and from which accounts, and to which organizations, was, ironically, irrelevant. The most valuable commodity traded on the stock market was information, and in the digital media era, misinformation and disinformation were the most dangerous weapons imaginable. Once Karen's posts went viral, and the "efficient market hypothesis" became operative, the news of Prism's philanthropy-inspired implosion spread like wildfire.

When Prism's investors and clients panicked—they were, without a doubt, the cretins blowing up Paul's phone—*Paul* panicked. Nobody, not even the most dangerous man on Wall Street, was immune to pressure. And when we ratcheted that pressure up to an unbearable level, and Paul signed the document I was currently holding in my hand, he had unwittingly agreed to more than just a simple retraction and revised NDA. He encased himself in legal carbonite—and sealed his fate.

Paul continued to stew and sulk and do fuck-all about his fragile feelings. A classic bully response to getting punched square in the mouth. He was completely fucked, and like all the people he'd victimized during his decades-long reign of terror, there wasn't a goddamned thing he could do about it. Poetic. Karmic. Cathartic.

I picked up the gym bag, walked toward Paul, and tossed it at his chest. He made a fumbling catch as I glided toward the sedan. I opened the passenger door and was moments from making my final escape.

"Stop right there," Paul said.

I turned around and saw the pistol pointed at my face. Paul had clearly held a gun before, and he looked mighty determined to use it. "You're not the first person to point that thing at me," I said. "I thought long and hard about using it on myself, but then I remembered I have too much to live for. Not sure I can say the same about you."

He pulled the trigger, but no bullet fired. He pulled again. Over and over and over, to no avail. He cocked his arm and threw the unloaded weapon at my head. I casually ducked as it sailed into the burnt grass on the other side of the road.

"Goodbye, Paul."

"You think you'll take me out?! I'm Paul fucking Kingsley! Who are you, Al?! A nobody! A bastard child! A worthless piece of shit!"

Standing alone in an empty field, ranting and raving at the top of his lungs and threatening to commit murder, Paul Kingsley looked absolutely unhinged. His truest colors revealed. With foam all but spewing from his mouth, he said, "You're a worthless piece of shit, Al! A worthless piece of shit!"

I climbed into the passenger seat of the Mercedes, closed the door, rolled down the window, and looked back at him. "My name is Ali Jafar, and my life is priceless."

Marvin drove us away.

# CAPITAL PUNISHMENT

Marvin dropped me off at the corner of Kearney and Pine. I strapped on my backpack, sprinted through the skyscraper's revolving glass doors, badged in at the security turnstile, and jogged to the elevators. Our planned media circus kicked off with a bang when The Cut ran a piece titled "Big Surprise: Hedge Fund Creep Paul Kingsley Sexually Assaulted a Woman in Tampa." Robbie's unshakable fealty had never quite made sense to me, and after the exposé cleared his name, the whole world knew why.

As the elevator doors closed, I clicked the link to a just-published story in Jezebel. Multiple porn actors described, in horrific detail, how Paul had repeatedly assaulted and exploited them at the Allure mansion. When the doors opened at the top floor I regretted not shooting him in the face when I had the chance.

I suppressed my disgust and refocused on the endgame. The office buzzed with frantic energy. Everyone knew the shit had hit the fan, but nobody understood how or why. A group of IT guys and miscellaneous analysts basked in their inevitable demises by pounding shots and passing blunts. The SPACs team furiously shredded documents and smashed laptops with the break-in-case-of-emergency axe. Phil from REITs lay half dead by the entrance to the men's room, caked in vomit and drenched in piss.

The overhead TVs featured every type of pundit speculating about what had really triggered "The Meltdown at Prism." My favorite theory claimed North Korean hackers had seized control of the fund and donated Paul's money to highlight the perils of privatization and free market capitalism.

When I arrived at my desk, Karen was neatly packing her personal items into a cardboard box and preparing to move into her shiny new office. I offered her my stupidest, most inviting grin, and wondered if I'd melted her frigid contempt once and for all.

"I'm *amazed* you didn't fuck this up," she said.

I shook my head and laughed. "I'm amazed you didn't double-cross us."

"I strongly considered it."

"What stopped you?" I said.

Karen scooped up her box and nodded toward the hallway. "Ready to sign your life away?"

"After you."

On our way down the long corridor to Paul's—check that, Brad's office—I heard Betty crying into her phone and two people humping in a vacant office. Both brought a smile to my face. I held open the heavy glass door for Karen and entered Brad's domain for the first and last time. He, Dennis, and Robbie were huddled at Paul's old desk, flanked by Gerry, the notorious "fixer." Some random Indian guy from IT was breaking into Paul's computer. *My, how the tables have turned.*

"You have the doc?" Brad asked me.

I twisted my backpack around, removed the clipboard, walked over, and attempted to hand it to him. Gerry intercepted and flipped through the pages. He chuckled to himself, then added his initials next to Paul's four signatures. After, he removed the lone staple and inserted the sheets of paper into the scanner he'd set up next to the humidor. We all watched in silence as the pages methodically entered and exited the machine. Once finished, Gerry switched to copy mode and started anew.

"Got it!" the Indian dude said excitedly.

I walked around the desk to watch him execute the final stages of Paul's seppuku. He opened Paul's email, downloaded the scanned PDF, renamed it "My Confession," inserted the file into a new email with the same subject line, and addressed the message to deb@wsj.com.

"Should I send it?" he asked.

"Are we good, Gerry?" Brad said.

Paul's former fixer paused, presumably for dramatic effect. "Congratulations, gentlemen—and lady. Prism Capital is officially under new management."

IT dude hit send, and the group erupted in celebratory cheers. Karen retreated to the humidor while the rest of us dispensed hugs and high fives with homoerotic impunity. Robbie broke down in tears. Dennis called for shots. Gerry lit a celebratory cigar. IT dude was just happy to be there. When the mood calmed, Brad bear-hugged me. He squeezed tight for altogether too long and thanked me over and over and over again, assuring me—and himself—that we'd done it. We'd really done it. We'd *finally* done it. With a few pieces of paper and some clicks of a mouse, we'd felled Brad's un-touchable father—the mad titan of the hedge fund industry. We'd caused a financial earthquake whose aftershocks would reverberate across Wall Street for decades. We'd freed ourselves.

Gerry passed around an affidavit and an NDA for everyone to sign, including himself. After we'd all inked our names, our legally binding amnesia was official: None of us knew why Paul cracked, why he leaked his own confession *and* NDAs to the press, or when he was last in his office, and, even if we did, we weren't at liberty to talk about it.

With this crucial component of the conspiracy complete, I needed to cover my own bases. Gerry passed me a handful of envelopes, each containing two printed copies plus a flash drive with a PDF version of Paul's suicide note. I wrote my mom's address on one and affixed it with an excessive amount of postage. After marking the others with their respective recipient's names, I stuffed the stack in my backpack.

"When're you talking to the *Journal*?" I asked Brad.

"Deb told me the exposé will go live this evening," he said. "My exclusive interview's tomorrow morning."

"Just make sure Karen takes point when discussing the new investment strategy."

"Technically, Al, I'm your boss again, and you can't tell me what to do."

"Guess I quit then."

Brad chuckled.

I checked the time on my phone. "I need to meet the Feds," I said, tempering the vibe.

"Hey, Al," Karen said from across the room. "Try not to get yourself killed, all right?"

"I didn't realize you cared."

"I don't," she said, flashing the subtlest of smirks.

Brad hugged me again, this time goodbye. "Whatever you need, Al. Whenever you need it."

$$$

At the corner of California and Battery, I removed the envelope addressed to my mom and dropped it inside the dented blue mailbox. Jennie and Preston sat in the adjacent Starbucks window. He was reading a paper copy of the *Journal* while she perused an issue of *Vogue*. Who were these people? And why had I overlooked their cartoonish behavior for so long? Jennie was gorgeous on the outside, sure, but I didn't know who she was or what she stood for on the inside. Perhaps that was the appeal. She wasn't sexy and mysterious, she was a stranger. Chasing after her all those years was just another elaborate form of self-sabotage. She couldn't reject me if she wasn't available.

I entered the coffee shop and sat beside her, then removed the stack of envelopes and set my backpack on the ground next to her oversize Prada purse. I shuffled them one by one so she could read the names I'd written: Joey (FBI), Damon, Miller (lawyer), and Jennie. I set Joey's aside, then stacked the others together and slid them inside her bag. I leaned in close and smelled cinnamon in her hair. "Please give my lawyer's copy to Damon, too."

She nodded and smiled and the garish "Dolce" and "Gabbana" of her brand-new glasses assaulted me. I thanked Preston, said goodbye to Jennie, and knew I'd never see them again.

A short walk later, I spotted Joey and Richie sitting on a park bench near the playground at Sue Bierman Park. Right where I wanted them. The Ferry Building bustled with people, and foot traffic along the Embarcadero was steadily gathering pace. If they decided to execute me, they'd have to do it in a very public venue. I removed my headphones as I approached, cutting short Inspectah Deck's legendary rhyme on "Triumph." They jumped up and jogged toward me, looking far from jovial.

"What in the flying fuck is going on, Al?" Joey said.

"I completed my task," I said, handing him the envelope. "I took down Paul Kingsley."

Joey ripped open the flap and shook the documents out. The flash drive fell to the sidewalk. Richie picked it up and slid it into his pocket. Joey handed him one of the printed copies of Paul's confession and they impatiently flipped through the pages.

"You should definitely read the whole thing," I said, "but I'll tell you the highlights. Paul Kingsley, in writing, as witnessed by his own attorney, *admitted* to the following misdeeds: insider trading, blackmail, securities fraud, stock market manipulation, wire fraud, sexually assaulting a woman in Tampa, Florida, and beating up multiple porn actresses.

"Wild, huh? But get this, according to his own sworn statement, *Paul* blacklisted Harold Shinawatra for blowing the whistle on Prism's past financial scandals. *Paul* ordered Dennis McNamara to secure material nonpublic information from his uncle in Congress. And *Paul* directed me to pursue black edge in order to rebuild my portfolio after the Icarus crash. Ironically, he threatened to blackmail *me* for the same crimes he induced Dennis to commit.

"But it gets better! Apparently, Paul couldn't live with his guilt any longer. To atone for his transgressions against society, he donated all of his personal wealth to charitable organizations, and bequeathed ownership of Prism Capital to his only son, Brad Kingsley.

"Finally, and you'll never believe this part, Paul agreed to indemnify all current and former Prism employees—me included—for any crimes committed under his watch, *and* declined all future opportunities to pursue criminal or civil litigation. That's all explained in the nondisclosure agreement.

"So, basically, *Paul* admitted to everything. You guys can arrest him when you're ready."

Joey fixed his gaze on the document and flipped the pages back and forth without uttering a sound.

Richie, not much for the fine print, laughed to himself. "I'll give you this, kid," he said, "you got some balls." He folded the paper in two. "How'd you get him to fess up?"

"I'd love to tell you guys, but I signed an NDA," I said, and winked.

Richie bobbed his head and cracked a smile. "What do you think, Joe? Should we shoot him?"

Joey didn't grasp the sarcasm, because he unholstered his handgun and pointed it directly at my forehead.

"You're the *second* person to point a gun at me today," I said. "With friends like these, who—"

Joey raised the pistol high above his head and I reflexively buried my face in my arms. He brought the butt of the weapon down with maximum force, which lacerated my forearm and opened a deep gash above my ear. "You fucked us!" he said. "You fucked us!"

He continued swinging. I did my best to cover my eyes. Each strike seemed like a blow from a sledgehammer. After he'd landed several solid hits, and I'd collapsed onto the ground, Richie pulled him off and restrained him and screamed at him to calm down. My vision blurred and shooting pains stabbed through my brain. Joey repeatedly said, "I'll fucking kill you! I'll fucking kill you! I'll fucking kill you!"

"Oh my God!" Keith shouted in the distance. "Those corrupt FBI agents are trying to kill that poor guy!"

It was an absurdly precise and laughably conspicuous assessment of the situation, which surely induced a prodigious amount of blood to spill from his nose. Keith repeated the same outrageous claim and encouraged everyone nearby to record and document Joey's abuse of power. Many complied. One concerned tech bro shouted, "Mothafuck tha po-lice!" and stooped down next to my splayed-out carcass and snapped some close-ups of my injuries.

Joey shoved him away and pointed the gun at him and threatened to shoot anyone who came too close. Battered but conscious, with blood pouring into my ear and streaking down my face, I smiled. A moment later, Joey and Richie lifted me by my arms and dragged me away from the crowd.

# THE WORLD IS YOURS

## *Saturday, April 16*

The opening of the interrogation room door startled me. My eyes strained from the synthetic overhead light and my face ached from the table I'd used as a pillow for the past who knows how many hours. The door closed behind Richie and he set a large McDonald's coffee and two breakfast sandwiches in front of me. Back to playing the good cop, I assumed. Considering I had thirty-six stiches in my skull—and a seriously fucked-up haircut—I refrained from making any more smart-assed quips.

I grabbed the coffee and removed the plastic lid and hastily took a sip. Just about every part of my body hurt, and since I was apparently an FBI hostage, imprisoned at an unknown facility, the future didn't look too bright. I focused on the positives: The newly broke and hopefully soon-to-be-indicted Paul Kingsley was *definitely* having a shittier day.

Richie sat quietly across from me while I ate the first sandwich. Sausage, egg, and cheese. An unbeatable flavor combination, ruined only by periodic whiffs of Richie's egregious body odor and my damp, sweaty crotch. I tried not to gag, and my mind teemed with questions. Simple ones, like: What time was it? But also more complex ones, like: Hadn't I been assaulted by a federal officer? And: Wasn't I being illegally held against my will? I crumpled the ocean-killing wrapper and set it on the table, then set to work on the second sandwich. A duplicate.

"How's your head?" Richie asked.

"Where's Joey?" I mumbled through synthetic foodstuffs.

Richie sighed and sipped his coffee. "He feels terrible about what happened."

I finished the second sandwich and washed down the grease. "What happens now?" I asked.

Richie's phone vibrated. He muttered something to himself, then stood and left. I stared at the claustrophobic room's beige walls and gray carpet and debated relieving myself in the corner. At least my caffeine headache was subsiding. I remembered to stay positive, and joyfully recalled the look on Paul's face when we vaporized his self-worth.

Richie barged back into the room. "Let's go, kid."

We walked down a series of long, depressing hallways, then ducked into a vacant office. Richie flipped on the lights, walked to the other side of the room's unused desk, and opened the center drawer. He gathered my phone, wallet, keys, and broken switchblade comb and handed them to me. Without a word we exited the office, navigated another circuitous route of corridors to an elevator, and rode to the ground floor. Richie stopped short of the building's main entrance.

"For what it's worth, you did good, kid." Richie shook my hand. "Just try to stay out of trouble from now on."

I looked at him, confused, and he nodded at the door. I didn't have to be told twice. Outside the spring sunshine warmed my face and the birds sang and the leaves sparkled like a sea of emeralds. It was like I'd walked onto the set of a goddamned Disney movie. I powered on my phone and looked behind me and to each side and waited for the FBI to violently rectify their clerical error. Dead battery. The only car in the lot, a jet-black SUV with tinted windows, parked horizontally across three open spaces, rolled toward the entrance and stopped in front of me. Then it made sense. The SWAT team inside would open fire and later claim I was a terrorist attempting to suicide bomb the facility.

The passenger window depressed and Damon's toothy grin surprised me. "Fuck you looking at?" he said, then exploded into gut-busting laughter. He exited the vehicle and dapped me up and hugged me tightly. Sporting a clean shave and a fresh fade, he clowned on my Cyndi Lauper–inspired hairstyle.

"Where's Paul?" I said.

"He had a very bad day," Damon said. "Last I heard, the FBI froze his remaining assets, put him on the no-fly list, and demanded he turn himself in." I was too happy to speak.

"Thanks to your girl Karen, the videos of your beatdown went mega-viral, too," he said. "Especially after the *Times* confirmed you were a Prism employee aiding an FBI investigation." I was too thrilled to laugh.

"It was a PR nightmare," he said. "I called your lawyer and she said the Southern District had already dropped all charges against you."

I was too stunned to say thank you.

"You did it, Al," he said. "You won."

A lifetime of frustration and disappointment and rage and joy and gratitude and relief swirled inside me and I broke down into tears. Clumsy, gasping, sobbing tears. Damon put his arm around me and told me it was okay. It was all good now. When I'd had my fill, I wiped my face on my suit sleeve and caught my breath, then we piled into the SUV and began the long drive back to San Francisco.

As we made our way onto I-80, Damon flipped the radio to the local hip-hop station and rhymed along to a track I'd never heard. They sure didn't make them like they used to. I cracked the passenger window, let the cool air rush through the remnants of my hair, and stared at the trees along the open road.

Like any good investment analyst, I took stock of my situation: no job, three high-grade concussions, multiple *Mortal Kombat*-inspired battle scars—plus, I didn't get the girl.

But I was *alive*.

And I was *free*.

Unencumbered for the first time. Freed from the shackles of false expectations. Freed from an industry—an entire ecosystem—built to exploit. Freed from a zero-sum contest designed to prey upon the weakest and the most vulnerable. Freed from one-percenter goals that were never mine. Freed from the faulty pretense that "winning" a corrupt and deceptive game would make my life feel meaningful.

I'd proved to myself my life was worth living. But what was worth living for? What did I value? What really mattered? I'd figure that out later.

First things first.

I'd book a flight to see my mom.

A flight home.

# Acknowledgments

W hile *Leverage* is a work of fiction, the mechanics of the novel are firmly rooted in the realities of the global financial system. Shorting stocks really is that ridiculous, hedge funds do routinely trade on illicit information—which is often passed along by industry insiders—and financial authorities and government agencies across the planet are at various turns complicit and/or overmatched.

Of course, to create a fun and fast-paced story, I omitted tedious and laborious details throughout the narrative. But rest assured, everything that happens in *Leverage* could happen in the "real world." A cursory glance at the latest headlines proves the day-to-day dealings of our opaque, globalized financial institutions are both much more banal and far more unbelievable.

With that out of the way, it's my distinct honor and privilege to thank the wonderful people who empowered me to write and publish this novel (those aren't the same thing).

First and foremost, an unquantifiable thank you to my wife and children for their unwavering support and endless patience. Everything I've accomplished begins with the three of you.

## ACKNOWLEDGMENTS

Big ups to my beta readers: Alex, Andrew, Cat, Dennard, Martin, and Meg. You lovely people have taught, inspired, and humbled me. Most important of all, you strengthened the director's cut of this batshit crazy novel, which undoubtedly put me on the batshit crazy path to publication.

Mega thanks to my agent Christopher Schelling for taking a chance on me, an unemployed dad with an emailable blog and unhealthy delusions of grandeur. You're a bastion of sanity and a consummate professional. Here's hoping *Leverage* is the first of many forays.

A massive, massive thank you to Peter Borland at Atria Books. I still can't believe a novel with my name on the cover resides on bookshelves. I'm so grateful you connected with my work, and your astute observations and keen insights helped me deliver the best possible version of *Leverage* to readers across the empire. We should do this again some time.

Blurbin' ain't easy, so an extra special shoutout to the brilliant authors who invested their time and energy reading, evaluating, and advocating for *Leverage*. The names adorning this novel are a veritable who's who of literary talent, which is both gratifying and humbling. Buy their books!

Much love to my fellow writers, creators, and collaborators across the internet (you know who you are). Your support and encouragement confirmed I was on the right path and motivated me to keep grinding, consequences be damned. The existence of this novel is a feather for your respective caps.

I owe an Icarus-size debt of gratitude to Oliver Bullough, John Carreyrou, Sheelah Kolhatkar, Michael Lewis, Dan McCrum, Andrew Ross Sorkin, and all the intrepid investigative journalists at *The Atlantic*, *The Economist*, the *Financial Times*, the *New Yorker*, and, of course, the *Wall Street Journal*. You amazingly talented people do the real work so that I can just make stuff up. If you stumble across this novel, please know you played a crucial role in its creation. And if we happen to meet in person one day, drinks are on me.

Last, and decidedly not least, *thank you* to all the readers who have spent or will spend their precious time and hard-earned money on *Leverage*. I'm extremely proud of the finished product, and I hope the novel's half as fun to read as it was to write.

Stay frosty out there.

—Amran